Welcome to Munsonville:

The People, Places, and Things of the BryonySeries

By Denise M. Baran-Unland

Cover art by Jennifer Wainwright

This book is lovingly dedicated to the reader, whoever you might be.

"Yes, Munsonville. A strange place of little consequence." Albert Brumfeldt in "Before The Blood."

CONTENTS

HOW TO USE THIS BOOK

"They" say all roads eventually lead to Rome.

"We" say all books and stories lead to Munsonville – if those books and stories are part of the BryonySeries.

Munsonville is a fictional fishing village in Northern Michigan, a place that draws people from across eras and continents deeply into its nets.

In fact, the majority of characters in the BryonySeries will eventually wander into Munsonville at some point. If not, they shall at least cross paths with those who do.

Maybe you'll become one of those people.

Among the pages of the BryonySeries books, you will meet many characters, visit many places, and encounter many things, so many you may not remember them all.

That's where this guidebook helps. Here are three ways you might like to use it.

One: Quickly look up a person, place, or thing that is vaguely familiar and refresh your recollections. Descriptions are deliberately vague to reduce spoilers. But descriptions do include the title of the book(s) where that person, place, or thing is found, in case an item piques your interest, and you want to read more.

Two: Scan all the entries in this guidebook as a sweeping introduction before picking up your first BryonySeries book.

Three: Read all the BryonySeries books first and then browse this guide to stir recollections of the journey.

Side note: This guidebook includes references for all BryonySeries books published through 2023. It may not include all references for books published after that date.

Nor does this guidebook include any BryonySeries books authored by Ed Calkins, Steward of Tara, for he may write his own guidebook one day.

Finally, this guidebook also does not include any of the references or imagery in the BryonySeries lyrical novel, "A Year of Shadows and Moonlight, Of Gathering Blooms in the Woods."

But this guidebook does contain plenty of literary references and much history: real history, pretend history, and all the in-between shades of both, seamlessly intermingled to create the BryonySeries world.

If you're just discovering the BryonySeries, you should know the series offers plenty of books for all ages, so you won't run out of reading material any time soon. The BryonySeries is so extensive, we've invented our own genre: phantasmic.

Phantasmic?

The Merriam-Webster dictionary defines "phantasm" as an illusion, a figment of the imagination, a product of fantasy, a ghost or specter, and something with a delusive appearance.

That best sums up the experience waiting for you.

There is no one right place to begin, no book you must read first, and no over-arching characters. Whatever book you pick up first is the right book for you to read first.

However, the BryonySeries does have one surprising universal narrator: you. That's because your interpretations of the stories you'll read will be unique to you and will unconsciously influence the way you mentally weave all the storylines.

Now, to echo the message of the "Munsonville" sign as folks drive into town, "Everyone is welcome here."

So book your room at Munsonville Inn (we recommend Room 27). And then pull up a chair, settle into its cushions with your favorite drink and snack from Sue's Diner, select a book – any book – and plan to stay awhile.

You might be glad you did.

Denise M. Baran-Unland

November 14, 2023

Bryonyseries.com.

PART ONE: PEOPLE

Abnicola the Great: A mysterious magician that performs at a harvest gathering on Fisher Farm. Appears in "Before The Blood: Bryony Marseilles" and referenced in "Before The Blood: Bryony Simons."

Ada: Daughter of Roger McLoughty. Appears in a short story in "Lycanthropic Summer."

Adam and Eve: Allegory Bryony Simons uses to describe her and John Simons' importance in the new Munsonville. Referenced in "Before The Blood: Bryony Simons."

Mary Addaway: Daughter of Patricia Addaway and adopted daughter of Gerald Miller Jr. Sister of Mary Addaway Miller and Larry Miller. Appears in "Visage," "House on Top of the Hill," and "Katie and the Big Fear." Mentioned in "Karla Joins In." See also Mary Miller.

Patricia Addaway: Gerald Miller Jr.'s love interest (and later wife) in "Katie and the Big Fear." Mother of Mary Addaway Miller, Sherry Addaway Miller, and Larry Miller. Mentioned in "Karla Joins in."

Amos Bronson Alcott: Father of author Louisa May Alcott. Referenced in "Before The Blood: Bryony Marseilles" and "Before The Blood: Bryony Simons."

Luke Allen: One of the Allen brothers. Mentioned once by name in "Before The Blood: Bryony Simons."

Mark Allen: One of the Allen brothers. Mentioned once by name in "Before The Blood: Bryony Simons."

Paul Allen: One of the Allen brothers, Mentioned once by name in "Before The Blood: Bryony Simons."

Titus Allen: One of the Allen brothers. Mentioned once by name in "Before The Blood: Bryony Simons."

Mr. Allen: Client of Kellen Wechsler in the 1940s. Referenced in **"Before The Blood: Kellen Wechsler."**

Amanda: One of the residents of the old candy factory in "Cornell Dyer and the Old Folks Home."

Amerigian: Poet of Ed Calkins, Steward of Tara. Referenced in "Bryony." Appears in "Staked!"

Charlie Anders: Stable groom at Simons Mansion. Briefly appears in "Bryony" and "Before The Blood: Bryony Simons."

Willie Anders: Stable boy at Simons Mansion. Briefly appears in "Bryony" and "Before The Blood: Bryony Simons."

Dr. Anderson: A regular doctor who practices in Jenson. Appears in "Bryony." Referenced in "Visage."

Hans Christian Anderson: Nineteenth century Danish writer of literary fairy tales. Referenced in "Before The Blood: Henry Matthews" and "Call of the Siren."

Apache: A group culturally related Native American tribes that eventually settled in the southwestern United States. Referenced in "Before The Blood: Bryony Marseilles."

Apollo: The Greek god of sun and light, known for his beauty, music, and poetry. Referenced in "Before The Blood: Kellen Wechsler."

Mr. Ardolf: Client of Cornell Dyer whose parakeet needs an exorcism. Appears briefly in "Cornell Dyer and the Old Folks Home."

Blair Ashmore: Resident of late nineteenth century Munsonville. First known husband of Neta Ashmore. Appears in "Before The Blood: Bryony Simons." Mentioned in "The Phoenix."

Neta Ashmore: Wife of Blair Ashmore. Arrives in Munsonville with her husband Blair in the late nineteenth century. Appears in "Before The Blood: Bryony Simons," "The Phoenix," "Call of the Siren," and "House on Top of the Hill." See also Neta Parks.

Raynelle Atkinson: The friend of Caitlin Miller's heart. Lives in California. Mentioned in "Call of the Siren" and "House on Top of the Hill."

John James Audubon: Ornithology and artist. Author of "Birds of America," which contains 435 life-size watercolors of his North American birds. He and his book are mentioned in "Before The Blood: Bryony Marseilles."

Augustus II the Strong: King of Poland and elector of Saxony. Lived in the seventeenth and eighteenth centuries. Mentioned in "Before The Blood: Kellen Wechsler."

Aunt Silly: Aunt of Caryn Rochelle. Sister of Dr. Fred Rochelle, veterinarian in Shelby, Michigan, and North Lyons, Michigan. Appears in "Lycanthropic Summer" and briefly in "House on Top of the Hill." See also Priscilla Matilda Rochelle.

Herr Otto Austein: Smug, middle-aged councilman wanting to know if Kellen would be returning to Deutsche Karl-Ferdinands-Universität. Appears briefly "Before The Blood: Kellen Wechsler."

Babs: Wannabe friend of Caryn Rochelle in "Lycanthropic Summer."

Emily Baldwin: Eldest daughter of New York tycoon Jacob King and Judith King. Sister of Agnes King. Wife of Nicholas Baldwin, cousin to the Vanderbilts. Appears briefly in "Before The Blood: John Simons," "Before The Blood: Henry Matthews," and "Before The Blood: Bryony Simons." See also Emily King

Nicholas Baldwin: Husband of Emily King Baldwin, cousin to the Vanderbilts. Mentioned in "Before The Blood: Henry Matthews" and "Before the Blood: Bryony Simons."

Todd Ballantine: Junior executive of R.C. Walter's advertising agency. Co-worker of Kellen Wechsler in the 1940s. Appears briefly in "Before The Blood: Kellen Wechsler."

Carl Bandersnacks: Fictional character in a short werewolf story by Caryn Rochelle in "Lycanthropic Summer."

Mr. Bankston: Owner or manager of the Wash 'n' Dry laundromat. Mentioned in "Before The Blood: Kellen Wechsler."

Duke of Baroyington: Fictional duke of a vague, fictional locale. Mentioned in "Before The Blood: Kellen Wechsler."

Strother Barker: Resident of Mary Singler's boarding house. Appears briefly in "Before The Blood: Henry Matthews."

Sam Barnes: A drifter. Co-founder of Sue's Diner. Husband of Sue Bass. Appears in "Call of the Siren" and "House on Top of the Hill."

Steve Barnes: Son of Steve and Sue Barnes. Lifelong Munsonville resident. Grew up working at Sue's Diner. Village maintenance man. Appears in "Bryony," Visage," "Staked!," "Call of the Siren," "House on top of the Hill," "Katie and the Big Fear," and "Brainy Ann." Mentioned in "Julie and the Too-Hard Homework."

Sue Barnes: Wife of Sam Barnes. Daughter of Susan Betts and Sally Bass. Mother of Steve Barnes. Co-founder of Sue's Diner. Appears briefly in "Before The Blood: Bryony Simons," The Phoenix," and "House on Top of the Hill." Protagonist in "Call of the Siren." Also known as Susan Grace Bass. See also Sue Bass.

P.T. Barnum: American showman and promoter. Mentioned in "Before The Blood: John Simons." Appears briefly in "Before The Blood: Bryony Simons."

Felicity Joy Bartlett: Girlfriend and wife of Andrew Helsby, John Simons' tutor. Mother of Priscilla Helsby, Emeline Helsby, and Little Andy Helsby. Appears in "Before The Blood: John Simons," "Before The Blood: Bryony Simons," and "Call of the Siren." See also Felicity Helsby

Sally Bass: One of the first residents of Munsonville. Wife of Theodore "Teddy" Bass. Mother of Sue Bass. Reputation for being "feisty" and the best cook and baker in the village. Appears in "Before The Blood: Bryony Marseilles," "Before The Blood: Bryony Simons," "The Phoenix," and "Call of the Siren."

Sue Bass: Wife of Sam Barnes. Daughter of Susan Betts and Sally Bass. Mother of Steve Barnes. Co-founder of Sue's Diner. Appears briefly in "Before The Blood: Bryony Simons," The Phoenix," and "House on Top of the Hill." Protagonist in "Call of the Siren." Also known as Susan Grace Bass. See also Sue Barnes.

Theodore "Teddy" Bass: One of the earliest residents of Munsonville. Wife of Sally Bass. Known for his carpentry and furniture-making skills. Co-owner of Bass & Betts woodshop. Appears in "Before The Blood: Bryony Marseilles," "Before The Blood: Bryony Simons," and (briefly) in "Summer Sisters." Mentioned in "Call of the Siren."

Mr. Basset: One of two checker players at the general store in "Cornell Dyer and the Eerie Lake."

Bastien: Stableman/driver at Aradia. Mentioned in "Before The Blood: Henry Matthews."

Elizabeth Bathory: Hungarian noblewoman and possible serial killer. Appears in all five volumes of "Before The Blood" (John Simons, Kellen Wechsler, Bryony Marseilles, Henry Matthews, and Bryony Simons) and "The Phoenix."

Julian Baynard: Instructed the adolescent Henry Matthews in all the subjects in the trivium. Briefly appears in "Before The Blood: Henry Matthews."

Emmet Beal: Tailor in a New York shop. Appears briefly in "Before The Blood: Kellen Wechsler."

Bob Beaton: Clerk at "Seventh Heaven" hotel at Paradise Falls. Appears in "Cornell Dyer and the Old Folks Home."

Miss Beatrice: Fiancé of Mortimer Rutherford. Appears briefly in "Before The Blood: John Simons."

Mr. Beaver: Mrs. Peabody's valet and driver in "Cornell Dyer and the Whispering Wardrobe."

Mrs. Beaver: Mrs. Peabody's cook and housekeeper in "Cornell Dyer and the Whispering Wardrobe."

Christine Lucille BeckmanShire: Cornell Dyer's sleuthing partner and love interest in "Cornell Dyer and the Old Folks Home."

Gretchen Bell: Wife of Algernon Demars. Teacher of the younger children at Thornton's first school. Teacher at Munsonville School. Mentioned in "Before The Blood: Bryony Marseilles." Appears briefly in "Before The Blood: Bryony Simons," "The Phoenix" and "Call of the Siren." See also Gretchen Demars.

Barbie Benton: Barbie Benton Miller. Girlfriend – and later wife – of Nate Miller. Appears in "Katie and The Big Fear" and possibly "House on Top of the Hill." Mentioned in "Karla Joins In."

Adele Belanger: Adele Marseilles: Wife of Reverend Galien Marseilles. Mother of Bryony Marseilles Simons, Mary Mae Marseilles, and Samuel George Marseilles. Avid reader. Poor health from scarlet fever. Appears in "Before The Blood: Bryony Marseilles." Mentioned in "Bryony" and "Before The Blood: Bryony Marseilles." See also Adele Marseilles.

Joanna Belanger: Wife of Milton Belanger, a Methodist minister in Detroit, Michigan. Mother of spinster Adele Belanger (later Adele Marseilles). Died of scarlet fever. Mentioned briefly in "Before the Blood: Bryony Marseilles" – but not by name.

Milton Belanger: Married to Joanna Belanger, who is never mentioned by her first name. Father of spinster Adele Belanger (later Adele Marseilles). Methodist minister in Detroit, Michigan.

Died of scarlet fever. Mentioned briefly in "Before the Blood: Bryony Marseilles."

Gretchen Bell: Girlfriend and later wife of Pastor Algernon Demars. See also Gretchen Demars. Appears in briefly "Before The Blood: Henry Matthews," "Before The Blood: Bryony Simons," "The Phoenix," and "Call of the Siren." Mentioned in "Before The Blood: Bryony Marseilles."

Miss Bessel: A secretary at R.C. Walters advertising agency in the 1940s. Appears in "Before The Blood: Kellen Wechsler."

The Beverlys: A family who is expecting their sixth baby, thus beating out the Wechslers, who only have five children. Mentioned in "Before The Blood: Kellen Wechsler."

Charlie Berry: The clerk behind the counter at the Five and Dime in "Cornell Dyer and the Old Folks Home."

Bessie: Servant in laundry room. Briefly appears in "Before The Blood: Bryony Simons."

Abe Betts: Son of Paulie and Ida Betts. Briefly appears in "Before The Blood: Bryony Simons."

Clarissa Betts: Wife of Sebastian Betts. Mentioned in "Before The Blood: Bryony Marseilles" and "Before The Blood: Bryony Simons." Appears briefly in "Call of the Siren."

Denny Betts: Oldest son of Phoebe and Sebastian Betts. Brother of Susan Betts. Mentioned in "Before The Blood: Bryony Marseilles" and "Call of the Siren."

Freddie Betts: Son of Phoebe and Sebastian Betts. Brother of Susan Betts. Appears in "Before The Blood: Bryony Marseilles." Mentioned in "Before The Blood: Bryony Simons."

Ida Betts: Daughter of Gus and Pearl Griffith. Sister of Harv Griffith. Mother of Abe Betts, Ned Betts, Peter Betts (stillbirth). Appears in "Before The Blood: Bryony Marseilles" and "Before The Blood: Bryony Simons." Referenced as "a Munsonville girl" in "Call of the Siren." See also Ida Griffith.

Milton Betts: Son of Phoebe and Sebastian Betts. Brother of Susan Betts. Husband of Lillian Hasset Betts. Appears in "Before The Blood: Bryony Marseilles," "Before The Blood: Bryony Simons" and "The Phoenix." Mentioned in "Call of the Siren."

Ned Betts: Son of Paulie and Ida Betts. Briefly appears in "Before The Blood: Bryony Simons."

Paulie Betts: Son of Phoebe and Sebastian Betts. Brother of Susan Betts. Husband of Ida Griffith Betts. Father of Abe Betts, Bed Betts, and Peter Betts (stillborn). Appears in "Before The Blood: Bryony Marseilles," "Before The Blood: Bryony Simons" and "The Phoenix." Mentioned in "Call of the Siren."

Peter Betts: Stillborn son of Paulie and Ida Betts. Briefly appears in "Before The Blood: Bryony Simons."

Phoebe Betts: Wife of Sebastian Betts and mother of Denny Betts, Paulie Betts, Robbie Betts, Milton Betts, Freddie Betts, and Phoebe Betts. Appears in "Before The Blood: Bryony Marseilles."

Robbie Betts: Son of Phoebe and Sebastian Betts. Brother of Susan Betts. Appears in "Before The Blood: Bryony Marseilles." Mentioned in "Before The Blood: Bryony Simons."

Sebastian Betts: Master carpenter who arrives in Munsonville in its early years. Co-owner of Bass & Betts woodshop. Attended University of Michigan. First-elected mayor of Munsonville. Husband of Phoebe Betts and Clarice Betts. Father of Denny Betts, Paulie Betts, Robbie Betts, Milton Betts, Freddie Betts, and Phoebe Betts. Appears in "Before The Blood: Bryony Marseilles," Before The Blood: Bryony Simons," and "Call of the Siren." Mentioned in "The Phoenix."

Susan Betts: Daughter of Phoebe and Sebastian Betts. Best friend of Bryony Simons. Infatuated with Erland Borgstrom. Fiancé of Boswell Alaster Pike Jr. Mother of Sue Bass. Appears in "Before The Blood: Bryony Marseilles" and "Before The Blood: Bryony Simons."

Bill: Ship worker. Briefly appears in "Before The Blood: Kellen Wechsler."

Billy: Worker in Emmet Beal's tailor shop. Briefly appears in "Before The Blood: Kellen Wechsler."

Kitty Blanchard: A real American stage actress who was popular in the 1870s and 1880s. Referenced in "Call of the Siren."

Professor Hugh Blanchard: Music professor at the fictional Wesley Music Conservatory. Appears in Before The Blood: John Simons." Mentioned in "Before The Blood: Henry Matthews."

Blossom: Henry Matthews pet name for Dr. Sidney Stone's housekeeper. Mentioned in "Before The Blood: Henry Matthews."

Gil Blurode: Very early resident of Munsonville. Appears in "Before The Blood: Bryony Marseilles." Mentioned in "Call of the Siren."

Boatman: Unnamed reference in Charon, the ferryman in Greek mythology who takes souls across the rivers Acheron and Styx. Appears briefly in "Cornell Dyer and the Eerie Lake."

Catarin Bohnhorst: Catarin Wechsler: Resident of Grotekop, Germany, during the 30 Years War. Wife of Kellen Wechsler. Mother of Allecke Wechsler, Marige Wechsler, Jurgen Wechsler, Otto Wechsler, Hilmar Wechsler (son), Eugell Wechsler, Alheit Wechsler, Leveke Wechsler, Ruprech Wechsler, Statius Wechsler, Ludolph Wechsler, Nolthe Wechsler, Maren Wechsler, Bartold Wechsler, Hilmar Wechsler (daughter), Peternella Wechsler, Apolonia Wechsler, Kungund Wechsler, Danchmer Wechsler, Carsten Wechsler, a daughter whose name was "known only to the angels" (along with others). Appears in "Before The Blood: Kellen Wechsler." See also Catarin Wechsler.

Marie-Rosa Bonheur: Nineteenth century French artist known for her realistic paintings and sculptures of animals. Mentioned in "Before The Blood: Henry Matthews."

Arvid Borgstrom: Scandinavian fisherman who moves to Munsonville with his twin sons Erland Borgstrom and Erasmus Borgstrom. Possible lover of Sally Bass. Hanged for the murder of his wife Astrid Borgstrom. Appears in "Before The Blood: Bryony Simons." Mentioned in "Call of the Siren."

Astrid Borgstrom: Wife of Arvid Borgstrom, mother of the twins Erland Borgstrom and Erasmus Borgstrom. Referenced as Astrid Borgstrom in "Before The Blood: Bryony Marseilles" and as Runa Borgstrom in "Call of the Siren." See also Runa Borgstrom.

Erasmus Borgstrom: Non-English speaking son of Arvid Borgstrom. Twin brother of Erland Borgstrom. Briefly infatuated with Susan Betts. Married to Myrna Cooper. Appears in "Before The Blood: Bryony Marseilles" and "Before The Blood: Bryony Simons." Mentioned in "Call of the Siren."

Erland Borgstrom: Non-English speaking son of Arvid Borgstrom. Twin brother of Erasmus Borgstrom. Object of Susan Betts infatuation. Infatuated with Millicent Gothart. Appears in "Before The Blood: Bryony Marseilles" and "Before The Blood: Bryony Simons." Mentioned in "Call of the Siren."

Runa Borgstrom: Wife of Arvid Borgstrom, mother of the twins Erland Borgstrom and Erasmus Borgstrom. Referenced as Astrid Borgstrom in "Before The Blood: Bryony Marseilles" and as Runa Borgstrom in "Call of the Siren." See also Astrid Borgstrom.

Dion Boucicault: Nineteenth century Irish actor and playwright. Mentioned in "Bryony" and "Before The Blood: Henry Matthews."

William-Adolphe Bouguereau: Nineteenth century French artist who painted realistic classical themes with an emphasis on the nude female body. Mentioned in "Before The Blood: Henry Matthews."

General Georges Boulanger: French general and politician. Mentioned in "Before The Blood: Kellen Wechsler."

Pierre Bourgot: Sixteenth century French werewolf. Mentioned in "Lycanthropic Summer."

Judge Wilson Brewer: Sentenced Arvid Borgstrom to be hanged for the murder of his wife Astrid Borgstrom. Mentioned in "Before The Blood: Bryony Marseilles."

Josiah Brewster: Minister in the fictional Cape Crag, Maine, in colonial times. Mentioned in "Cornell Dyer and the Missing Tombstone."

Bridget: Domestic in the Jenson home of Dr. Sidney Stone. Briefly appears in "Before The Blood: Bryony Simons."

Morton Brooks: Butler at Simons Mansion. Appears briefly in "Bryony" and "Before The Blood: Bryony Simons.

Benjamin "Benjy" "Ben" Brown: son of nineteenth century Munsonville lumberjack Ben Brown. Mother is Laurel Brown. Sister of Lila Brown. Appears briefly in "Before The Blood: Bryony Simons." Mentioned in "Call of the Siren."

Ebenezer "Benny" Brown: Nineteenth century juggler at Hewes Music Hall in lower Manhattan. Appears in "Before The Blood: John Simons."

Joey Brown: Classmate of Melissa Marchellis at Munsonville School. Descendent of nineteenth century lumberjack Ben Brown. Son of Reverend Robert "Bobby" Brown and Mabel Brown.

Laurel Brown: Wife of Ben Brown. Mother of Lila Brown and Benjy Brown. Appears in "Before The Blood: Bryony Simons" and mentioned in "Call of the Siren."

Lila Brown: Daughter of Ben and Laurel Brown. Schoolteacher at Munsonville School. Married to Addison Drake. See also Lila Drake. Appears in "Before The Blood: Bryony Simons" and "Call of the Siren."

Matilda Brown: Daughter of Stuart Drake and Belinda Brake. Wife of lumberjack Benjy Brown. Mother of Ritchie Brown and Robbie

Brown. Works as a cook in Sue's Diner. Appears in "Before The Blood: Bryony Marseilles," "Before The Blood: Bryony Simons," "Call of the Siren," and "House on Top of the Hill." See also Matilda Drake.

Ritchie Brown: Son of Benjy and Matilda Drake Brown. Mentioned in "Call of the Siren." Appears in "House on To of the Hill."

Robbie Brown: Son of Benjy and Matilda Drake Brown. Mentioned in "Call of the Siren."

Albert Brumfeldt: Nineteenth century publisher and friend, colleague of Lord Girard. Mentioned in "Bryony." Appears in "Before The Blood: Henry Matthews," briefly in "Before The Blood: Bryony Simons," and in "The Phoenix."

Leland Buchanan: Business associate of Albert Brumfeldt and Lord Girard. Appears in "Before The Blood: Henry Matthews" and "Before The Blood: Bryony Simons."

Pearl S. Buck: A twentieth century American novelist, best known for "The Good Earth, for which Buck received the Pulitzer Prize in 1932. Mentioned in "Bryony."

Herr Builtemeyer: A councilman Seulobitz, a fictional town in Germany. Briefly appears in "Before The Blood: Kellen Wechsler."

Bumpy: One of the renegade Viking duo Gruff and Bumpy, who stole a treasure chest. Also known as. Olaf the Bumpy. Appears in "Cornell Dyer and the Missing Tombstone."

Burchard: Field laborer. Mentioned in "Before The Blood: Kellen Wechsler."

Burgermeister of Seulobitz: Mayor of a fictional town in Germany and the first to strike a bargain with Kellen Wechsler. Appears in "Before The Blood: Kellen Wechsler."

Celia Burneretta: The spoiled little sister of Elizabeth Burneretta, a piano student of John Simons. Briefly appears in "Before The Blood: John Simons."

Elizabeth Burneretta: A piano student of John Simons. Briefly appears in "Before The Blood: John Simons."

Mercy Burneretta: The spoiled little sister of Elizabeth Burneretta, a piano student of John Simons. Briefly appears in "Before The Blood: John Simons."

Rose Burneretta: The mother of Elizabeth Burneretta, a piano student of John Simons. Briefly appears in "Before The Blood: John Simons."

George Burroughs: Photographer at the New York Gazette. Mentioned in "Before The Blood: Henry Matthews."

Madelaine Burton: Sister of Molly Burton, one of the Never Robbers. Wife of Mike Olsen. Grandmother to supernatural super sleuth Cornell Dyer. The originator of the Madelaine effect. Appears in "Cornell Dyer and the Never Robbers." See also Madelaine Olsen.

Molly Burton: The newest and the youngest of the four Never Robbers. Sister of Madelaine Burton Olsen. Appears in "Cornell Dyer and the Never Robbers." Also appears briefly in "Cornell Dyer and the Eerie Lake."

Lord Byron: Full name is George Gordon Byron. English poet, most famous for "Don Juan." Author of the 183 poem "The Giaour," which is mentioned in "Before The Blood: Henry Matthews."

Mrs. Cady: Owner of a slop shop (a real nineteenth century store that sold ready-made, inexpensive clothing for me), who contacted out sewing work to Henry Matthews' mother and sisters. "Before The Blood: Henry Matthews."

Bishop Cafferty: One of the four Never Robbers. Appears in "Cornell Dyer and the Never Robbers."

Patti Cakes: Wannabe friend of Caryn Rochelle in "Lycanthropic Summer."

Ed Calkins, Steward of Tara: a real, sixty-something, proud of his Irish-heritage computer programmer and amateur writer who has also spent his entire life working in newspaper circulation. Years ago, Calkins invented a "ruthless dictator" alter ego, also known as "The Steward of Tara." With Calkins' permission, BryonySeries author Denise M. Baran-Unland furthered altered him to create a minor character in "Bryony," making Calkins the first Irish vampire of any significance. Of course, Calkins claims "Bryony" is really all about him, so he's held his own book signings, which he is calls, "The Ed Calkins Tour." There must be some truth in his sentiments, because Calkins' plot importance does grow with each novel in the original BryonySeries trilogy. Calkins is the author of "Ruthless" (his backstory) and "Denise M. Baran-Unland's Irish Genealogy." He also shares his writings on the BryonySeries blog. He appears in "Bryony," "Visage," and "Staked!"

Cameraman of Christmas Future: Briefly appears in "Cornell Dyer and the Flu."

Miss Bethany Ann Calloswick: A science teacher at Sunnystorm School in "Cornell Dyer and the Calcium Deficient Bones."

Mr. Carlson: Bus driver for Munsonville School. Appears in "Bryony:

Andrew Carnegie: American industrialist and philanthropist. Mentioned in "Before The Blood: John Simons

Lewis Carroll: Author of "Alice in Wonderland," "Through the Looking Glass." Referenced in "Before The Blood: Henry Matthews in terms of the Queen of Hearts (John Tenniel illustration) and "The Mock Turtle's Song."

Carol: Wannabe friend of Caryn Rochelle in "Lycanthropic Summer."

Johann Carolos: German publisher of the first newspaper called, "Relation aller Fürnemmen und gedenckwürdigen Historien" or "Account of all distinguished and commemorable stories." The World Association of Newspapers recognizes "The Relation" as the world's first newspaper. Referenced in "Before The Blood: Kellen Wechsler."

Carrynne: Fictional alter ego of Caryn Rochelle in "Lycanthropic Summer."

Dr. Donald Carter: Full-time dentist in Jenson. Part-time dentist in Munsonville, where he lives. Married to Laverne Carter. Father of Leslie Carter and Greg Carter. Appears in "House on Top of the Hill" and "Brainy Ann."

Greg Carter: Son of Donald Carter and Laverne Carter. Brother of Leslie Carter. Bus boy at Munsonville Inn. Student teacher at

Munsonville School. Appear in "Bryony," "House on Top of the Hill," and "Brainy Ann."

Leslie Carter: Waitress at Sue's Diner. Daughter of Donald Carter and Laverne Carter. Sister of Gregory Carter, who is the student teacher in "Bryony." Appears in "House on Top of the Hill," and "Brainy Ann."

Laverne Carter: Socialite wife of Dr. Donald Carter. Brings 1950s tea parties to Munsonville. Mother of Leslie Carter and Greg Carter. Appears in "House on Top of the Hill" and "Brainy Ann."

Herr Willeken Casendorppe: Alter ego of Kellen Wechsler and phony nephew of the Burgermeister of Seulobitz, mayor of a fictional town in Germany. Kellen uses this in "Before The Blood: Kellen Wechsler."

Seymour Cassidy: Oblate of the fictional St. Romanos Monastery in the Kurd Mountains. Renowned pianist and piano teacher. Appears in "Before The Blood: John Simons," "Before The Blood: Kellen Wechsler," and "Before The Blood: Henry Matthews." Mentioned in "Before The Blood: Bryony Marseilles" and "Before The Blood: Bryony Simons." Also known as Maestro.

Mrs. Catterling: Housekeeper to the to-good-to-be-true Watson family, where three of its children were piano students of John Simons. Briefly mentioned in "Before The Blood: John Simons."

Charlie Charleston: Supernatural super sleuth Cornell Dyer's guide in "Cornell Dyer and the Flu."

Charles: Domestic at Abbott Simons' Fifth Avenue home. Briefly appears in "Before The Blood: John Simons."

Charon: The ferryman in Greek mythology who takes souls across the rivers Acheron and Styx. Appears briefly in "Cornell Dyer and the Eerie Lake."

Chaucer: Full name is Geoffrey Chaucer, author of The Canterbury Tales, seventeen tales that a fictional group of pilgrims tell as a story competition. Known as the "father of English literature" and the "father of English poetry."

Chrissy: A little girl that Cara Miller, older sister of Katie Miller, occasionally babysits. Mentioned briefly in "Katie and the Big Fear."

Markham Churn: Beulah County assessor. Mentioned briefly in "Before The Blood: Bryony Marseilles."

George Clare: Nineteenth century journalist from Gevaudan, France. He lives as a vagabond with his family, forever seeking "the big story." Secondary character in "The Phoenix."

Isabella Clare: Heiress and wife to George Clare. Secondary character in "The Phoenix."

Marie Clare: George and Isabella's twelve-year-old daughter. Protagonist in "The Phoenix.

Mrs. Claridon: A society woman mentioned briefly in "Before The Blood: John Simons."

Astor G. Clarke: Head of the English Department in the mid to late nineteenth century at Jenson College of the Liberal Arts and member of the Munsonville Society for the Humanities. Appears in several volumes of "Before The Blood: Bryony Marseilles, Henry Matthews, and Bryony Simons.

June Clements: Librarian at Munsonville Library. Appears in "Bryony," "Staked!," "House on Top of the Hill," and "Julie and the Too-Hard Homework."

President Grover Cleveland: United States president from 1885 to 1889 and from 1893 to 1897. Invites John Simons to play at The White House in "Before The Blood: Bryony Simons."

François-Henri Clicquot: French organ builder in the eighteenth century. Mentioned briefly in "Before The Blood: Kellen Wechsler."

Old Mrs. Clutterbuck: Eleanor's caretaker in "Cornell Dyer and the Eerie Lake."

Felix Coates: Reported on the Hudson River Valley's abundant grape crop. Mentioned briefly in "Before The Blood: Henry Matthews."

Jared Cole: Sheriff for Livingston County. Evansville is in Livingston County. Mentioned by name in "Before The Blood: Henry Matthews."

Robert "Bob" Collyer: American Unitarian clergyman, who presided over P.T. Barnum's funeral services. "We will try the matter and see how it works" was a response he often gave his wife. Appears in "Before The Blood: Bryony Simons."

Colpa: Official wife of the fictional Ed Calkins, Steward of Tara, artist, and art mentor to Laura Jones, one of Melissa Marchellis' friends from Grover's Park. Mentioned in "Bryony" and "Visage." Appears briefly in "Staked!" Also known as Colpa Ivanovich.

Contessa de la Palacio: A fictional client of the renowned fictional piano master Seymour Cassidy.

Gertrude Cook: A guest at Spencer Inn on Christmas Eve. Married to Gunther Cook. Briefly appears in "Before The Blood: John Simons."

Gunther Cook: A guest at Spencer Inn on Christmas Eve. Married to Gertrude Cook. Briefly appears in "Before The Blood: John Simons."

Pastor Fletcher Cooke: Pastor in Cape Crag, Maine. Appears in "Cornell Dyer and the Missing Tombstone."

Ann Cooper: Wife of Jack Cooper. Born and raised in Munsonville. Mother of Lauren Cooper and Trenton Cooper. Appears as Ann Cooper in "Visage" and "Staked!" See also Ann Dalton.

Bob Cooper: Fisherman and owner of Sue's Diner. Son of Mitchell and Ruth Cooper. Appears in "Bryony" and "House on Top of the Hill."

Jack Cooper: Son of Bob and Janice Cooper. Appears in "Brainy Ann," Julie and the Too-Hard Homework," Katie and the Big Fear," "Bryony," "Visage," "Staked!"

Erin Cooper: One of the ministering spirits. Wife of Miles Cooper. Mother of Mary Katherine Cooper and Mitchell Eugene Cooper. Daughter of Eugene and Kate Miller. Sister of Alannah Miller Hasset, Briana Miller, Caitlín Miller, Dana Miller Harper, Fiona Miller, Isleen Miller, and Ailbe Miller. Good with flowers. Appears in "Before The Blood: Bryony Marseilles, "Before The Blood: Bryony Simons, and "Call of the Siren." See also Erin Miller

Matt Cooper: Son of Mitch and Mary Cooper. Brother to Mona Cooper Griffith, Myrna Cooper Dalton, Miles Cooper, and Maudie Cooper. Appears briefly in "Before The Blood: Bryony Simons."

Mary Cooper: Wife of Mitchell Cooper. Sister-in-law of Eugene Miller and Kate Miller. Mother of Mona Cooper Griffith, Myrna Cooper Dalton, Matt Cooper, Miles Cooper, and Maudie Cooper. Appears briefly in "Before The Blood: Bryony Simons" and "Call of the Siren."

Mitchell Cooper: Husband of Mary Cooper. Brother-in-law of Eugene Miller and Kate Miller. Father of Mona Cooper Griffith, Myrna Cooper Dalton, Matt Cooper, Miles Cooper, and Maudie Cooper. Sings cowboy songs with Eugene Miller on Munson Day. Appears briefly in "Before The Blood: Bryony Simons."

Mary Katherine Cooper: Daughter of Miles and Erin Miller Cooper. Sister of Mitchell Eugene Cooper. Died in childhood. Mentioned briefly in "Call of the Siren."

Mitchell Eugene Cooper: Son of Miles and Erin Miller Cooper. Brother of Mary Katherine Cooper. Wife of Ruth Cooper. Father of Bob Cooper. Appears in "Call of the Siren" and "House on Top of the Hill."

Maudie Cooper: Daughter of Mitch and Mary Cooper. Youngest sister to Mona Cooper Griffith, Myrna Cooper Dalton, Matt Copper, Miles Cooper. Appears briefly in "Before The Blood: Bryony Simons" and "Call of the Siren."

Miles Cooper: Son of Mitch and Mary Cooper. Brother to Mona Cooper Griffith, Myrna Cooper Dalton, Matt Cooper, and Maudie

Cooper. Appears briefly in "Before The Blood: Bryony Simons" and "Call of the Siren."

Mona Cooper: Daughter of Mitch and Mary Cooper. Sister to Myrna Cooper Dalton, Matt Copper, Miles Cooper, and Maudie Cooper. Appears briefly in "Before The Blood: Bryony Simons" and "Call of the Siren." See also Mona Griffith.

Myrna Cooper: Daughter of Mitch and Mary Cooper. Sister to Mona Cooper Griffith, Matt Copper, Miles Cooper, and Maudie Cooper. Wife of William Dalton. Mother of Kathleen Dalton and Robert Dalton. Appears briefly in "Before The Blood: Bryony Simons" and "Call of the Siren." See Also Myrna Dalton

Douglas "Doug" Copeland: Owner of Munsonville Inn. Husband of Marion "Merry" Copeland. Father of Evelyn Copeland Chandler. Appears in "Call of the Siren" and "House on Top of the Hill."

Marion "Merry" Copeland: Owner of Munsonville Inn. Wife of Doug Copeland, and mother of Evelyn Copeland Chandler. Appears in "Call of the Siren" and "House on Top of the Hill."

Falconer Cremmins: Employee of Hewes Music Hall. Suspected of arson. Mentioned in "Before The Blood: John Simons."

Joe Culpter: Business associate of Owen Munson and Clyde Fisher. Husband of Miranda Culpter. Mentioned by name in "Before The Blood: Bryony Marseilles."

Miranda Culpter: Wife of Joe Culpter. Mentioned by name in "Before The Blood: Bryony Marseilles."

Cumans: A nomadic Turkic people from present-day southern Russia in the tenth to thirteenth centuries.

Priscilla Cummings: A sullen Bible study student in Jenson College. She wore an oversized man's suit and a bowler and chewed Blackjack gum. Appears in "Before The Blood: Henry Matthews."

Lady Harriet Cumnor: A character in Elizabeth Gaskell's "Wives and Daughters." Mentioned by name in "Before The Blood: Bryony Marseilles."

Erika Cusatelli: A character who appears in a short story in "Lycanthropic Summer."

Anna Czarnecki: Young daughter of Bryga Czarnecki, housekeeper at Simons Mansion. Wife of Peter Marchellis. Mother of Frank Marchellis. Grandmother of Melissa Marchellis and Brian Marchellis. Appears in "Bryony," "Staked!," "Before The Blood, Bryony Simons," "The Phoenix," "Call of the Siren," and "House on Top of the Hill." See also Anna Marchellis.

Bryga Czarnecki: Housekeeper for Abbott Simons and (later) John Simons at Simons Mansion. Appears in "Bryony," "Staked!," "Before The Blood: John Simons," and "Before The Blood: Bryony Simons." Mentioned by name in "The Phoenix."

Richard Dadd: Painter of 'The Fairy Feller's Master-Stroke." Mentioned by name in "Before The Blood: Henry Matthews."

Dagobert: Hessian solder. Appear in "Cornell Dyer and the 'Mistical' Being."

Ann Dalton: Munsonville girl, the first to befriend Melissa Marchellis. Daughter of Rob Dalton and May Dalton. Sister to Clay Dalton. Appears in "Bryony," "Visage," "Staked!," and "Brainy Ann."

Clay Dalton: Munsonville boy and best friend of Brian Marcellis. the first to befriend Melissa Marchellis. Son of Rob Dalton and Mae Dalton. Brother to Ann Dalton. Appears in "Bryony" and "Brainy Ann." Mentioned in "Staked!"

May Dalton: Wife of Rob Dalton. Mother of Ann Dalton and Clay Dalton. Daughter of Jan Swenson and Colette Swenson. Sister of Gabe Swenson. Appears in "Bryony," Lycanthropic Summer," "Julie and the Too-Hard Homework," Katie and the Big Fear," Brainy Ann," and "House on Top of the Hill." See also May Swenson.

Robert "Rob" Dalton: Husband of May Dalton. Father of Ann Dalton and Clay Dalton. Appears in "Bryony," Lycanthropic Summer," "Julie and the Too-Hard Homework," Katie and the Big Fear," Brainy Ann," and "House on Top of the Hill."

William "Bill" Dalton: Reporter for The Munsonville Times. Husband of Myrna Cooper Dalton. Father of Kathleen Dalton and Robert Dalton. Appears in "Call of the Siren" and "House on Top of the Hill."

Ethan Damien: A doctor who hired John Simons to play piano for a party. Mentioned in "Before The Blood: John Simons."

Danika: Friend of Henry Matthews. Appears briefly in "Bryony."

Dick Darrow: Caryn Rochelle's prom date in "Lycanthropic Cummer."

Lila Davis: Woman who cooks and cleans for John Simons in exchange for piano lessons for her daughter Mary Davis. Appears briefly in "Before The Blood: John Simons."

Mary Davis: Daughter of Lila Davis. Mentioned "Before The Blood: John Simons."

Tillie Davis: Sister of Lila Davis. She also cooks and cleans for John Simons in exchange for piano lessons for her son Teddy Davis. Appears briefly in "Before The Blood: John Simons."

Teddy Davis: Son of Tillie Davis. Mentioned "Before The Blood: John Simons."

Claude Debussy: French composer of the late nineteenth and early twentieth centuries. Mentioned in "Before The Blood: Kellen Wechsler" and "Before The Blood: Bryony Simons."

Delbert: A resident of Paradise Falls in "Cornell Dyer and the Old Folks Home."

Eugène Delacroix: French Romantic artist. Mentioned in "Before The Blood: Henry Matthews."

Sister Maria DeLourdes: The other name of Agnes King. Referenced this way in "Before The Blood: Bryony Simons" and "The Phoenix."

Algernon Demars: Former student of Rev. Galien Marseilles. Theology teacher and leader of a Bible study at Jenson College. Open first school in Thornton. Member of the Munsonville Society for the Humanities. Husband of Gretchen Bell Demars. Pastor at Munsonville Congregational Church. Mayor of Munsonville. Appears in "Before The Blood: Bryony Marseilles," "Before The Blood: Henry Matthews," "Before The Blood: Bryony Simons," The Phoenix," and "Call of the Siren."

Gretchen Demars: Wife of Algernon Demars. Teacher of the younger children at Thornton's first school. Teacher at Munsonville School. Mentioned in "Before The Blood: Bryony Marseilles." Appears briefly in "Before The Blood: Bryony Simons," "The Phoenix" and "Call of the Siren." See also Gretchen Bell.

Lou Denison: Insurance salesman. Munsonville village board member. Husband of Lydia Harper, daughter of Jasper Harper and Dana Miller Harper. Appears briefly in "Call of the Siren" and "House on Top of the Hill."

Mrs. Denison: Algebra II and grammar teacher at Munsonville School. Appears in "Bryony."

Mr. Dexter: Butcher in Jenson. Mentioned in "Before The Blood: Henry Matthews."

Dick: Boy worker on a cargo ship. Appears briefly in "Before The Blood: Kellen Wechsler."

Charles Dickens: Social critic and regarded by some as the greatest novelist of the nineteenth century. Mentioned in "Before The Blood: John Simons" and "Before the Blood: Bryony Simons."

Emily Dickinson: Nineteenth century American poet, who was unknown in life and lauded for her importance in American poetry after her death. Mentioned in "Bryony."

Marlene Dietrich: German American motion-picture actress from the 1910s to the 1970s. Mentioned in "Before The Blood: Kellen Wechsler."

Bert Dobbins: Mediocre comedian at Hewes Music Hall. Appears in "Before The Blood: John Simons."

Gustave Doré: French artist, best known for illustrating Dante's "Inferno." Mentioned in "Before The Blood: Bryony Simons."

Fyodor Dostoyevsky: Russian novelist, best known for "Crime and Punishment" (1866) and "The Brothers Karamazov (1880)." Mentioned in "Before The Blood: Henry Matthews."

Jacques Doucet: French fashion designer and known as the pioneer of haute couture. Mentioned in "Call of the Siren."

Mayor Dick Dougherty: Farmer. Mayor of Evansville. Husband of Meg Dougherty. Appears in "Before The Blood: Henry Matthews."

Meg Dougherty: Wife of Dick Dougherty. Gossip and good cook. Appears in "Before The Blood: Henry Matthews."

Addison Drake: Eldest son of Stuart Drake and Belinda Drake. Eventual owner of Drake's General Store. Married to Lila Brown Drake. Appears on "Before The Blood: Bryony Marseilles," "Before The Blood: Bryony Simons," "Call of the Siren," and "House on Top of the Hill."

Alexander "Alex" Drake: Munsonville barber. Son of Paul Drake and Phyllis Drake. Sister of Amanda Drake. Husband of Elizabeth "Betty" Drake." Father of Samuel Drake and Sheldon Drake. Mentioned in "Call of the Siren." Appears in "House on Top of the Hill."

Amanda Drake: Daughter of Paul Drake and Phyllis Drake. Sister of Amanda Drake. Wife of Ailbe Miller. Mother of Gerald Miller after three stillbirths. Appears in "Call of the Siren" and "House on Top of the Hill."

Barbara Drake: Wife of Sam Drake. Mother of Julie Drake. Appears in "Julie and the Too-Hard Homework." Appears briefly in "Bryony," "Lycanthropic Summer," "Katie and the Big Fear," "Brainy Ann," and "House on Top of the Hill."

Belinda Drake: Daughter of Patrick Solomon. Wife of Stuart Drake, owner of Drake's Store. Mother of Addison Drake, Norton Drake, and Matilda Drake. Appears in "Before The Blood: Bryony Marseilles," "Before the Blood: Bryony Simons," and "Call of the Siren."

Lila Drake: Daughter of Ben and Laurel Brown. Schoolteacher at Munsonville School. Married to Addison Drake. See also Lila Brown. Appears in "Before The Blood: Bryony Simons" and "Call of the Siren."

Julie Drake: Daughter of Sam Drake and Barbara Drake. Friends with Ann Dalton, Katie Miller, Melissa Marchellis. Wife of David Drake (David's name is never mentioned, except that he took Julie's last name when they were married). Julie and David are both psychologists. Appears in "Bryony," "Visage," "Staked!," "House on Top of the Hill," "Julie and the Too-Hard Homework," "Katie and the Big Fear," and "Brainy Ann."

Matilda Drake: Daughter of Stuart Drake and Belinda Brake. Wife of lumberjack Benjy Brown. Mother of Ritchie Brown and Robbie Brown. Works as a cook in Sue's Diner. Appears in "Before The Blood: Bryony Marseilles," "Before The Blood: Bryony Simons," "Call of the Siren," and "House on Top of the Hill." See also Matilda Brown.

Maggie Drake: Daughter of Joe Harper and Linda Harper. Sister of Percy Harper and Jasper Harper. Wife of Norton Drake. Works at

Munsonville Inn. Mentioned in "Before The Blood: Bryony Marseilles." Appears briefly in "Before The Blood: Bryony Simons." Appears in "Call of the Siren."

Norton Drake: Youngest son of Stuart Drake and Belinda Drake. Eventual owner of Drake's General Store. Married to Maggie Harper Drake. Appears on "Before The Blood: Bryony Marseilles," "Before The Blood: Bryony Simons," and "Call of the Siren."

Paul Drake: Illegitimate son of Stuart Drake. Wife of Phyllis Drake. Father of Amanda Drake Miller and Alexander Drake. Barber at Munsonville Inn.

Sam Drake: Son of Alexander Drake and Josephine Goddard Drake. Husband to Barbara Drake. Father of Julie Drake. Appears briefly "Visage." Appears in "Julie and the Too-Hard Homework," "Katie and the Big Fear," and "Brainy Ann."

Stuart Drake: Husband to Belinda Solomon Drake. Father of Paul Drake, Addison Drake, Norton Drake, and Belinda Drake. Owner of Drake's Store. "Appears in "Before The Blood: Bryony Marseilles."

Lucille DuBois: Hires supernatural super sleuth Cornell Dyer. Appears in "Cornell Dyer and the Missing Tombstone."

Howard Dumond: John Simons' valet. Mentioned in "Bryony." Appears briefly in "Before The Blood" Bryony Simons."

Danny the Dustman: Associate of the Matthews' family. Appears briefly in "Before The Blood: Henry Matthews."

Cornell Dyer: Supernatural super sleuth who travels around the United States in a motor home solving supernatural mysteries. Wife of Katie Miller Dyer. Father to Karla Dyer. Briefly mentioned in

"Staked!" Appears in "Visage" and all of The Adventures of Cornell Dyer chapter books. Also known as Professor Cornell Dyer (Cornell prefers this name).

Karla Dyer: Best friend to John-Peter Simotes. Daughter of Cornell Dyer and Katie Miller Dyer. Has extrasensory abilities. Appears in "Staked!" and "Karla Joins In."

Katie Dyer: Daughter of Gerald and Katie Miller. Sister of Gerald Miller Jr., Al Miller, Ben Miller, Russ Miller, Will Miller, Eric Miller, Pete Miller, Nate Miller, and Cara Miller Larvey. Widow of supernatural super sleuth Cornell Dyer. Mother of Karla Dyer. Graduate of Molly Blake School of Beauty in Jenson. Works at Klever Cuts in Jenson. Appears in "Bryony," "Visage," "Staked!," "Katie and the Big Fear," "Julie and the Too-Hard Homework," "Brainy Ann," "Karla Joins In," and "House on Top of the Hill." See also Katie Miller.

Catherine Eddowes: One of Jack the Ripper's victims. Mentioned in "Before The Blood: Henry Mathews."

Thomas Edison: American businessman and inventor. Mentioned in "Before The Blood: John Simons," Before The Blood: Kellen Wechsler," and "Before The Blood: Bryony Simons."

Gustave Eiffel: A French civil engineer best known for the Eiffel tower. Mentioned in "Before The Blood: Kellen Wechsler."

Adah Elbert: Daughter and caretaker of Jasper Harper and Dana Miller Harper. Wife of Dickie Elbert. Mother of Joan Elbert. Appears in "House on Top of the Hill."

Dickie Elbert: Accountant. Member of Munsonville's Village Board. Married to Adah Harper Elbert. Father for Joan Elbert, the

Miss Elbert who later teaches at Munsonville School. Appears briefly in "Call of the Siren." Appears in "House on Top of the Hill."

Joan Elbert: The spinster Miss Elbert who teaches at Munsonville School. Appears in "House on Top of the Hill," "Bryony" and "Staked!"

Eleanor: Love of interest of Jack in "Cornell Dyer and the Eerie Lake."

Ralph Waldo Emerson: American essayist, philosopher, and poet. Mentioned in "Before The Blood: Bryony Marseilles

Sam Engerson: Stablemaster at Simons Mansion. Briefly mentioned in "Bryony" and "Before The Blood: Bryony Simons."

Ephraim: The name given to Seymour Cassidy by the monks at St. Romanus Monastery. Mentioned in "Before The Blood: Kellen Wechsler."

Charles Erler: Homesteader who spends Christmas Eve at Spencer Inn. Mentioned in "Before The Blood: John Simons."

Auguste Escoffier: French culinary artist and inventor of 5,000 recipes. Known as "the king of chefs and the chef of kings." Mentioned in "Before The Blood: Kellen Wechsler" and "Before The Blood: Bryony Simons."

Estelle: Servant girl at Arcadia. Appears in "Before The Blood: Henry Matthews."

Margaret "Ma" Evans: Early resident of Cape Crag, Maine. Housekeeper of Josiah Brewster. Appears in "Cornell Dyer and the Missing Tombstone."

Frost Fairy: A character in "Cornell Dyer and the Whispering Wardrobe."

Falko: A resident of the fictional Grotekop, Germany. Briefly appears in "Before The Blood: Kellen Wechsler."

Fanny: Servant at the Jenson home of Dr. Hiram Rush and his wife Amelia Rush. Appears briefly in "Before The Blood: Henry Matthews."

Alex Fate: Munsonville hack driver. Second husband of Linda Harper Fate. Appears in "Before The Blood: Bryony Marseilles," "Before The Blood: Henry Matthews," "Before The Blood: Bryony Simons," and "Call of the Siren." Mentioned in "The Phoenix."

Linda Fate: Wife of Joe Harper and Alex Fate. Mother of Maggie Harper Drake, Percy Harper, and Jasper Harper. A cook with her daughter Maggie Harper at Simons Mansion and Munsonville Inn. Appears in "Before The Blood: Bryony Simons" and "Call of the Siren." See also Linda Fate.

Jim Feigel: Munsonville postmaster. Husband of Vicki Feigel. Father of Tommy Feigel. Appears in "House on Top of the Hill" and "Brainy Ann."

Tommy Feigel: Munsonville handyman. Son of Jim Feigel and Vicki Feigel. Appears in "House on Top of the Hill," "Katie and the Big Fear," and "Brainy Ann."

Vicki Feigel: Munsonville postal worker Wife of Jim Feigel. Mother of Tommy Feigel. Appears in "House on Top of the Hill," "Katie and the Big Fear," and "Brainy Ann."

Marshall Field: American entrepreneur and the founder of the Chicago-based department stores known as Marshall Field and Company. Mentioned in "Before The Blood: Henry Matthews."

Nancy Fish: Second wife of P.T. Barnum. Married to Barnum by famed American Unitarian preacher Robert Collyer. Appears in "Before The Blood: Bryony Simons."

Clyde Fisher: Cowboy. Early resident of Munsonville. Good friend of Owen Munson. Great uncle of James Fisher and family. Founder of Fisher Farm. Appears in "Before The Blood: Bryony Marseilles" and "Before The Blood: Bryony Simons." Mentioned briefly in "Bryony." Also known as Old Man Fisher and Grandpa Clyde.

Daisy Fisher: Daughter of James Fisher and Maybelle Fisher. Sister of Rose Fisher, Lilac Fisher, Iris Fisher, Heather Fisher, Marigold Fisher, Jasmine Fisher, and Violet Fisher. Tomboy. Appears in "Before The Blood: Bryony Marseilles." Mentioned in "Before The Blood: Bryony Simons" and "Call of the Siren."

Heather Fisher: Daughter of James Fisher and Maybelle Fisher. Sister of Rose Fisher, Daisy Fisher, Lilac Fisher, Iris Fisher, Marigold Fisher, Jasmine Fisher, and Violet Fisher. Loves to sing. Honorary cowgirl, Appears in "Before The Blood: Bryony Marseilles." Mentioned in "Before The Blood: Bryony Simons" and "Call of the Siren."

Iris Fisher: Daughter of James Fisher and Maybelle Fisher. Sister of Rose Fisher, Daisy Fisher, Lilac Fisher, Heather Fisher, Marigold Fisher, Jasmine Fisher, and Violet Fisher. Engaged to Leo Hasset. Pretty in an ethereal way. Loves flowers. Appears in "Before The Blood: Bryony Marseilles." Mentioned in "Before The Blood: Bryony Simons" and "Call of the Siren."

James Fisher: Early resident of Munsonville. Nephew to Clyde Fisher. Husband of Maybelle Fisher. Father of Rose Fisher, Lilac Fisher, Daisy Fisher, Iris Fisher, Heather Fisher, Marigold Fisher, Jasmine Fisher, and Violet Fisher. Owner of Fisher Farm. Mayor of Munsonville. Mentioned briefly in "Bryony" and "The Phoenix." Appears in "Before The Blood: Bryony Marseilles," "Before The Blood: Bryony Simons," and "Call of the Siren."

Jasmine Fisher: Daughter of James Fisher and Maybelle Fisher. Sister of Rose Fisher, Daisy Fisher, Lilac Fisher, Iris Fisher, Heather Fisher, Marigold Fisher, and Violet Fisher. Appears in "Before The Blood: Bryony Marseilles," "Before The Blood: Bryony Simons" and "Call of the Siren."

Lilac Fisher: Daughter of James Fisher and Maybelle Fisher. Sister of Rose Fisher, Daisy Fisher, Iris Fisher, Heather Fisher, Marigold Fisher, Jasmine Fisher, and Violet Fisher. Gentle and shy. Appears in "Before The Blood: Bryony Marseilles." Mentioned in "Before The Blood: Bryony Simons" and "Call of the Siren."

Marigold Fisher: Daughter of James Fisher and Maybelle Fisher. Sister of Rose Fisher, Daisy Fisher, Lilac Fisher, Iris Fisher, Heather Fisher, Jasmine Fisher, and Violet Fisher. Appears in "Before The Blood: Bryony Marseilles," "Before The Blood: Bryony Simons" and "Call of the Siren."

Maybelle Fisher: Early resident of Munsonville. Wife of James Fisher. Father of Rose Fisher, Lilac Fisher, Daisy Fisher, Iris Fisher, Heather Fisher, Marigold Fisher, Jasmine Fisher, and Violet Fisher. Mentioned briefly in "Bryony" and "The Phoenix." Appears in "Before The Blood: Bryony Marseilles," "Before The Blood: Bryony Simons," and "Call of the Siren."

Old Man Fisher: See Clyde Fisher.

Rose Fisher: Oldest daughter of James Fisher and Maybelle Fisher. Sister of Lilac Fisher, Daisy Fisher, Iris Fisher, Heather Fisher, Marigold Fisher, Jasmine Fisher, and Violet Fisher. Engaged to Leo Hasset. Appears in "Before The Blood: Bryony Marseilles." Mentioned in "Before The Blood: Bryony Simons" and "Call of the Siren."

Violet Fisher: Daughter of James Fisher and Maybelle Fisher. Sister of Rose Fisher, Daisy Fisher, Lilac Fisher, Iris Fisher, Heather Fisher, Marigold Fisher, and Jasmine Fisher. Appears in "Before The Blood: Bryony Marseilles," "Before The Blood: Bryony Simons" and "Call of the Siren."

Rev. Preston Fithian: Fictional preacher from Ohio, referenced in "Before The Blood: Bryony Marseilles."

F. Scott Fitzgerald: A twentieth century American short story writer and novelist, especially known for his novel "The Great Gatsby." Mentioned in "Bryony."

Mrs. Fitzgerald: Fifth and sixth grade teacher at Munsonville School. Appears in "Julie and the Too-Hard Homework" and "Brainy Ann."

Herr Curth Flechtemann: Sausage-stuffer in the fictional Grotekop, Germany. Appears briefly in "Before The Blood: Kellen Wechsler."

Flynn: Owner and cook in a diner enroute to Paradise Falls in "Cornell Dyer and the Old Folks Home."

Mariano Fortuny: Spanish polymath, artist and fashion designer. Mentioned in "Call of the Siren."

Bryson Fox: Owner of Munsonville Inn. Appears in "Call of the Siren."

Francois: Henry Matthews' art teacher at Arcadia. Mentioned in "Before The Blood: Henry Matthews."

Wyndham Franklin: Raised Morgan horses in New Haven Connecticut. Engaged to Martha Spencer. Briefly appears in "Before The Blood: John Simons."

Gladys Fredericks: Cook at Simons Mansion. Mentioned in "Bryony" and "Before The Blood: Bryony Simons."

Joe Fredericks: Head gardener at Simons Mansion. Mentioned in "Bryony."

Jason Frye: Classmate of Melissa Marchellis, Shelly Gallagher, Laura Jones, and Kimberly Whitney in Grovers Park. Works part-time at Pizza Express. Overseas missionary. Pastor at Munsonville Congregational Church. Love interests included Laura Jones and Melissa Marchellis. Appears in "Bryony," "Visage," "Staked!" and "House on Top of the Hill."

Horace Fuller: Editor of the Evansville Courier. Appears in "Before The Blood: Henry Matthews" and briefly in "The Phoenix."

Gabriel: Angel. Briefly and fictionally appears in "Before The Blood: Henry Matthews."

Shelly Gallagher: Friend of Melissa Marchellis, Shelley Gallagher, Laura Jones, and Kimberly Whitney in Grovers Park. Appears in

"Bryony," "Visage," "Staked!," "Changes for Shelly," A Room for Laura," and "Melissa and the Hidden Treasure."

Mr. Ganley: Owner of a used car lot in Jenson. Mentioned in "Katie and the Big Fear."

Gilles Garnier, The Werewolf of Dole: Sixteenth century French werewolf. Appears in "Lycanthropic Summer."

Elizabeth Gaskell: Author of "Wives and Daughters." Mentioned in "Before The Blood: Bryony Marseilles."

Mayor Gazelle: Appears in "Cornell Dyer and the Eerie Lake."

George: Boy worker on a cargo ship. Appears in "Before The Blood: Kellen Wechsler."

Georges: Henry's valet at Arcadia. Appear briefly in "Before The Blood: Henry Matthews."

Geronimo: An Apache leader and medicine man. Mentioned in "Before The Blood: John Simons."

Gibbs: Butler at Abbott Simons' Fifth Avenue home. Husband of Janie Gibbs. Father of Nora Gibbs. Appears briefly in "Before The Blood: John Simons."

Janie Gibbs: Cook at Abbott Simons' Fifth Avenue home. Wife of Gibbs. Mother of Nora Gibbs. Appears briefly in "Before The Blood: John Simons."

Nora Gibbs: Housemaid at Abbott Simons' Fifth Avenue home. Daughter of Gibbs and Janie Gibbs. Appears briefly in "Before The Blood: John Simons."

Gilmore and his Brass Band: Patrick Gilmore was a real American bandmaster and innovator in instrumentation. Leader of the New York 22nd Regiment Band (also called Gilmore's Band), which toured Europe. Mentioned in "Before The Blood: John Simons."

Ghost Girl: Sue Bass' nickname for Anna Czarnecki Marchellis. Appears in "Call of the Siren." See also Anna Czarnecki and Anna Marchellis.

Goosey Girl: Caitlin Miller's pet name for Sue Bass in "Call of the Siren."

Jeannine Girad: Husband of Louis Girard. Mother of Lawrence and Louise Girard/Caroline Matthews. Mentioned in "Before The Blood: Henry Matthews."

Lawrence "Lord" Girard: Powerful behind-the-scenes businessman. Lover of Albert Brumfeldt. Son of Louis Girard and Jeannine Girard. Brother of Louise Girard/Caroline Matthews. Appears in "Before The Blood: Henry Matthews." Mentioned (as Lord Girard) in "Before The Blood: John Simons" and "Before The Blood: Bryony Simons." Appears in flashback in "The Phoenix." Also known as Lord Girard.

Lord Girard: See Lawrence "Lord" Girard.

Louis Girard: Wife of Jeannine Girard. Father to Lawrence Girard and Louise Girard/Caroline Matthews. Mentioned in "Before The Blood: Henry Matthews."

Louise Girard: Daughter of Louis Girard and Jeannine Girard. Sister of Lawrence Girard. Wife of Harold Matthews. Mother of Henrietta "Etta" Matthews Markham, Charlotte "Lottie" Matthews, Margaret "Maggie" Matthews, Elizabeth "Lizzie" Matthews,

Katherine "Kitty" Matthews, and Henry "Hankie" Matthews Appears in "Before The Blood: Henry Matthews." See also Caroline Matthews.

Dr. Tilton Gladstone: Doctor at Jenson Memorial Hospital. Mentioned in "Call of the Siren." Appears briefly in "Before The Blood: Henry Matthews."

Vincent Van Gogh: Dutch painter. He created 2100 pieces of art in a decade. Approximately 860 of them were oils he painted in the last two years of his life. Mentioned in "Before The Blood: Kellen Wechsler" and "Before The Blood: Bryony Simons."

Abigail Goodwin: A witch in Cape Crag, Maine in "Cornell Dyer and the Missing Tombstone."

Dr. Edwin Gothart: A doctor who practices in Munsonville and Jenson Memorial Hospital. Physician to Elizabeth Bathory. Strong knowledge of hematology (blood and blood disorders). Appears in "Before The Blood: John Simons," "Before The Blood: Kellen Wechsler," "Before The Blood: Bryony Marseilles," "Before The Blood: Henry Matthews," "Before The Blood: Bryony Simons," "The Phoenix," "Call of the Siren," "House on Top of the Hill," "Snowbell," "Bryony," "Visage," and "Staked!" See also Dr. Brandon Gradthorn, Dr. Arnold Hartgerd, Dr. Alvin Thradgort, and Dr. Abner Rothgard.

Millicent Gothart: Supposed daughter of Dr. Edwin Gothart. Fiancé of Dr. Martin Parks. Infatuated with Henry Matthews. Object of infatuation of Erland Borgstrom. Appears in "Before The Blood: John Simons," "Before The Blood: Kellen Wechsler," "Before The Blood: Bryony Marseilles," "Before The Blood: Henry Matthews,"

"Before The Blood: Bryony Simons," "The Phoenix," "Call of the Siren," and "Staked!"

Jay Gould: American railroad magnate and financier. Business associate of Abbott Simons. Mentioned in "Before The Blood: John Simons."

Dr. Brandon Gradthorn: A doctor who practices in Munsonville and Jenson Memorial Hospital. Physician to Elizabeth Bathory. Strong knowledge of hematology (blood and blood disorders). Appears in "Before The Blood: John Simons," "Before The Blood: Kellen Wechsler," "Before The Blood: Bryony Marseilles," "Before The Blood: Henry Matthews," "Before The Blood: Bryony Simons," "The Phoenix," "Call of the Siren," "House on Top of the Hill," "Snowbell," Bryony," "Visage," and "Staked!" See also Dr. Edwin Gothart, Dr. Arnold Hartgerd, Dr. Alvin Thradgort, and Dr. Abner Rothgard.

Grandpa Clyde: See Clyde Fisher

Grandpa Mo: Nickname for Mike Olsen, the grandfather of supernatural super sleuth Cornell Dyer. Husband of Madelaine Burton Olsen. Appears in "Cornell Dyer and The Flu" and "Cornell Dyer and the Never Robbers." See also Mike Olsen.

Chauncey Granville: Chair of the math department at Jenson College. Appears briefly at a Bible study in "Before The Blood: Henry Matthews."

Doby Green: Also known as Dobie Green. Newspaper contractor. Appears in "Before The Blood: Henry Matthews.

Colin T. Greene: Also known as Colin Greene, Esquire and Sir Colin Greene. One of Lord Girard's attorneys. Husband of Elaine

Greene. Jenson resident. Appears in "Before The Blood: Henry Matthews."

Elaine Greene: Devoted and overbearing wife of Colin T. Greene. Jenson resident. Appears in "Before The Blood: Henry Matthews."

Gus Griffith: Munsonville lumberjack. Wife of Pearl Griffith. Father of Harvey Griffith and Ida Griffith Betts. Possibly had an affair with Sally Bass. Appears in "Before The Blood: Bryony Marseilles" and "Before The Blood: Bryony Simons,"

Harvey Griffth: Munsonville lumberjack. Husband of Mona Cooper Griffith. Appears in "Before The Blood: Bryony Marseilles" and "Before The Blood: Bryony Simons,"

Ida Griffth: Daughter of Gus Griffith and Pearl Grifith. Brother of Harvey Griffith. Wife of Paulie Betts. Mother of Abe Betts, Ned Betts, and Peter Betts. Appears in "Before The Blood: Bryony Marseilles" and "Before The Blood: Bryony Simons." Mentioned as "a Munsonville girl" in "Call of the Siren."

Pearl Griffith: Wife of Gus Griffith. Mother of Harvey Griffith. Mother of Ida Griffith. Has tuberculosis. Came to Munsonville for better air to fight the disease. Appears in "Before The Blood: Bryony Marseilles."

Gruff (Urag the Gruff): One of two renegade Vikings, along with Olaf the Bumpy, in "Cornell Dyer and the Missing Tombstone.

Virgil Gundersmith: Fiddler at Hewes Music Hall in Lower Manhattan. Wears checks and a white cowboy hat. Appears in "Before The Blood: John Simons."

Dick Hamilton: Richard F. "Tody" Hamilton, real publicist for P.T. Barnum and Barnum and Bailey's Greatest Show on Earth. Coined the phrase "mastodonic marvel" for Jumbo the elephant. Appears in "Before The Blood: Bryony Simons."

Hankie: Pet name for Henry Matthews during boyhood in "Before The Blood: Henry Matthews."

Hannah: Cook for Dr. Sydney Stone of Jenson. Appears briefly in "Before The Blood: Henry Matthews.

Dana Harper: One of the ministering spirits. Wife of Jasper Harper. Mother of Joey Harper, Adah Harper Elbert, Lydia Harper Denison, Phoebe Harper Joyce, Esther Harper Carter, Chloe Harper Rogers, Daughter of Eugene and Kate Miller. Sister of Alannah Miller Hasset, Briana Miller, Caitlín Miller, Erin Miller Cooper, Fiona Miller, Isleen Miller, and Ailbe Miller. Works at Munsonville Inn and (later) Sue's Diner. Appears in "Before The Blood: Bryony Marseilles, "Before The Blood: Bryony Simons, and "Call of the Siren." See also Dana Miller.

Jasper Harper: Lame son of Joe Harper and Linda Harper Fate. Brother of Percy Harper and Maggie Harper Drake. Husband of Dana Miller Harper. Father of Joey Harper, Adah Harper Elbert, Lydia Harper Denison, Phoebe Harper Joyce, Esther Harper Carter, Chloe Harper Rogers, Daughter of Gerald and Kate Miller. Mentioned in "Before The Blood: Bryony Marseilles." Appears in "Before The Blood: Bryony Simons, and "Call of the Siren."

Joe Harper: Munsonville fisherman. Husband of Linda Harper. Father of Maggie Harper, Percy Harper, and Jasper Harper. Mentioned in "Before The Blood: Bryony Simons" and "Call of the Siren."

Joe "Joey" Harper: The oldest son of Jasper Harper and Dana Miller Harper. Appears in "Call of the Siren." May appear in "House on Top of the Hill."

Linda Harper: Wife of Joe Harper and Alex Fate. Mother of Maggie Harper Drake, Percy Harper, and Jasper Harper. A cook with her daughter Maggie Harper at Simons Mansion and Munsonville Inn. Appears in "Before The Blood: Bryony Simons" and "Call of the Siren." See also Linda Fate.

Maggie Harper: Daughter of Joe Harper and Linda Harper. Sister of Percy Harper and Jasper Harper. Wife of Norton Drake. A cook with her mother at Simons Mansion and Munsonville Inn.

Percy Harper: Oldest son of Joe Harper and Linda Harper. Brother of Maggie Harper Drake and Jasper Harper. Appears in "Before The Blood: Bryony Simons."

Jean Harlow: Real American actress and sex symbol in the 1930s. Mentioned in "Before The Blood," Kellen Wechsler."

Lisa Harding: Host of Kellen Wechsler who visits Melissa Marchellis in her dreams. Appears in "Bryony." See also Imelda.

Genevieve Harrington: Wife of international investor Marshall Harrington. Appears in "Before The Blood: John Simons, "Before The Blood: Henry Matthews," and "Before The Blood: Bryony Simons."

Marshall Harrington: International investor. Husband of Genevieve Harrington. Appears in "Before The Blood: John Simons, "Before The Blood: Henry Matthews," and "Before The Blood: Bryony Simons." Appears very briefly in "Bryony."

President Benjamin Harrison: The twenty-third president of the United States (1889 to 1893). Mentioned in "Before The Blood: Henry Matthews" and "Before The Blood: Bryony Simons."

Mayor Carter Harrison: Real mayor of Chicago (1879 until 1887). Appears very briefly in "Before The Blood: Henry Matthews."

Dr. Arnold Hartgerd: A doctor who practices in Munsonville and Jenson Memorial Hospital. Physician of Elizabeth Bathory. Strong knowledge of hematology (blood and blood disorders). Appears in "Before The Blood: John Simons," "Before The Blood: Kellen Wechsler," "Before The Blood: Bryony Marseilles," "Before The Blood: Henry Matthews," "Before The Blood: Bryony Simons," "The Phoenix," "Call of the Siren," "House on Top of the Hill," "Snowbell," "Bryony," "Visage," and "Staked!" See also Dr. Brandon Gradthorn, Dr. Edwin Gothart, Dr. Alvin Thradgort, and Dr. Abner Rothgard.

Beverly Hartley: A psychiatrist in the fictional movie "Dream Ghouls" and object of heroine worship for Julie Drake in "Julie and the Too-Hard Homework."

Alannah Hasset: One of the ministering spirits. Wife of Leo Hasset. Mother of Eugenia Hasset, Veronica Hasset, and Olivia Hasset, all married with unknown last names. Eldest daughter of Gerald and Kate Miller. Sister of Briana Miller, Caitlín Miller, Dana Miller Harper, Erin Miller Cooper, Fiona Miller, Isleen Miller, and Ailbe Miller. Appears in "Before The Blood: Bryony Marseilles, "Before The Blood: Bryony Simons," "The Phoenix," and "Call of the Siren." See also Alannah Miller.

Eugenia Hasset: Daughter of Leo Hasset and Alannah Hasset. Sister of Veronica Hasset and Olivia Hasset. Attended the Girls

High School of Boston, married a man from Boston, and raised her family in Boston. Mentioned in "Call of the Siren."

Leo Hasset: Husband of Alannah Miller Hasset. Father of Eugenia Hasset, Veronica Hasset, and Olivia Hasset, all married with unknown last names. Eldest son of Richard "Dick" Hasset and Lula Hasset. Brother to Lillian Hasset Betts and Luther Hasset. Works at The Munsonville Times, which his family owns. Mayor of Munsonville.

Lula Hasset: Wife of Richard "Dick" Hasset. Mother of Lillian Hasset Betts, Leo Hasset, and Luther Hasset. Sister of Isabella Clare. Good friends with Boswell Pike and Janet Pike and Algernon Demars and Gretchen Demars. Works at the family-owned The Munsonville Times. Appears in "Before The Blood: Bryony Marseilles," "Before The Blood: Bryony Simons," "The Phoenix," and "Call of the Siren."

Luther Hasset: Youngest son of Richard "Dick" Hasset and Lula Hasset. Brother to Lillian Hasset Betts and Luther Hasset. Works at the family owned The Munsonville Times, eventually serving as its editor. Lifelong infatuation with Bryony Marseilles Simons. Insomniac. Lover of Sue Bass. Biological father of Steve Barnes.

Olivia Hasset: Daughter of Leo Hasset and Alannah Hasset. Sister of Eugenia Hasset and Veronica Hasset. Attended the Girls High School of Boston, married a man from Boston, and raised her family in Boston. Mentioned in "Call of the Siren."

Veronica Hasset: Daughter of Leo Hasset and Alannah Hasset. Sister of Alannah Hasset and Eugenia Hasset. Attended the Girls High School of Boston, married a man from Boston, and raised her family in Boston. Mentioned in "Call of the Siren."

Richard "Dick" Hasset: Husband of Lula Hasset: Father of Lillian Hasset Betts, Leo Hasset, and Luther Hasset. Best friends with George Clare. Good friends with Boswell Pike and Janet Pike and Algernon Demars and Gretchen Demars. Owns The Munsonville Times. Appears in "Before The Blood: Bryony Marseilles," and "Before The Blood: Bryony Simons." Mentioned in The Phoenix" and "Call of the Siren."

Hattie: Kept track of the laundry staff at Simons Mansion in "Bryony."

Jake Haunch: Part of a family of cigarette makers and sellers. Best piano student of John Simons. Appears briefly in "Before The Blood: John Simons."

Miss Havisham: Wealthy spinster in the Charles Dickens novel "Great Expectations." Lives in a crumbling mansion amidst her decaying wedding feast and forever wearing her wedding gown because she was once jilted at the altar. Bryony Simons privately assigns the nickname to Agnes King in "Before The Blood: Bryony Simons."

Mrs. Haunch: Mother of Jake Haunch, John Simons' best piano studio. Runs a cigarette operation. Appears briefly in "Before The Blood: John Simons."

Bart Hayes: Husband of Flossie Hayes. Deputy sheriff of Evansville. Father of four children. Appears in "Before The Blood: Henry Matthews."

Flossie Hayes: Wife of Bart Hayes, deputy sheriff of Evansville. Mother of four children. Appears in "Before The Blood: Henry Matthews."

Herr Gundel Heidenrich: Councilman at Seulobitz, Germany. Appears briefly in "Before The Blood: Kellen Wechsler."

G.W.F. Hegel: Real nineteenth century German philosopher. Mentioned briefly in "Before The Blood: Bryony Simons."

Andrew Helsby: Private tutor of John Simons. Wife of Felicity Joy Barlett Helsby. Father of Priscilla Helsby. Emeline Helsby, and Little Andy Helsby. Brother to Thomas Helsby. Lives in Queens, New York, and Lower Manhattan, New York. Appears in "Before The Blood: John Simons" and "Before The Blood: Bryony Simons."

Andy Helsby: Youngest child of Andrew Helsby and Felicity Joy Bartlett Helsby. Appears in "Before The Blood: Bryony Simons." Also known as Little Andy.

Emeline Helsby: Daughter of Andrew Helsby and Felicity Joy Bartlett Helsby. Sister of Priscilla Helsby and Little Andy Helsby. Appears in "Before The Blood: Bryony Simons" and "Call of the Siren."

Felicity Helsby: Wife of Andrew Helsby. Mother of Priscilla Helsby, Emeline Helsby, and Little Andy Helsby. Appears in "Before The Blood: John Simons," ""Before The Blood: Bryony Simons" and "Call of the Siren."

Priscilla Helsby: Daughter of Andrew Helsby and Felicity Joy Bartlett Helsby. Sister of Emeline Helsby and Little Andy Helsby. Appears in "Before The Blood: Bryony Simons" and "Call of the Siren."

Thomas Helsby: Brother of Andrew Helsby. Appears very briefly in "Before The Blood: John Simons."

Ernest Hemmingway: A twentieth century American journalist and writer. His novel "The Old Man and the Sea," which was published in 1952, won a Pulitzer Prize for fiction in 1953 and a Nobel Prize for literature in 1954. Mentioned in "Bryony."

Henchal family: Owners of The Munsonville Times who suddenly left town. Mentioned in "Katie and the Big Fear." Further developed in "House on Top of the Hill."

Henry the Coward: Nickname Bryony Simons bestows on Henry Matthews in "Before The Blood: Bryony Simons." Henry takes ownership of the name in "Bryony."

Miss Georgette Herpstedder: Hired to teach the older children in the first public school in Thornton. Mentioned in "Before The Blood: Bryony Simons."

Herrmann the Great: Alexander Hermann, a real French magician, who performed at the Chicago Opera House in April 1894. John and Bryony Simons see him perform in "Before The Blood: Bryony Simons.

Hessians: Name for the German troops who fought with the British Army during the Revolutionary War. Appear briefly in "Cornell Dyer and the 'Mistical' Being."

Clarice Hewes: Dear-mute wife of Dana Hewes, owner of Hewes Music Hall. Appears in "Before The Blood: John Simons."

Dana Hewes: Wife of Clarice Hewes. Owner of Hewes Music Hall (with an underground opium den) in Lower Manhattan. Appears in "Before The Blood: John Simons."

Mrs. Higgensworth: Member of the Relief and Aid Society in Chicago. Makes great tripe soup. Mentioned in "Before The Blood: Henry Matthews."

Hippocrates: Classical Greek doctor and father of modern medicine. Mentioned in "Before The Blood: Bryony Marseilles."

Mrs. Samuel Hodgeston and her daughter Miss Elspeth Hodgeston: Mentioned briefly in The Munsonville Times in "Before The Blood: Bryony Marseilles" after becoming injured when riding home from a tea.

Sherman A. Homes: Sherlock Holmes parody character. Part of a trio of supernatural super sleuths that include Cornell Dyer and Dr. Jim Wipston. Appears in "Cornell Dyer and the Howls of Basketville."

Mr. Hoarse: John's nickname for a guest at Spencer Inn. Appears briefly in "Before The Blood: John Simons."

Mr. Hogley: Plays checkers with Mr. Basset at the general store in "Cornell Dyer and the Eerie Lake."

Savannah Holloway: Mysterious widow of railroad magnate and robber baron Warren Holloway. Hires John Simons as her sole farmhand. Appears in "Before The Blood: John Simons, "Before The Blood: Bryony Simons," and "A Year of Shadows and Moonlight, of Gathering Blooms in the Woods." Mentioned in "The Phoenix." Also known as Widow Holloway.

Warren Holloway: Railroad magnate and robber baron. Mentioned in "Before The Blood: John Simons, "Before The Blood: Henry Matthews," and "Before The Blood: Bryony Simons."

Rev. Obadiah Hopkins: A fictional blind preacher from Mississippi. Mentioned in "Before The Blood: Bryony Marseilles."

Mrs. Horsehair: Runs a boarding home in "Cornell Dyer and the Eerie Lake."

Michael Housely: Dean of Jenson College. Appears briefly in "Before The Blood: Henry Matthews."

Mrs. Hullis: Client of supernatural super sleuth Cornell Dyer. Appears briefly in "Cornell Dyer and the Old Folks Home."

Henrik Ibsen: Real nineteenth century Norwegian playwright. Best known for "A Doll's House" and "Peer Gynt."

Idel: Poor co-worker in the fields with Kellen Wechsler. Appears briefly in "Before The Blood: Kellen Wechsler."

Ilsabe: Kellen's blind paternal grandmother in "Before The Blood: Kellen Wechsler."

Imelda: Host of Kellen Wechsler. Visits Melissa Marchellis in her dreams. Appears in "Bryony." See also Lisa Harding.

Robert Ingersoll: American lawyer, orator, and writer with the nickname of the "Great Agnostic." Bryony Simons hears him speak at the Auditorium Theatre in Chicago while on her honeymoon with John Simons. Mentioned in "Before The Blood: Bryony Simons."

Theodore Irving: A former alcoholic beau of Henry's cousin Emma, who also attacked her. Mentioned in "Before The Blood: Henry Matthews."

Colpa Ivanovich: Official wife of the fictional Ed Calkins, Steward of Tara, artist, and art mentor to Laura Jones, one of Melissa Marchellis' friends from Grover's Park. Mentioned in "Bryony" and "Visage." Appears briefly in "Staked!" Also known as just "Colpa."

Jack of All Trades: Friend and guide of Cornell Dyer in "Cornell Dyer and the Eerie Lake" and "Cornell Dyer and the Flu."

Jack the Ripper: Real unidentified serial killer in 1888 the Whitechapel district, London, England. Mentioned in "Before The Blood: Henry Matthews."

Alfred Jackson: Cousin to Dana Hewes. Manager at Hewes Music Hall. Second coachman at Simons Mansion. Often seen drinking, drunk, or both. Appears in "Bryony," "Before The Blood: John Simons," and "Before The Blood: Bryony Simons."

James: A footman at Simons Mansion in "Bryony" and "Before The Blood: Bryony Simons."

Gordon James: President of First Bank of Shelby. Appears in "Lycanthropic Summer."

Mr. Janitor: Character in "Cornell Dyer and the Calcium-Deficient Bones" and "Cornell Dyer and the Howls of Basketville."

Jacque Jean-Baptiste: Henry Matthew's gardener at Little Arcadia, Henry Matthews' greenhouse. Appears in "Before The Blood: Henry Matthews."

William Jenney: Nineteenth century engineer and architect who helped shape Chicago's skyline. Mentor of architect and urban planner Daniel Burham. Designed The Home Insurance Building in 1885, one of the world's first skyscrapers, which stood on LaSalle

Street between Adams and Monroe, from 1885 until its demolition in 1931. Appears briefly in "Before The Blood: Henry Matthews."

Jezebels: The name given by Judith Store in "Before The Blood: Henry Matthews" to any woman who relinquishes her calling to marriage and motherhood.

Tom Jenkins: Head coachman at Simons Mansion. Appears briefly in "Bryony" and "Before The Blood: Bryony Simons."

Jessyca: A blind embroidery artist and seer in "Call of the Siren."

Mrs. Joad: Mrs. George Curling Joad. A real person who won the croquet championship in the women's division in 1869, the first time the championship opened to women. Her husband, George Curling Joad, won the men's championship.

Joe: Appears in two short stories in "Lycanthropic Summer."

Mrs. Johnston: 1940s neighbor of the Wechsler family. Afraid of mice and patient of Dr. Alvin Thradgort. Mentioned in "Before The Blood: Kellen Wechsler."

Becky Jones: Best friend and roommate to Sylvia Manning, client of supernatural super sleuth in "Cornell Dyer and the Necklace of Forgetfulness."

Gertrude "Trudi" Jones: Bryony Simons' personal maid. Appears in "Bryony" and "Before The Blood" Bryony Simons." Mentioned in "Visage."

Laura Jones: Friend of Melissa Marchellis, Shelly Gallagher, and Kimberly Whitney. Sibling of many. Infatuated with Jason Frye. Artist and student of Colpa Ivanovich at Artemis Rose Art College.

Appears in "Bryony," "Visage," "Staked!," "House on Top of the Hill," "A Room for Laura," "Changes for Shelly," and "Melissa and the Hidden Treasure."

Jim Kaden: Railroad worker and border at Mary Singler's rooming house in Evansville. Eventually marries Mary Singler on Valentine's Day. Appears briefly in "Before The Blood: Henry Matthews."

Mary Kaden: Runs a rooming house in Evansville. Henry Matthews' occasional lover. Eventually marries Jim Kaden, a railroad worker and border at her house, on Valentine's Day. Appears briefly in "Before The Blood: Henry Matthews." See also Mary Singler.

Kant: Immanuel Kant. Real German philosopher of the eighteenth century. Mentioned in "Before The Blood: Bryony M<Marseilles."

Veronica Keating: Early resident of Munsonville. Strong supporter of Boswell Pike as mayor. Mother of Victor Keating, who was born severely handicapped and died shortly after birth. Died by mutual suicide with husband and identical twin Virgil Keating. Appears briefly in "Before The Blood: Bryony Marseilles."

Victor Keating: Only child of identical twins and spouses Virgil Keating and Vernoica Keating. Died shortly after birth. Mentioned in "Before The Blood: Bryony Marseilles."

Virgil Keating: Early resident of Munsonville. Strong supporter of Boswell Pike as mayor. Mother of Victor Keating, who was born severely handicapped. Died by mutual suicide with wife and identical twin Veronica Keating. Appears briefly in "Before The Blood: Bryony Marseilles."

Thomas à Kempis: Real fifteenth century Christian theologian. Best known for his work, "Imitation of Christ." Brief excerpt appears in "Before The Blood: Bryony Marseilles."

Clay Kendall: Evansville banker, a bachelor known for nervousness and shaking hands. Appears briefly in "Before The Blood: Henry Matthews."

Agnes King: Daughter of Jacob King and Judith King. Sister of Emily King. Fiancée of Henry Matthews. Spends time with her aunt at the Cloistered Dominican Nuns of the Perpetual Rosary in Lancaster, of which she eventually becomes a member. Inherited her mother's albinism. Appears in "Before The Blood: John Simons," "Before The Blood: Kellen Wechsler," "Before The Blood: Henry Matthews," "Before The Blood: Bryony Simons," and "The Phoenix." Also known as Sister Maria DeLourdes.

Emily King: Eldest daughter of New York tycoon Jacob King and Judith King. Sister of Agnes King. Wife of Nicholas Baldwin, cousin to the Vanderbilts. Inherited mother's albinism. Appears briefly in "Before The Blood: John Simons," "Before The Blood: Henry Matthews," and "Before The Blood: Bryony Simons." See also Emily Baldwin

Jacob King: Tycoon and robber baron of unknown industry. Husband of Judith King. Father of Emily King Baldwin and Agnes King. Business associate of Lord Girard, Albert Brumfeldt, Warren Holloway, Carlton Mandeville, and Abbott Simons. Appears in "Before The Blood: Kellen Wechsler," "Before The Blood: Henry Matthews," and "Before The Blood: Bryony Simons." Mentioned in "Before The Blood: John Simons" and "The Phoenix."

Judith King: An albino and invalid wife of Jacob King. Mother of Emily King and Agnes King. Appears in "Before The Blood: Kellen Wechsler" and "Before The Blood: Henry Matthews."

King Matthias: King of Hungary and Croatia from 1458 to 1490. Mentioned "Bryony."

Joan Klinger: Boarder at Mary Singler's rooming house in Evansville and fan of Henry Matthews' short stories in the Evansville Courrier. Appears briefly in "Before The Blood: Henry Matthews."

Cecily Knowles: Widow of Earl Knowles, business associate of Lord Girard, Albert Brumfeldt, Warren Holloway, and Abbott Simons. Mentioned in "Before The Blood: Henry Matthews."

Earl Knowles: Business associate of Lord Girard, Albert Brumfeldt, Warren Holloway, and Abbott Simons. Mentioned in "Before The Blood: Henry Matthews."

Rev. Barnabus P. Kramer of Fairmount: Fictional church pastor. Mentioned in The Munsonville Times in "Before The Blood: Bryony Marseilles.:

George Krase: Lovesick character in a short story in "Lycanthropic Summer."

Kristoph: A Hessian who appears in "Cornell Dyer and the 'Mistical' Being."

Sally Lafayette: A can-can dancer at Hewes Music Hall in Lower Manhattan. Appears briefly in "Before the Blood: John Simons."

Landry: The male lead character in George Sand's nineteenth century novel, "La Petite Fadette."

Cuddy Lane: A ventriloquist at Hewes Music Hall in Lower Manhattan. Appears in "Before The Blood: John Simons" and "Before The Blood: Kellen Wechsler."

Mr. Langley: Owner of a slop shop (nineteenth century store that sold ready-made, inexpensive clothing for me), who contracted out sewing work to Henry Matthews' mother and sisters in "Before The Blood: Henry Mathews."

Cara Larvey: Daughter of Gerald and Katie Miller. Sister of Gerald Miller Jr., Al Miller, Ben Miller, Russ Miller, Will Miller, Eric Miller, Pete Miller, Nate Miller, and Katie Miller Dyer. Married to Judy Warman Miller. Wife of Phil Larvey, firefighter for the Beulah County Fire Department. Mother of Megan Larvey. Sings at Munsonville Congregational Church. Bakes good cookies. Appears in "Visage," Katie and the Big Fear," and "House on Top of the Hill." "Mentioned in "Karla Joins In." See also Cara Miller.

Phil Larvey: Firefighter at Beulah County Fire Department, which later opens an office in Munsonville. Husband of Cara Miller Larvey. Father of Megan Larvey. Appears briefly in "Staked!" Mentioned in "Karla Joins In."

Jozsef Lenke: Husband to Sophia Lenke. Adopted father of Anna Czarnecki. Bookkeeper for a hardware store in Detroit. Lives with his family in an apartment above the store. Owns a fishing village in Munsonville. Mentioned in "Staked!" and "Call of the Siren." Appears in "House on Top of the Hill."

Sophia Lenke: Wife to Jozsef Lenke. Adopted mother of Anna Czarnecki. Good friend and correspondent of Neta Ashmore, who arranged the adoption. Lives with her family in an apartment above the store. Owns a fishing village in Munsonville. Mentioned in "Staked!" Appears in "The Phoenix," "Call of the Siren," and "House on Top of the Hill."

Mrs. Librarian: A character in "Cornell Dyer and the Calcium-Deficient Bones."

Fr. Franz Lieber: Pastor of St. Adelbert Catholic Church in Jenson. Briefly appears in "Before The Blood: Henry Matthews."

Jenny Lind: Swedish opera singer dubbed the "Swedish Nightingale." Mentioned in "Before The Blood: John Simons" and "Before The Blood: Bryony Simons."

Linda: Wannabe friend of Caryn Rochelle in "Lycanthropic Summer."

Lionel: Married man looking for women at a bar in a short story in "Lycanthropic Summer."

Mary Lister: Housekeeper to Rev. Alexis Panchuk, pastor at the fictional St. Athanasius Church in Detroit, Michigan. Appears in "Bryony" and "House on Top of the Hill."

Mr. Lockwood: A man helplessly caught up in a flirtation with Bess Masters Mandeville at a party. Appears briefly in "Before The Blood: Henry Matthews."

Lothair III of Supplinburg: A real king of Germany in 1125. Mentioned in "Before The Blood: Kellen Wechsler."

Mrs. Lovell: Housekeeper for Leopold and Leona Russell in New York. They were previously business associates of Abbott Simons until their reversal of fortune. But they kept their Fifth Avenue home by taking select boarders. Appears briefly in "Before The Blood: John Simons."

Minerva Lute: The prim young lady in a faded print dress and crisp bonnet enjoying apricot snuff during a Bible study at Jenson College. Appears in "Before The Blood: Henry Matthews."

Maestro: See Seymour Cassidy

Major: Drunken neighbor of Henry Matthews' family and guardian to Bess Masters (later Mandeville). Appears in "Before The Blood: Henry Matthews."

Carlton Mandeville: Husband to Bess Masters Mandeville. Business associate of Lord Girard, Albert Brumfeldt, Warren Holloway, Carlton Mandeville, and Abbott Simons. Publisher of the New York Gazette. Appears in "Before The Blood: Henry Matthews" and "Before The Blood: Bryony Simons."

Elizabeth Mandeville: Wife of Carlton Mandeville. Occasional lover Herny Matthews. Best friend of Henry's sister Maggie Matthews. Ward of major. Also known as Lady Elizabeth Mandeville and Good Queen Bess. Appears in "Before The Blood: Henry Matthews." See also Bess Masters.

Sylvia Manning: Client of supernatural super sleuth in "Cornell Dyer and the Necklace of Forgetfulness."

Louis Marche: Fictional French fashion designer in the nineteenth century. Referenced in "The Phoenix" and "Call of the Siren."

Anna Marchellis: Young daughter of Bryga Czarnecki, housekeeper at Simons Mansion. Wife of Peter Marchellis. Mother of Frank Marchellis. Grandmother of Melissa Marchellis and Brian Marchellis. Appears in "Bryony," "Staked!," "Before The Blood, Bryony Simons," "The Phoenix," "Call of the Siren," and "House on Top of the Hill." See also Anna Czarnecki and Ghost Girl.

Brian Marchellis: Son of Frank Marchellis and Darlene Marchellis. Stepson of Steve Barnes. Husband of Cindy Caswell Marchellis. Father of Deanna Marchellis, Ellie Marchellis, and Fawn Marchellis. Graduate of Joliet Junior College's culinary arts department. Owner of cleaning company. Eventual owner of Sue's Diner. Refused to own another pet after one dog (Scooter) and two cats (Snowbell and Charcoal) died tragic deaths. Appears in "Bryony," "Visage," "Staked!" and "House on Top of the Hill."

Darlene Marchellis: Widow of Frank Marchellis. Wife of Steve Barnes. Mother of Melissa Marchellis Simotes Wechsler and Brian Marchellis. Freelance writer. Appears in "Bryony," "Visage," "Staked!," "House on Top of the Hill," "Melissa and the Hidden Treasure," and possibly "A Room for Laura," and "Changes for Shelly."

Frank Marchellis: Husband of Darelene Marchellis. Son of Peter Marchellis and Anna Czarnecki Marchellis. Photo journalist and world traveler. Insulin-dependent diabetic and double amputee, who died of kidney failure. Appears in "House on Top of the Hill," "Melissa and the Hidden Tresure," and possibly "A Room for Laura," and "Changes for Shelly." Mentioned in "Bryony," "Visage," and "Staked!"

Melissa Marchellis: 1970s teen who traded her blood with Victorian vampire and pianist John Simons for a trip back into time as his wife Bryony Marseilles Simons. Wife of John Simotes, Kellen Wechsler, and Jason Frye. Mother of John-Peter Simotes. Daughter of Frank Marchellis and Darlene Marchellis. Sister of Brian Marchellis. Stepdaughter of Steve Barnes. Daughter-in-law of Marvin Simotes and Carol Simotes. Protagonist of "Bryony" and "Visage." Appears in "Staked!," "House on Top of the Hill" and briefly in "Karla Joins In."

Peter Marchellis: Husband of Anna Czarnecki Marchellis. Father of Frank Marchellis. Butcher in Detroit, Michigan. Pioneer real estate broker, which is where he made his money. Bought Simons Manion in 1955 with the intention of restoring it. Appears in "House on Top of the Hill." Mentioned in "Bryony," "Staked!" and possible "Melissa and the Hidden Treasure."

Marilyn: Instructor at Molly Blake School of Beauty. Hired supernatural super sleuth Cornell Dyer to perform a séance. Appears in "Cornell Dyer and the Flu." Reference (name omitted) in "Visage."

Adelaide Markham: Eldest child of William Markham and Etta Matthews Markham. Sister of Emma Markham, Giselle Markham, Archer Markham, and Wyatt Markham. First cousin of Henry Matthews. Student at Woman's Hospital Medical College. First female biology professor at Jenson College. Appears in "Before The Blood: Henry Matthews."

Archer Markham: Eldest son of William Markham and Etta Matthews Markham. Brother of Adelaide Markham, Emma Markham, Giselle Markham, and Wyatt Markham. First cousin of Henry Matthews. Passionate about studying law. Scrupulous in morals. Appears in "Before The Blood: Henry Matthews."

Emma Markham: Daughter of William Markham and Etta Matthews Markham. Sister of Adelaide Markham, Giselle Markham, Archer Markham, and Wyatt Markham. First cousin of Henry Matthews. Teaches at Mary Our Holy Mother Catholic School. Life goal is getting married. Appears in "Before The Blood: Henry Matthews."

Etta Markham: Daughter of Harold Matthews and Caroline Matthews/Louise Girard. Sister of Charlotte (Lottie) Matthews, Margaret (Maggie) Matthews, Elizabeth (Lizzie) Matthews, Katherine (Kitty) Matthews, and Henry (Hankie) Matthews. Seamstress. Wife of William Markham. Mother of Adelaide Markham., Emma Markham, Giselle Markham, Archer Markham, and Wyatt Markham. Bookkeeper. Brother-in-law to Henry Matthews. Lives in a third floor apartment with her family in a Chicago brownstone. Appears in "Before The Blood: Henry Matthews. See also Etta Matthews and Etta Markham

Giselle Markham: Daughter of William Markham and Etta Matthews Markham. Sister of Adelaide Markham, Emma Markham, Archer Markham, and Wyatt Markham. Teaches art to schoolchildren. Student at the Art Institute in Chicago. Appears in "Before The Blood: Henry Matthews."

William Markham: Husband of Etta Matthews Markham. Adopted father of Adelaide Markham. Father of Emma Markham, Giselle Markham, Archer Markham, and Wyatt Markham. Bookkeeper. Brother-in-law to Henry Matthews. Lives in a third-story apartment in a Chicago brownstone with his family. Appears in "Before The Blood: Henry Matthews.

Wyatt Markham: Youngest son of William Markham and Etta Matthews Markham. Sister of Adelaide Markham, Giselle

Markham, Archer Markham, and Wyatt Markham. First cousin of Henry Matthews. His father's unofficial apprentice. Fascinated with insects. Appears in "Before The Blood: Henry Matthews."

Herr Johannes Markwart: The suspicious councilman who wanted to know the name of the university where Kellen had supposedly taught in "Before The Blood: Kellen Wechsler."

Christopher Marlowe: Rea; English playwright and poet in the poet Elizabethan era. Mentioned in "Before The Blood: Henry Matthews."

Adele Marseilles: Wife of Reverend Galien Marseilles. Mother of Bryony Marseilles Simons, Mary Mae Marseilles, and Samuel George Marseilles. Avid reader. Poor health from scarlet fever. Appears in "Before The Blood: Bryony Marseilles." Mentioned in "Bryony" and "Before The Blood: Bryony Marseilles." See also Adele Belanger.

Bryony Marseilles: Birth name was Bryonia. Daughter of Reverend Galien Marseilles and Adele Marseilles. Wife of John Simons. Mother of an unnamed son. Best friend of Susan Betts. Adopted niece of Orville Parks and Bertha Parks. Love interest of Luther Hasset and Henry Matthews. Only child but adopts the Fisher girls as her Summer Sisters. Infatuated with Owen Munson and Henry Matthews. Identifies with Lake Munson. Poor health due to chlorosis. Appears in "Before The Blood: Bryony Marseilles," "Before The Blood: Henry Matthews," and "Before The Blood: Bryony Simons." Appears in flashback in "The Phoenix." Appears briefly in "Bryony" and "Staked!" Mentioned in "Visage," "Call of the Siren," Brainy Ann," "Julie and the Too-Hard Homework," and "Katie and the Big Fear." See also Bryony Simons

Galien Marseilles (Reverend): Husband of Adele Belanger Marseilles. Father to Bryony Marseilles Simons, Mary Mae Marseilles, and Samuel George Marseilles. Former pastor of the fictional Saints Peter and Paul Catholic Church in Detroit, Michigan. Pastor of Munsonville Congregational Church. Former teacher of Algernon Demars. Neta Ashmore's lover. Loves reading works by Charles Spurgeon. Appears in "Bryony," "Before The Blood: Bryony Marseilles," "Before The Blood: Henry Matthews," "Before The Blood: Bryony Simons." Appears briefly in "The Phoenix." Mentioned in "Call of the Siren."

Mary Mae Marseilles: Stillbirth daughter of Reverend Galien and Adele Belanger Marseilles. Mentioned in "Before The Blood: Bryony Marseilles."

Samuel George Marseilles: Stillbirth son of Reverend Galien and Adele Belanger Marseilles. Mentioned in "Before The Blood: Bryony Marseilles."

Rhoda Mason: Waitress at the no-name diner in "Cornell Dyer and the 'Mistical' Being."

William E. Mason: Chicago lawyer and U.S. Senator in the late nineteenth century. Bryony Simons hears him speak at the Auditorium Theatre in Chicago while on her honeymoon with John Simons. Mentioned in "Before The Blood: Bryony Simons."

Bess Masters: Wife of Carlton Mandeville. Occasional lover Henry Matthews. Best friend of Henry's sister Maggie Matthews. Ward of major. Also known as Lady Elizabeth Mandeville and Good Queen Bess. Appears in "Before The Blood: Henry Matthews." See also Bess Masters.

Harold Masters: Henry Matthews' alter ego. Mystery author. Off and on teacher at Munsonville School. Appears in "Bryony" and "House on Top of the Hill." Mentioned in "Visage," "Staked!" and "Karla Joins In."

Roger Masury: Photographer in Jenson. Photography teacher in Chicago. Photographed Henry Matthews in a variety of clothing and Giselle Markham nude. Appears in "Before The Blood: Henry Matthews."

Bernie Mather: Early lumberjack resident of Munsonville, with fiery red hair and a strong tenor voice. Appears in "Before The Blood: Bryony Marseilles." Mentioned in "Call of the Siren."

Caroline Matthews: Also known as Louise Girard. Daughter of Louis Girard and Jeannine Girard. Sister of Lawrence Girard. Wife of Harold Matthews. Mother of Henrietta "Etta" Matthews Markham, Charlotte "Lottie" Matthews, Margaret "Maggie" Matthews, Elizabeth "Lizzie" Matthews, Katherine "Kitty" Matthews, and Henry "Hankie" Matthews Appears in "Before The Blood: Henry Matthews." See also Louise Girard.

Charlotte (Lottie) Matthews: Daughter of Harold Matthews and Caroline Matthews/Louise Girard. Sister of Henrietta (Etta) Matthews Markham, Margaret (Maggie) Matthews, Elizabeth (Lizzie) Matthews, Katherine (Kitty) Matthews, and Henry (Hankie) Matthews. Seamstress. Mother's helper. Content to live at home always. Appears in "Before The Blood: Henry Matthews."

Elizabeth (Lizzie) Matthews: Daughter of Harold Matthews and Caroline Matthews/Louise Girard. Sister of Henrietta (Etta) Matthews Markham, Charolotte (Lottie) Matthews, Margaret (Maggie) Matthews, Katherine (Kitty) Matthews, and Henry

(Hankie) Matthews. Expert seamstress who strives to own her own tailor shop one day. Appears in "Before The Blood: Henry Matthews."

Etta Matthews: See Henrietta (Etta) Matthews and Etta Markham.

Harold Matthews: Possible pseudonym. Renegade from gypsy caravan. Wife of Caroline Matthews/Louise Girard. Father of Henrietta "Etta" Matthews Markham, Charlotte "Lottie" Matthews, Margaret "Maggie" Matthews, Elizabeth "Lizzie" Matthews, Katherine "Kitty" Matthews, and Henry "Hankie" Matthews. Street musician. Chimney sweep. Newspaper distributor. Guitarist. Beer drinker. Opportunist. Appears in "Before The Blood: Henry Matthews."

Henrietta (Etta) Matthews: Daughter of Harold Matthews and Caroline Matthews/Louise Girard. Sister of Charlotte (Lottie) Matthews, Margaret (Maggie) Matthews, Elizabeth (Lizzie) Matthews, Katherine (Kitty) Matthews, and Henry (Hankie) Matthews. Seamstress. Wife of William Markham. Mother of Adelaide Markham., Emma Markham, Giselle Markham, Archer Markham, and Wyatt Markham. Bookkeeper. Brother-in-law to Henry Matthews. Lives in a third floor apartment with her family in a Chicago brownstone. Appears in "Before The Blood: Henry Matthews. See also Etta Matthews and Etta Markham

Henry (Hankie) Matthews: Son of Harold Matthews and Caroline Matthews/Louise Girard. Brother of Henrietta (Etta) Matthews Markham, Charlotte (Lottie) Matthews, Margaret (Maggie) Matthews, Elizabeth (Lizzie) Matthews, and Katherine (Kitty) Matthews. Father's helper. Avid reader. Nephew and ward of Lawrence "Lord" Girard." Fiancé of Agnes King. Reporter for the New York Gazette. Asthmatic. Friend of John Simons. House steward at Simons Mansion. Cousin to Markam children. Appears in "Bryony," "Before The Blood: John Simons," "Before The Blood: Kellen Wechsler," "Before The Blood: Henry Matthews," "Before The Blood: Bryony Simons," "The Phoenix," and "Call of the Siren." Appears in flashback in "Staked!" Mentioned in "Visage." See also Harold Masters.

Katherine (Kitty) Matthews: Daughter of Harold Matthews and Caroline Matthews/Louise Girard. Sister of Henrietta (Etta) Matthews Markham, Charlotte (Lottie) Matthews, Margaret (Maggie) Matthews, Elizabeth (Lizzie) Matthews, and Henry (Hankie) Matthews. Not shocked at scandal or smut. Wants to marry a kind man and raise a family in a little country house with a white picket fence. Appears in "Before The Blood: Henry Matthews."

Kitty Matthews: See Katherine (Kitty) Matthews

Lizzie Matthews: See Elizabeth (Lizzie) Matthews

Lottie Matthews: See Charlotte (Lottie) Matthews

Maggie Matthews: See Margaret (Maggie) Matthews.

Margaret (Maggie) Matthews: Daughter of Harold Matthews and Caroline Matthews/Louise Girard. Sister of Henrietta (Etta) Matthews Markham, Charlotte (Etta) Matthews, Elizabeth (Lizzie) Matthews, Katherine (Kitty) Matthews, and Henry (Hankie) Matthews. Seamstress. Wants to be rich, fashionable, and beautiful. Appears in "Before The Blood: Henry Matthews."

Guy de Maupassant: Real nineteenth century French short story writer. Mentioned in "Before The Blood: Bryony Marseilles."

Archbishop John McClosky: Real first American-born Archbishop of New York and second archbishop in the diocese. He served from 1864 until his death in 1885. Appears briefly in "Before The blood: John Simons."

Francis McCloud: Editor of the fictional New York Gazette. Appears briefly in "Before The Blood: Henry Matthews." Mentioned in "Before The Blood: John Simons."

Flossie McGee: Male impersonator at Hewes Music Hall in Lower Manhattan. Suffers from gastritis. Lives on gruel and cigarettes. Appears in "Before The Blood: John Simons."

Jim McGinnis: Real name was James Anthony McGinnis. Associate of P.T. Barnum. Owner and manager of The Barnum and Bailey Greatest Show on Earth. Appears in "Before The Blood: Bryony Simons."

Ruth McGinnis: Wife of Jim McGinnis. Her name before marriage was Ruth Louisa McCaddon. Appears in "Before The Blood: Bryony Simons."

Roger McLoughty: A worn-down dad in a short story in "Lycanthropic Summer."

Dirk Meadows: Pantomime dame at the fictional Hews Music Hall in Lower Manhattan, New York. Appears in "Before The Blood: John Simons."

Irving Mendel: Resident of Evansville. Married to Polly Mendel. Father of thirteen children. Hangs out in the tavern. Obese. Henry Matthews privately calls him Wooly Mammoth. Appears in "Before The Blood: Henry Matthews."

Polly Mendel: Resident of Evansville. Married to Irving Mendel. Mother of thirteen children. Obese. Henry Matthews privately calls her Polly Manatee. Appears in "Before The Blood: Henry Matthews."

Mephistopheles: Demon in German folklore, first appearing in the in the anonymous "Historia von D. Johann Fausten" in the sixteenth century and then in other stories in the Faust legend. Mentioned in "Before The Blood: Bryony Marseilles" and "Before The Blood: Henry Matthews" in reference to a character who physically resembles him.

Metta: Mother of Kellen Wechsler. Lover of soldier Brandt Wechsler. Resident of Grotekop. Appears in "Before The Blood: Kellen Wechsler."

Mildred: A housemaid at Simons Mansion in "Bryony" and "Before The Blood: Bryony Simons."

Al Miller: Son of Gerald and Katie Miller. Brother of Gerald Miller Jr., Ben Miller, Russ Miller, Will Miller, Eric Miller, Pete Miller, Nate Miller, Cara Miller Larvey, and Katie Miller Dyer. Math teacher, then principal, at Jenson High School. Married with children. Appears in "Visage," Katie and the Big Fear," and "House on Top of the Hill." Mentioned in "Karla Joins In."

Ailbe Miller: Son of Eugene Miller and Kate Miller. Brother of Alannah Miller Hasset, Briana Miller, Caitlín Miller, Dana Miller Harper, Erin Miller Cooper, Fiona Miller, and Isleen Miller. Married to Amanda Drake Miller. After three stillbirths, he becomes the father of Gerald Miller. Pastor at Munsonville Congregational Church. Appears in "Before The Blood: Bryony Simons" (as an infant), ""Call of the Siren," and "House on Top of the Hill." Mentioned in "Katie and the Big Fear."

Alannah Miller: One of the ministering spirits. Wife of Leo Hasset. Mother of Eugenia Hasset, Veronica Hasset, and Olivia Hasset, all married with unknown last names. Eldest daughter of Gerald and Kate Miller. Sister of Briana Miller, Caitlín Miller, Dana Miller Harper, Erin Miller Cooper, Fiona Miller, Isleen Miller, and Ailbe Miller. Appears in "Before The Blood: Bryony Marseilles, "Before The Blood: Bryony Simons," "The Phoenix," and "Call of the Siren." See also Alannah Hasset.

Ben Miller: Son of Gerald and Katie Miller. Brother of Gerald Miller Jr., Al Miller, Russ Miller, Will Miller, Eric Miller, Pete Miller, Nate Miller, Cara Miller Larvey, and Katie Miller Dyer. History teacher, then principal, at Jenson Junior High School. Married with children. Appears in "Visage," Katie and the Big Fear," and "House on Top of the Hill." Mentioned in "Karla Joins In."

Briana Miller: One of the ministering spirits. Daughter of Eugene and Kate Miller. Sister of Alannah Miller Hasset, Caitlín Miller, Dana Miller Harper, Erin Miller Cooper, Fiona Miller, Isleen Miller, and Ailbe Miller. Caretaker of Geroge Clare and Orville Parks. Opens first health care office in Munsonville, despite lack of formal training. Appears in "Before The Blood: Bryony Marseilles, "Before The Blood: Bryony Simons," "The Phoenix," and "Call of the Siren."

Caitlin Miller: One of the ministering spirits. Daughter of Eugene and Kate Miller. Sister of Alannah Miller Hasset, Briana Miller, Dana Miller Harper, Erin Miller Cooper, Fiona Miller, Isleen Miller, and Ailbe Miller. Caretaker of Sue Bass. Special friend of Raynelle

Atkinson. Appears in "Before The Blood: Bryony Marseilles, "Before The Blood: Bryony Simons, and "Call of the Siren." Mentioned in "House on Top of the Hill."

Cara Miller: Daughter of Gerald and Katie Miller. Sister of Gerald Miller Jr., Al Miller, Ben Miller, Russ Miller, Will Miller, Eric Miller, Pete Miller, Nate Miller, and Katie Miller Dyer. Wife of Phil Larvey, firefighter for the Beulah County Fire Department. Sings at Munsonville Congregational Church. Bakes good cookies. Appears in "Visage," Katie and the Big Fear," and "House on Top of the Hill." Mentioned in "Karla Joins In." See also Cara Larvey.

Dana Miller: One of the ministering spirits. Wife of Jasper Harper. Mother of Joey Harper, Adah Harper Elbert, Lydia Harper Denison, Phoebe Harper Joyce, Esther Harper Carter, Chloe Harper Rogers, Daughter of Eugene and Kate Miller. Sister of Alannah Miller Hasset, Briana Miller, Caitlín Miller, Erin Miller Cooper, Fiona Miller, Isleen Miller, and Ailbe Miller. Works at Munsonville Inn and (later) Sue's Diner. Appears in "Before The Blood: Bryony Marseilles, "Before The Blood: Bryony Simons, and "Call of the Siren." See also Dana Harper.

Eric Miller: Son of Gerald and Katie Miller. Brother of Gerald Miller Jr., Al Miller, Ben Miller, Russ Miller, Will Miller, Pete Miller, Nate Miller, Cara Miller Larvey, and Katie Miller Dyer. Sells used cars in Jenson. Unmarried. Appears in "Visage," Katie and the Big Fear," "House on Top of the Hill," and "Kara Joins In."

Erin Miller: One of the ministering spirits. Wife of Miles Cooper. Mother of Mary Katherine Cooper and Mitchell Eugene Cooper. Daughter of Eugene and Kate Miller. Sister of Alannah Miller Hasset, Briana Miller, Caitlín Miller, Dana Miller Harper, Fiona Miller, Isleen Miller, and Ailbe Miller. Good with flowers. Appears in "Before The Blood: Bryony Marseilles, "Before The Blood: Bryony Simons, and "Call of the Siren." See also Erin Cooper.

Eugene Miller: Husband of Kate Miller. Brother-in-law of Mitch Cooper and Mary Cooper. Father of the ministering spirits: Alannah Miller Hasset, Briana Miller, Caitlín Miller, Dana Miller Harper, Erin Miller Cooper, Fiona Miller, Isleen Miller, and Ailbe Miller. Sang cowboy songs with Mitch at Munson Day. Appears in "Before The Blood: Bryony Marseilles" and "Before The Blood: Bryony Simons."

Fiona Miller: One of the ministering spirits. Daughter of Eugene and Kate Miller. Sister of Alannah Miller Hasset, Briana Miller, Caitlín Miller, Dana Miller Harper, Erin Miller Cooper, Isleen Miller, and Ailbe Miller. Nonverbal. Sharpshooter. Defender of Briana Miller. Appears in "Before The Blood: Bryony Marseilles, "Before The Blood: Bryony Simons, and "Call of the Siren."

Gerald Miller Jr.: Eldest son of Gerald and Katie Miller. Brother of Al Miller. Ben Miller, Russ Miller, Will Miller, Eric Miller, Pete Miller, Nate Miller, Cara Miller Larvey, and Katie Miller Dyer. Fisherman. Married and divorced from Patricia "Patty" Addaway Miller. Father of Mary Miller, Sherry Miller, and Larry Miler. Appears in "Visage," Katie and the Big Fear," "House on Top of the Hill," and "Karla Joins In."

Gerald Miller Sr.: Son of Ailbe Miller and Amanda Drake Miller. Husband of Kathleeen Dalton Miller. Father of Gerald Miller Jr., Al Miller, Ben Miller, Russ Miller, Will Miller, Eric Miller, Pete Miller, Nate Miller, Cara Miller Larvey, and Katie Miller Dyer. Bookkeeper for the family fishing business. Lifelong fisherman. Appears in "Visage," Katie and the Big Fear," "House on Top of the Hill," and "Karla Joins In."

Glenn Miller: American composer, trombone player, big band conductor, and recording artist. Mentioned in "Before The Blood: Kellen Wechsler."

Isleen Miller: One of the ministering spirits. Daughter of Eugene and Kate Miller. Sister of Alannah Miller Hasset, Briana Miller, Caitlín Miller, Dana Miller Harper, Erin Miller Cooper, Fiona Miller, and Ailbe Miller. Caretaker of her mother. Appears in "Before The Blood: Bryony Marseilles, "Before The Blood: Bryony Simons, and "Call of the Siren."

Kate Miller: Husband of Eugene Miller. Sister-in-law of Mitch Cooper and Mary. Mother of the ministering spirits: Alannah Miller Hasset, Briana Miller, Caitlín Miller, Dana Miller Harper, Erin Miller Cooper, Fiona Miller, Isleen Miller, and Ailbe Miller. Cheerful, servant leader, and motherly. Appears in "Before The Blood: Bryony Marseilles," "Before The Blood: Bryony Simons," "The Phoenix," and "Call of the Siren."

Katie Miller: Daughter of Gerald and Katie Miller. Sister of Gerald Miller Jr., Al Miller, Ben Miller, Russ Miller, Will Miller, Eric Miller, Pete Miller, Nate Miller, and Cara Miller Larvey. Widow of supernatural super sleuth Cornell Dyer. Mother of Karla Dyer. Graduate of Molly Blake School of Beauty in Jenson. Works at Klever Cuts in Jenson. Appears in "Bryony," "Visage," "Staked!," "Katie and the Big Fear," "Julie and the Too-Hard Homework," "Brainy Ann," Karla Joins In," and "House on Top of the Hill." See also Katie Dyer.

Kathleen Miller: Daughter of William Dalton and Myrna Cooper. Husband of Gerald Miller Sr. Mother of Gerald Miller Jr., Al Miller, Ben Miller, Russ Miller, Will Miller, Eric Miller, Pete Miller, Nate Miller, Cara Miller Larvey, and Katie Miller Dyer. Bookkeeper for the family fishing business. Appears in "Visage," Katie and the Big Fear," "House on Top of the Hill," and "Karla Joins In."

Larry Miller: Son of Gerald Miller Jr. and Patricia Addaway Miller. Brother of Mary Addaway Miller and Sherry Addaway Miller. Fisherman. Appears in "Visage," "House on Top of the Hill," "Katie and the Big Fear," and "Karla Joins In." See also Mary Addaway.

Mary Miller: Daughter of Patricia Addaway and adopted daughter of Gerald Miller Jr. Sister of Sherry Addaway Miller and Larry Miller. Appears in "Visage," "House on Top of the Hill," and "Katie and the Big Fear." Mentioned in "Karla Joins In." See also Mary Addaway.

Nate Miller: Son of Gerald and Katie Miller. Brother of Gerald Miller Jr., Al Miller, Ben Miller, Russ Miller, Will Miller, Eric Miller, Pete Miller, Cara Miller Larvey, and Katie Miller Dyer. Fisherman. Widower. Previously married to Barbie Benton. Appears in "Visage," Katie and the Big Fear," "House on Top of the Hill," and Mentioned in "Karla Joins In."

Pete Miller: Son of Gerald and Katie Miller. Brother of Gerald Miller Jr., Al Miller, Ben Miller, Russ Miller, Will Miller, Eric Miller, Nate Miller, Cara Miller Larvey, and Katie Miller Dyer. Bookkeeper for the family fishing business. Teaches first at Jenson Elementary School and then high school biology at Munsonville School. Unmarried. Appears in "Visage," Katie and the Big Fear," and "House on Top of the Hill." Mentioned in "Karla Joins In."

Russ Miller: Son of Gerald and Katie Miller. Brother of Gerald Miller Jr., Al Miller, Ben Miller, Will Miller, Eric Miller, Pete Miller, Nate Miller, Cara Miller Larvey, and Katie Miller Dyer.

76

Married to Judy Warman Miller. Publisher and editor of The Munsonville Times. Appears in "Visage," Katie and the Big Fear," and "House on Top of the Hill." Mentioned in "Karla Joins In."

Sherry Miller: Daughter of Patricia Addaway and adopted daughter of Gerald Miller Jr. Sister of Sherry Addaway Miller and Larry Miller. Appears in "Visage," "House on Top of the Hill," and "Katie and the Big Fear." Mentioned in "Karla Joins In." See also Sherry Addaway.

Will Miller (Officer): Son of Gerald and Katie Miller. Brother of Gerald Miller Jr., Al Miller, Ben Miller, Russ Miller, Eric Miller, Pete Miller, Nate Miller, Cara Miller Larvey, and Katie Miller Dyer. Munsonville police officer. Appears in "Bryony," "Visage," Katie and the Big Fear," and "House on Top of the Hill." Mentioned in "Karla Joins In."

Polly Milton: Main character in Louisa May Alcott's 1869 novel "An Old-Fashioned Girl." Appears in literary form in "Before The Blood: Bryony Marseilles."

Ministering Spirits: The nickname for the daughters of Eugene Miller and Kate Miller: Alannah Miller Hasset, Briana Miller, Caitlín Miller, Dana Miller Harper, Erin Miller Cooper, Fiona Miller, and Isleen Miller. The nickname is based on Hebrews 1:14: "Are they not all ministering spirits, sent forth to minister for them who shall be heirs of salvation?" Referenced in "Before The Blood: Bryony Marseilles," "Before The Blood: Bryony Simons," and "Call of the Siren."

Mike "Jed" Minton: Wife of Sissy Minton and boarder at Mary Singler's Evansville rooming house in "Before The Blood: Henry Matthews."

Sissy Minton: Husband of Jed Minton and boarder at Mary Singler's Evansville rooming house in "Before The Blood: Henry Matthews."

Claude Monet: Real nineteenth and twentieth century French impressionist known for his seascapes. Mentioned in "Before The Blood: Henry Matthews" and "The Phoenix."

Mongols: A nomadic group of tribes with a common language that rose to great military achievement under the leadership of Genghis Khan. Mentioned in "Bryony" and "Before The Blood: Henry Matthews."

Philibert Montot: Sixteenth century French werewolf. Mentioned in "Lycanthropic Summer."

Livy Mooney: Evansville resident. Wife of Todd Mooney. Eldest daughter of Sheriff Tom Platt and Nancy Platt. Sister of Babbie Platt. Mentioned in "Before The Blood: Henry Matthews." See also Livy Platt.

Todd Mooney: Evansville schoolmaster. Husband of Livy Platt Monney. Appears briefly in in "Before The Blood: Henry Matthews."

Miss Fanny Moore: Guest at Spencer Inn with her sister Polly Moore on Christmas Eve. Mentioned in "Before The Blood: John Simons."

Miss Polly Moore: Guest at Spencer Inn with her sister Fanny Moore on Christmas Eve. Mentioned in "Before The Blood: John Simons."

Michael Morchester: Main character in the fictional movie "Dream Ghouls." Seen in "Julie Drake and the Too-Hard Homework."

Dr. Morgan: A primary care doctor who practices in Jenson. Appears in "Staked!"

Dr. Mroviak: Family physicians for Jozsef Lenke and Sophia Lenke in Detroit, Michigan. Treated their adopted daughter Anna by encouraging plenty of trips back to Munsonville for fresh air. Mentioned in "Staked!" and "The Phoenix."

Randolph Mueller: Former manager for world-renowned pianist Seymour Cassidy. Appears briefly in "Before The Blood: Bryony Simons."

Kenneth Tyler Müller: Sullen grandson of Rosemary Müller in "Cornell Dyer and the 'Mistical' Being."

Rosemary Müller: Hires supernatural super sleuth to banish a ghost in "Cornell Dyer and the 'Mistical' Being."

Mary Mulligan: A nurse from Jenson who occasionally helps with the care of Pearl Griffth, Denny Betts, and the Fisher girls. Mentioned in "Before The Blood: Bryony Marseilles."

Owen Munson: Scottish-Italian founder of the fictional fishing village Munsonville in Northern Michigan. The impetus for Munsonville's economy. Former cowboy. Often seen and heard singing cowboy songs. Even tempered. Good friends with Boswell Pike and Clyde Fisher.

Mr. Murdoch: Fictional store manager of Steinway & Sons, a German American piano company, founded in 1853 in Manhattan,

York and became renowned for its high quality pianos. Appears briefly in "Before The Blood: John Simons."

The Murphys: Irish family who contracted out sewing work and wound up with typhoid. Mentioned in "Before The Blood: Henry Matthews."

Mutti: Means "Mommy" in German. Used in "Before The Blood: Kellen Wechsler."

Janet Myers: Forthright Boston schoolteacher who travels to Munsonville to become Boswell Pike's mail-order bride. Adopted Mother of Boswell Pike Jr. and Iris Pike. Mother of Edgar Pike, Claude Pike, and Blanche Pike. Founder of the first public school in Munsonville. Appears in "Before The Blood: Bryony Marseilles." See also Janet Pike.

Nellie: A scullery maid at Simons Mansion in "Bryony" and "Before The Blood: Bryony Simons."

Donahue Nelson: Mentioned in The Munsonville Times in "Before The Blood: Bryony Marseilles." Had his boots and seventy dollars stolen.

Never Robbers: A trio of bandits plus one who travel through time robbing banks that don't exist – and supernatural super sleuth Cornell Dyer's motor home in "Cornell Dyer and the Never Robbers."

Captain Newington: Captain of a cargo ship. Mentioned in "Before The Blood: Kellen Wechsler

Cyrus Newton: Seedy owner of Munsonville Inn. Unsuccessfully runs for mayor. Appears briefly in "Before The Blood: Bryony

Marseilles," "Before The Blood: Bryony Simons," "The Phoenix," and "Call of the Siren."

Old Nick: Christian nickname for the devil. Used in "Before The Blood: Bryony Marseilles," "Before The Blood: Bryony Simons," "The Phoenix," and "Summer Sisters."

Nina: Servant at the Jenson home of Dr. Hiram Rush and Amelia Rush. Appears briefly in "Before The Blood: Henry Matthews."

Madelaine Olsen: Sister of Molly Burton, one of the Never Robbers. Wife of Mike Olsen. Grandmother to supernatural super sleuth Cornell Dyer. The originator of the Madelaine effect. Appears in "Cornell Dyer and the Never Robbers." See also Madelaine Burton.

Mike Olsen: One of the Never Robbers. Wife of Madelaine Burton Olsen. Grandfather of supernatural super sleuth Cornell Dyer. Appears in "Cornell Dyer and The Flu" and "Cornell Dyer and the Never Robbers." See also Grandpa Mo.

Oma: German word for "grandmother." Used in "Before The Blood: Kellen Wechsler."

Opa: German word for "father." Used in "Before The Blood: Kellen Wechsler."

Ott: Formerly homeless, non-verbal man who identifies as a dog. Protector of Mrs. Variola, the shopkeeper in Leland Hills, Illinois. Appears in "Before The Blood: Henry Matthews."

Tanya O'Toole: Appears in a short story in "Lycanthropic Summer."

Tom Overbeck: Jeweler in Jenson. Mentioned in "Call of the Siren."

Fr. Alexis Panchuk (Reverend): Pastor at the fictional St. Athanasius Church in Detroit, Michigan. Appears in "Bryony" and "House on Top of the Hill."

Bertha Parks: Early resident of Munsonville. Wife of fisherman Orville Parks. Mother to Dr. Martin Parks. Adopted aunt of Bryony Marseilles Simons. Housekeeper to Reverend Galien Marseilles, pastor of Munsonville Congregational Church. Appears in "Bryony," "Before The Blood: Bryony Marseilles," "Before The Blood: Henry Matthews," "Before The Blood: Bryony Simons," "The Phoenix," and "Call of the Siren."

Dr. Martin Parks: Boston vivisectionist. Proponent of blood transfusions. Colleague of Dr. Edwin Gothart. Fiancé of Millicent Gothart. Son of Orville Parks and Bertha Parks. Husband of Neta Ashmore Parks. Appears in "Before The Blood," Bryony Simons," "The Phoenix," and "Call of the Siren."

Neta Parks: Wife of Blair Ashmore. Arrives in Munsonville with her husband Blair in the late nineteenth century. Appears in "Before The Blood: Bryony Simons," "The Phoenix," "Call of the Siren," and "House on Top of the Hill." See also Neta Ashmere.

Orville Parks: Early resident of Munsonville. Fisherman known for his tall fish stories. Married to Bertha Parks. Father to Dr. Martin Parks. Adopted uncle of Bryony Marseilles Simons. Appears in "Bryony," "Before The Blood: Bryony Marseilles," "Before The Blood: Henry Matthews," "Before The Blood: Bryony Simons," "The Phoenix," and "Call of the Siren."

Paxton: A domestic in Abbott Simons' home. Appears briefly in "Before The Blood: John Simons."

Mrs. Peabody: A client of supernatural super sleuth Cornell Dyer in "Cornell Dyer and the Whispering Wardrobe." Also known as Mrs. Claus.

Raymond Peabody: New York restaurant owner that hires pianist John Simons to play for immigrants coming into Castle Garden. Appears in "Before The Blood: John Simons."

Donald B. Pemberton: Historian at Cape Crag, Maine, in "Cornell Dyer and the Missing Tombstone."

Penelope: The favorite niece of the Squire of Levonshire. Appears in "Before The Blood: Kellen Wechsler."

Pericles: Greek general, orator, and statesman, orator, and general during the Golden Age of Athens: 480 to 404 BCE. Mentioned in "Before The Blood: Bryony Marseilles."

Miles Perry: Dashing student in tan pinstriped suit and yellow chrysanthemum in his lapel at Bible study at Jenson College. Appears in "Before The Blood: Henry Matthews."

Peter the Werewolf: Also known as Peter the Wild Boy. During the 18th century, he lived a feral life in the woods near Hamelin, Germany. The daughter-in-law of King George I in England had Peter brought to Great Britain, was he received care and lived to be an old man. Most likely had the rare genetic disorder Pitt–Hopkins syndrome. Mentioned "Lycanthropic Summer."

Philippe: Stableman at Arcadia. Appears in "Before The Blood: Henry Matthews."

Baby Boy Pike: Unnamed child of Boswell Pike and Susannah Pike, either stillborn or dying shortly after birth. Mentioned in "Before The Blood" Bryony Marseilles" and "Before The Blood: Bryony Simons."

Blanche Pike: Youngest child of Mayor Bosell Pike and Janet Meyers Pike. Stepsister of Boswell Pike Jr. and Iris Pike. Sister of Edgar Pike and Claude Pike. Loves her caretaker Ida Griffith. Appears in "Summer Sisters" and "Before The Blood: Bryony Marseilles."

Boswell Pike: Appointed by Owen Munson as first mayor of Munsonville. Philosophy teacher at Jenson College. Husband of Susannah Pike and Janet Meyers Pike. Father of Boswell Pike Jr., Iris Pike, an unnamed son, Edgar Pike, Claude Pike, and Blanche Pike. Appears in "Before The Blood: Bryony Marseilles," "Before The Blood: Henry Matthews," and "Before The Blood: Bryony Simons." Mentioned inn "The Phoenix" and "Call of the Siren."

Boswell Pike Jr.: Eldest son of Mayor Bosell Pike and Susanna Pike. Stepson of Janet Meyers Pike. Brother of Iris Pike. Stepbrother of Edgar Pike, Claude Pike, and Blanche Pike. Nemesis and fiancé of Susan Betts. Hated by Susan Betts and Bryony Marseilles. Hopes to be Munsonville's mayor. English teacher at Jenson College. Appears in "Summer Sisters," "Before The Blood: Bryony Marseilles," "Before The Blood: Bryony Simons," and "Call of the Siren."

Claude Pike: Unruly son of Boswell Pike and Janet Meyers Pike. Stepbrother of Boswell Pike Jr. and Iris Pike. Brother of Edgar and Blanche Pike. Appears in "Before The Blood: Bryony Marseilles."

Edgar Pike: Unruly son of Boswell Pike and Janet Meyers Pike. Stepbrother of Boswell Pike Jr. and Iris Pike. Brother of Claude and Blanche Pike. Appears in "Before The Blood: Bryony Marseilles."

Iris Pike: Eldest daughter of Mayor Bosell Pike and Susanna Pike. Stepson of Janet Meyers Pike. Sister of Boswell Pike Jr., whom she adores. Stepsister of Edgar Pike, Claude Pike, and Blanche Pike. Goes blind from measles and later attends Perkins School Perkins School for the Blind in Watertown, Massachusetts. Appears in "Summer Sisters," and "Before The Blood: Bryony Marseilles."

Janet Pike: Forthright Boston schoolteacher who travels to Munsonville to become Boswell Pike's mail-order bride. Adopted Mother of Boswell Pike Jr. and Iris Pike. Mother of Edgar Pike, Claude Pike, and Blanche Pike. Founder of the first public school in Munsonville. Appears in "Before The Blood: Bryony Marseilles." See also Janet Meyers.

Susanna Pike: Early resident of Munsonville. First wife of Boswell Pike. Mother of Boswell Pike Jr., Iris Pike, and an unnamed baby boy. Appears briefly in "Before The Blood: Bryony Marseilles."

Allen Pinkerton: Nineteenth century private investigator and founder of the Pinkerton National Detective Agency. Mentioned in "Before The Blood: Henry Matthews."

Dr. Piper: The hospital doctor that treated Sylvia Manning and supernatural super sleuth Cornell Dyer in "Cornell Dyer and the Necklace of Forgetfulness."

Babbie Platt: Special needs daughter of Sheriff Tom Platt and Nancy Platt. Appears in "Before The Blood: Henry Matthews."

Livy Platt: Evansville resident. Wife of Todd Mooney. Eldest daughter of Sheriff Tom Platt and Nancy Platt. Sister of Babbie Platt. Mentioned in "Before The Blood: Henry Matthews." See also Livy Mooney.

Nancy Platt: Wife of Sheriff Tom Platt. Mother of Livy Platt Mooney and Babbie Platt. Owner of Sweet Puffs, a mysterious white kitten with aquamarine eyes. Appears in "Before The Blood: Henry Matthews."

Sheriff Tom Platt: Sheriff of Evansville. Husband of Nancy Platt. Father of Livy Platt Mooney and Babbie Platt. Appears in "Before The Blood: Henry Matthews."

Polly Plese: A can-can girls at Hewes Music Hall in Lower Manhattan, New York. Appears in "Before The Blood: John Simons."

Louis Prang: Nineteenth century Polish-American lithographer and printer and immigrant from Germany. Known as the "Father of the American Christmas Card." Mentioned in "Before The Blood: John Simons."

Prince of Wales: Mentioned in "Before The Blood: John Simons," "Before The Blood: Kellen Wechsler," and "Before The Blood: Bryony Simons"

Mr. Principal: Principal of Sunnystorm School in "Cornell Dyer and the Calcium-Deficient Bones."

Mrs. Pruitt: A neighbor of the 1940s Wechsler family in "Before The Blood: Kellen Wechsler."

Mr. Puffin: Client of supernatural super sleuth Cornell Dyer in "Cornell Dyer and the Old Folks Home."

Obadiah Quill: Pantomime dame at Hewes Music Hall in Lower Manhattan, New York. Appears in "Before The Blood: John Simons."

Arthur Rackham: Real English book illustrator. Mentioned in "Before The Blood: Bryony Simons."

Randy: Love interest of Carrynne, the fictional alter ego of Caryn Rochelle in "Lycanthropic Summer."

Herr Gottfried Rantzouen: A vegetable merchant in the fictional Grotekop, Germany. Appears briefly in "Before The Blood: Kellen Wechsler."

Becky Sue Rawlins: Wife of Evansville tavern owner Eli Rawlins and promoter of birth control. Mother of Eli Rawlins Jr. Appears briefly in "Before The Blood: Henry Matthews."

Eli Rawlins: Evansville tavern owner and promoter of birth control. Married to Becky Sue Rawlins. Father of Eli Rawlins Jr. Appears briefly in "Before The Blood: Henry Matthews."

Eli Rawlins Jr.: Baby boy of Evansville tavern owner Eli Rawlins and Becky Sue Rawlins, both promoters of birth control. Appears briefly in "Before The Blood: Henry Matthews."

Mr. Realtor: Eager to sell a home on 311 Reed Street to supernatural super sleuth Cornell Dyer in "Cornell Dyer and the Calcium-Deficient Bones."

Miss Receptionist: Works at Sunnystorm School in "Cornell Dyer and the Calcium-Deficient Bones."

Terrance Rees: President of Rees Trading Company. Appears briefly in "Before The Blood: Kellen Wechsler."

Cesar Ritz: Nineteenth century Swiss hotelier, youngest of thirteen children, and founder of the Hôtel Ritz in Paris and the Ritz and Carlton Hotels in London. Mentioned in "Before The Blood: Kellen Wechsler."

Robert: A footman at Simons Mansion in "Bryony" and "Before The Blood: Bryony Simons."

Joe Roberts: Project manager for Simons Mansion. Appears in "Bryony" (briefly) and "House on Top of the Hill."

Jack Robinson: A mythical person from the eighteenth century who kept his social visits extremely short. That led to the expression "faster than you can say Jack Robinson." Mentioned in "Before The Blood: Henry Matthews."

Caryn Alaina Rochelle: Teen girl in the early 1960s who promised herself she would write the world's greatest werewolf love story by the time she turned eighteen. Protagonist of "Lycanthropic Summer."

Dr. Fred Rochelle: Gentle and compassionate veterinarian with offices in two fictional villages: Lyons Park, Michigan, and Shelby, Michigan. Known for his sensitivity to animals. Sister to Priscilla "Aunt Silly" Rochelle and father to Caryn Rochelle, teen protagonist of "Lycanthropic Summer." Also known as Frederick Allan Rochelle.

Priscilla Matilda Rochelle: Outlandish jewelry maker for the tourist shops in Shelby (where she lives) and Munsonville, both fictional villages in North Michigan. Sister of Dr. Fred Rochelle. Aunt of Caryn Rochelle, teen protagonist of "Lycanthropic Summer." See also Aunt Silly.

Shirley Marguerite Rochaminster Rochelle: Rich ex-wife of veterinarian Dr. Fred Rochelle. Mother of Caryn Rochelle, teen protagonist of "Lycanthropic Summer."

Rockefeller: John Davison Rockefeller Sr, a real philanthropist and first billionaire in United States history. Mentioned in "Before The Blood: Henry Matthews."

James Roosevelt: Real vice president of the real Chemical Bank of New York. Appears briefly in "Before The Blood: John Simons."

Mr. Rosenbaum: Employer of William Markham, husband of Etta Matthews Markum, sister of Henry Mattews. Appears briefly in "Before The Blood: Henry Matthews.

Rosie: Soup-making fortuneteller/witch. Appears in "Lycanthropic Summer."

Titus Rousseau: Provided instruction in the quadrivium to the adolescent Henry Matthews in "Before The Blood: Henry Matthews."

Dr. Abner Rothgard: A doctor who practices in Munsonville and Jenson Memorial College. Physician of Elizabeth Bathory. Strong knowledge of hematology (blood and blood disorders). Appears in "Before The Blood: John Simons," "Before The Blood: Kellen Wechsler," "Before The Blood: Bryony Marseilles," "Before The Blood: Henry Matthews," "Before The Blood: Bryony Simons,"

"The Phoenix," "Call of the Siren," "House on Top of the Hill," "Snowbell, "Bryony," "Visage," and "Staked!" See also Dr. Brandon Gradthorn, Dr. Arnold Hartgerd, Dr. Alvin Thradgort, and Dr. Edwin Gothart.

Jacques Roulet, The Werewolf of Angers: Sixteenth century French werewolf. Appears in "Lycanthropic Summer."

Anton Rubinstein: Real Russian virtuoso pianist. Through a contract with Steinway & Sons piano company, Rubinstein toured the United States from 1872 to 1873 season, giving 200 concerts. Mentioned in "Before The Blood: John Simons."

Amelia Rush: Vivacious and somewhat scatterbrained wife of Jenson surgeon Dr. Hiram Rush. Mother of Victorian Rush and Parker Rush. Appears in "Before The Blood: Henry Matthews."

Dr. Hiram Rush: Jenson surgeon. Husband of Amelia Rush. Father of Victoria Rush and Parker Rush. Appears in "Before The Blood: Henry Matthews."

Parker Rush: Toddler son of Dr. Hiram Rush and Amelia Rush. Brother of Victoria Rush. Appears briefly in "Before The Blood: Henry Matthews."

Victoria Rush: Slightly plump daughter of Dr. Hiram Rush and Victorian Rush of Jenson, Michigan. Popular with her father's medical students. Object of Henry Matthews' infatuation. Taught Henry to dance. Appears in "Before The Blood: Henry Matthews."

Mr. Rutgers: head of the school board in a short story in "Lycanthropic Summer."

Lonnie Russell: Obese, rich, spoiled, lazy piano student of John Simons. Son of Leopold Russell and Leona Russell. Mentioned in "Before The Blood: John Simons."

Leona Russell: Wife of Leopold Russell, who had a reversal of fortune and wound up taking boarders in their Fifth Avenue home. Mother of Lonnie Russell. Lover of Henry Matthews. Appears in "Before The Blood: John Simons," Before The Blood: Henry Matthews," and "Before The Blood: Bryony Simons."

Leopold Russell: Amassed wealth in turpentine, had a reversal of fortune and rented out rooms in his Fifth Avenue home. Husband of Leona Russell. Father of Lonnie Russell. Appears in "Before The Blood: John Simons," Before The Blood: Henry Matthews," and "Before The Blood: Bryony Simons."

Della Rutherford: Willowy wife of New York piano manufacturer Herbert Rutherford. Mother of Mortimer Rutherford. Hired John Simons to play for her twenty-fifth anniversary. Appears in "Bryony," "Before The Blood: John Simons," Before The Blood: Henry Matthews," and "Before The Blood: Bryony Simons."

Herbert Rutherford: New York piano manufacturer. Wife of Della Rutherford. Father of Mortimer Rutherford. Reluctantly hired John Simons to play for her twenty-fifth anniversary. Appears in "Before The Blood: John Simons," Before The Blood: Henry Matthews," and "Before The Blood: Bryony Simons." Mentioned in "Bryony."

Mortimer Rutherford: Pretentious son of New York piano manufacturer Herbert Rutherford and Della Rutherford. Persuades John Simons to play for his parents' twenty-fifth wedding anniversary in exchange for a cut of the profits to satisfy gambling debts. Engaged to "Mis Beatrice." Appears in "Before The Blood: John Simons."

Ruthie: Appears in a short story in "Lycanthropic Summer" and works in Dr. Fred Rochelle's veterinarian office in Shelby, also in "Lycanthropic Summer." Also appears as a waitress at Sue's Diner in "Ruthless."

Billy Salter: Caretaker of the grounds in Munsonville. Sister to Ginne Salter, waitress at Sue's Diner. Appear I House at the Top of the Hill." Mentioned in "Katie and the Big Fear."

Dr. Samuelson: Veterinarian in Munsonville. Appears in "Bryony," "Staked!," and "House on Top of the Hill."

Jay Sanderson: Evansville farmer and church pastor. Married to Rita Sanderson. Childless. Adopted father of the three remaining children of Sheriff Deputy Bart Hayes and his wife Flossie Hayes. Appears briefly in "Before The Blood: Henry Matthews."

Rita Sanderson: Wife of Evansville farmer and church pastor Jay Sandusky. Married to Rita Sanderson. Childless. Adopted mother of the three remaining children of Sheriff Deputy Bart Hayes and his wife Flossie Hayes. Caretaker of Livy Mooney. Mentioned in "Before The Blood: Henry Matthews."

George Sands: Real female French nineteenth century novelist. Mentioned in "Before The Blood: Bryony Marseilles."

Michael Sandusky: Thornton resident. Father of Mrs. Miranda Culpter, wife of Joe Culpter, who was a business associate of Owen Munson, Clyde Fisher, and (most likely) James Fisher. Mentioned in "Before The Blood: Bryony Marseilles."

Sandy: Wannabe friend of Caryn Rochelle in "Lycanthropic Summer."

Laech Herr Schapmester: Also known as Mr. Hal Laech. Former friend of Brandt Wechsler. Nemesis and persecutor of Kellen Wechsler. Appears in "Before The Blood: Kellen Wechsler."

Mr. School Board President: Appears briefly in this role in "Cornell Dyer and the Calcium-Deficient Bones."

Shealtiel, father of Zerubbabel: Biblical figure. Mentioned in "Before The Blood: Henry Matthews."

Miss School Secretary: Appears briefly in this role in "Cornell Dyer and the Calcium-Deficient Bones."

Sea Legs Stu: Worker on a cargo ship. Appears briefly in "Before The Blood: Kellen Wechsler."

Sebbie: Nickname Phoebe Betts uses for her husband Sebastian Betts in "Before The Blood: Bryony Marseilles."

Fanny Shaw: Female secondary character in Louisa May Alcott's 1869 novel "An Old-Fashioned Girl." Appears in literary form in "Before The Blood: Bryony Marseilles."

Tom Shaw: Main male character in Louisa May Alcott's 1869 novel "An Old-Fashioned Girl." Appears in literary form in "Before The Blood: Bryony Marseilles."

Abbott Simons: Full name is Farlow (or Farrow) Abbott Simons. Wealthy financier. Lives on Fifth Avenue, New York. Business associate of Lord Girard, Marshall Harrington, Herbert Rutherford, Bartholomew Smythe, and Albert Brumfeldt. Wife of Lucetta

Spencer Simons, Father of Adrianna Simons and John Simons. Staunch Catholic. Stubbornly attends Old St. Patrick Cathedral and refuses to recognize the new cathedral as the archdiocesan seat. Appears in "Before The Blood: John Simons" and briefly in "Before The Blood: Kellen Wechsler," "Before The Blood: Henry Matthews," and "Before The Blood: Bryony Simons." Mentioned in "Bryony."

Adrianna Simons: Infant daughter and firstborn child of Abbott Simons and Lucetta Spencer Simons. Dies moments after birth. Lives as a star watching over her younger brother John Simons, according to Lucetta. Appears very briefly in flashback and star form in "Before The Blood: John Simons" and in star form only in "Before The Blood: Bryony Simons."

Bryony Simons: Birth name was Bryonia. Daughter of Reverend Galien Marseilles and Adele Marseilles. Wife of John Simons. Mother of an unnamed son. Best friend of Susan Betts. Adopted niece of Orville Parks and Bertha Parks. Love interest of Luther Hasset and Henry Matthews. Only child but adopts the Fisher girls as her Summer Sisters. Infatuated with Owen Munson and Henry Matthews. Identifies with Lake Munson. Poor health due to chlorosis. Appears in "Before The Blood: Bryony Marseilles," "Before The Blood: Henry Matthews," and "Before The Blood: Bryony Simons." Appears in flashback in "The Phoenix." Appears briefly in "Bryony" and "Staked!" Mentioned in "Visage," "Call of the Siren," Brainy Ann," "Julie and the Too-Hard Homework," and "Katie and the Big Fear." See also Bryony Marseilles

John Simons: Youngest child and only son of Abbott Simons and Lucetta Spencer Simons. World-renowned pianist and composer. Husband of Bryony Marseilles Simons. Host of Kellen Wechsler, his manager. Owner of Simons Mansion. Vampire after death.

Appears in "Before The Blood: John Simons," "Before The Blood: Kellen Wechsler," "Before The Blood: Henry Matthews," "Before The Blood: Bryony Simons," "The Phoenix," "Bryony," "Visage," and "Staked!" Mentioned by name in "Brainy Ann," "Julie and the To-Hard Homework," "Katie and the Big Fear," and "Karla Joins In."

Lucetta Simons: Wife of Abbott Simons. Mother of Adrianna Simons and John Simons, whom she adores and often hand-feeds. Daughter of Everett Spencer and Prudence Spencer. Sister of Eleanor Spencer Wilson, Martha Spencer, and Christine Spencer. Avid gardener, with plants and vines growing all over the bedroom. Appears in "Before The Blood: John Simons." Mentioned in "Before The Blood: Bryony Simons" and "Bryony." See also Lucetta Spencer.

Mary Singler: Runs a rooming house in Evansville. Henry Matthews' occasional lover. Eventually marries Jim Kaden, a railroad worker and border at her house, on Valentine's Day. Appears briefly in "Before The Blood: Henry Matthews." See also Mary Kaden.

Lady Siron: Guest at Jacob King's spacious townhome overlooking Kensington Gardens in London England. Married to Lord Siron. Flirted with Lord Windlser at a tea party. Appears briefly in "Before The Blood: Kellen Wechsler."

Lord Siron: Guest at Jacob King's spacious townhome overlooking Kensington Gardens in London England. Appears briefly in "Before The Blood: Kellen Wechsler."

Sisters of Mercy: Founded and operated the fictional St. Joseph Orphanage for Boys in Hartford, Connecticut. Mention in "Before The Blood: John Simons"

Sitting Bull: Political and spiritual leader of the Sioux tribes, whom he united to relentlessly fight against white men's control of the land. Mentioned in "Before The Blood: John Simons."

Donovan Smith: Librarian with liberal leanings, who hosts politically charged lectures in "Before The Blood: Henry Matthews."

Bartholomew Smythe: Sickly and very old business associate of Abbott Simons, Marshall Harrington, Lord Girard, Albert Brumfeldt, Warren Holloway, and Herbert Rutherford. Eccentric art collector. Husband of Edwina Smythe. Patient of Dr. Edwin Gothart and Dr. Martin Parks. Calls up P.T. Barnum in a séance. Appears in "Before The Blood: John Simons," "Before The Blood: Henry Matthews," "Before The Blood: Bryony Simons," "Call of the Siren," and "Bryony."

Edwina Smythe: Wife of Bartholomew of Edwina Smythe. Eccentric art collector. Patient of Dr. Edwin Gothart and Dr. Martin Parks. Calls up P.T. Barnum in a séance. Appears in "Before The Blood: John Simons," "Before The Blood: Henry Matthews," "Before The Blood: Bryony Simons," "Call of the Siren," and "Bryony."

Elspeth Smythe: Granddaughter of Bartholomew Smythe and Edwina Smythe. Appears briefly "Before The Blood: Bryony Simons" and "Bryony."

Meredyth Smythe: Granddaughter of Bartholomew Smythe and Edwina Smythe. Appears briefly "Before The Blood: Bryony Simons" and "Bryony."

Belinda Solomon: Daughter of Patrick Solomon. Wife of Stuart Drake, owner of Drake's Store. Mother of Addison Drake, Norton Drake, and Matilda Drake. Appears in "Before The Blood: Bryony Marseilles," "Before the Blood: Bryony Simons," and "Call of the Siren." See also Belinda Drake.

Patrick Solomon: Early resident of Munsonville. Sick with consumption. Widower. Father of Belinda Solomon Drake. Appears in "Before The Blood: Bryony Simons." Mentioned in "Call of the Siren."

John Philip Sousa: Real nineteenth century American composer, conductor, and recording artist. His music appears briefly in "Before The Blood: Bryony Simons."

Brinsley Spencer: Minister. Father of Everett Spencer. Husband of Corina Spencer. Mentioned briefly in "Before The Blood: John Simons."

Christine Spencer: Youngest daughter of Everett Spencer and Prudence Spencer. Sister of Eleanor Spencer Wilson, Martha Spencer, and Lucetta Spencer Simons. Vanished forever after running off with a guest from Spencer Inn. Appears in "Before The Blood: John Simons."

Corina Spencer: See Granny Spencer.

Eleanor Spencer: Eldest daughter of Everett Spencer and Prudence Spencer. Heir and owner/operator of Spencer Inn. Wife of Ralph Wilson. Childless. Sister of Lucetta Spencer Simons, Martha

Spencer, and Christine Spencer. Sober personality. Suffers from headaches. Appears in "Before The Blood: John Simons." See also Eleanor Wilson.

Everett Spencer: Son of Brinsley Spencer and Corina Spencer. Owner/operator of Spencer Inn. Wife of Prudence Spencer. Father of Eleanor Spencer Wilson, Lucetta Spencer Simons, Martha Spencer, and Christine Spencer. Piano player. Jolly and even-tempered. John Simons maternal grandfather. Also known as Papa Everett. Appears in "Before The Blood: John Simons."

Granny Spencer: Wife of Brinsley Spencer, among others. Mother of Everett Spencer, among others. Lives in a hut in the woods. Extensive garden inside and out. Reclusive and eccentric. Appears in "Before The Blood: John Simons."

Lucetta Spencer: Wife of Abbott Simons. Mother of Adrianna Simons and John Simons, whom she adores and often hand-feeds. Daughter of Everett Spencer and Prudence Spencer. Sister of Eleanor Spencer Wilson, Martha Spencer, and Christine Spencer. Avid gardener, with plants and vines growing all over the bedroom. Appears in "Before The Blood: John Simons." Mentioned in "Before The Blood: Bryony Simons" and "Bryony." See also Lucetta Spencer.

Martha Spencer: Daughter of Everett Spencer and Prudence Spencer. Sister of Elanor Spencer Wilson. Lucetta Spencer Simons, and Christine Spencer. Engaged to Wyndham Franklin, who raised Morgan horses in New Haven Connecticut. Appears in "Before The Blood: John Simons."

Prudence Spencer: Wife of Everett Spencer. Mother of Eleanor Spencer Wilson, Lucetta Spencer Simons, Martha Spencer, and

Christine Spencer. Primary cook and housekeeper of Spencer Inn. Jolly personality. Also known as Mama Prudie. Appears in "Before The Blood: John Simons."

Mitchell Spurm: Victim of arson in his barn, five miles north of Jenson. Mentioned in "Before The Blood: Bryony Marseilles."

Johanna Spyri: Real author of "Heidi," a bestselling children's fiction/Swiss literature story of a young girl raised in the Alps by her grandfather known as the Alm-Uncle. Referenced in "Before The Blood: Bryony Marseilles."

Squire of Levonshire: Owned a large parcel of land that Kellen Wechsler wanted for himself. Has a favorite niece named Penelope. Lives in Meredith Manor. Hosted a Michaelmas celebration on his grounds. Appears in "Before The Blood: Kellen Wechsler." See also Thomas Thackery.

St. Francis of Assisi: Real wealthy son of a cloth merchant who forsook his wealth for a life of poverty and devotion to God. Mentioned in "Before The Blood: John Simons" in reference to the dramatic way he rejected his upbringing: stripping naked and hugging a leper.

St. Ladislaus: King of Hungary from 1077 and King of Croatia from 1091. Mentioned in "Bryony."

Randolph Monroe McCallister St. Martin: Rich man from North Lyons who disappeared with his wife and son soon after the son's birth. Appears in "Lycanthropic Summer" and "House on Top of the Hill."

Randolph Monroe McCallister St. Martin the Third: Son of Randolph Monroe McCallister St. Martin and Delores St. Martin.

Disappears after birth with his parents. Appears in "Lycanthropic Summer" and "House on Top of the Hill."

Delores Gevaudan St. Martin: Wife of Randolph Monroe McCallister St. Martin. Identifies with werewolves. Appears in "Lycanthropic Summer" and "House on Top of the Hill."

James Stanford: Leland Buchanan: Business associate of Albert Brumfeldt and Lord Girard. Appears in "Before The Blood: Henry Matthews" and "Before The Blood: Bryony Simons."

Father Stanislaus: Pastor at the fictional Mary Our Holy Mother Catholic Church in Chicago, who tells Emma Markham, Henry Matthews' niece, that she should offer up teaching at the school as a sacrifice to God instead of expecting wages. Mentioned in "Before The Blood: Henry Matthews."

Mr. Steering: Shopkeeper at Marbleheart, Ohio, in "Cornell Dyer and the Eerie Lake."

William Steinway: Head of Steinway & Sons. Master piano designer. Founder of Steinway Hall. Hires John Simons to play piano. Appears in "Before The Blood: John Simons."

Gary Stevenson: Business associate of 1940s at Kellen Wechsler. R. C. Walter's advertising agency. Husband of Jeanette Stevenson. Accepting of Kellen's mistress, Margaret Vollbauer. Appears in "Before The Blood: Kellen Wechsler."

Jeannette Stevenson: Wife of Gary Stevenson. Thinly tolerates Kellen's mistress, Margaret Vollbauer. Appears in "Before The Blood: Kellen Wechsler."

Mrs. Stickney: Housekeeper at Caryn Rochelle's North Lyons, Michigan, home in "Lycanthropic Summer."

Frank R. Stockton: A nineteenth century American writer of short stories and children's stories, best known for "The Lady of the Tiger?" Mentioned in "Bryony."

Archibald Stone: Vulgar and popular piano player at Hewes Music Hall in Lower Manhattan, New York. Ne'er to do cousin of Dr. Sidney Stone. Appears in "Before The Blood: John Simons" and "Before The Blood: Kellen Wechsler." Mentioned in "Before The Blood: Bryony Simons."

Judith Stone: Stuffy and pretentious wife of Dr. Sidney Stone. Appears in "Before The Blood: Henry Matthews."

Dr. Sidney Stone: Eminent Jenson physician in skill, stature, and social standing. Business associate of Lord Girard. Treats Henry Matthews' asthma. Member of the Munsonville Society for the Humanities. Archetype of "old medicine" clinging to its traditions and stubbornly refusing modern medicine, including blood transfusions. By turns polished, snarky, and provoking. Appears in "Before The Blood: Bryony Marseilles," "Before The Blood: Henry Matthews," and "Before The Blood: Bryony Simons."

August Strindberg: A Swedish writer and painter (1849 to 1912). Referenced in "Before The Blood: Bryony Marseilles."

Peter Stumpf: German farmer and serial killer who was accused of werewolfery. He was executed on October 31, 1589. Also known as the Werewolf of Bedburg. Mentioned in "Lycanthropic Summer."

William Stroudley: Nineteenth century English locomotive engineer, whose latest work appeared at the Exposition Universelle (World's Fair) in 1889 in Paris, France. Mentioned in "Before The Blood: Kellen Wechsler."

Mr. Stump: Mysterious old man in "Cornell Dyer and the Eerie Lake."

Mr. Superintendent: Superintendent of Sunnystorm School in "Cornell Dyer and the Calcium-Deficient Bones."

Colette Swenson: Wife of Jan Swenson. Mother of Gabe Swenson and Mae Swenson Dalton. Appears in "House on Top of the Hill."

Gabe Swenson: Son of Jan Swenson and Colette Swenson. Brother of Mae Swenson Dalton. Works for Beulah County sheriff's department and Munsonville Police Department. Mentor of Will Miller. Appears in "Bryony," "House on Top of the Hill," and "Brainy Ann."

Jan Swenson: Beulah County sheriff. Husband of Colette Swenson. Father of Gabe Swenson and Mae Swenson Dalton. Appears in "Call of the Siren," "House on Top of the Hill," and "Brainy Ann."

May Swenson: Wife of Rob Dalton. Mother of Ann Dalton and Clay Dalton. Daughter of Jan Swenson and Colette Swenson. Sister of Gabe Swenson. Appears in "Bryony," Lycanthropic Summer," "Julie and the Too-Hard Homework," Katie and the Big Fear," Brainy Ann," and "House on Top of the Hill." See also May Dalton.

Algernon Charles Swinburne: Real nineteenth century English poet and literary critic. Mentioned in "Before The Blood: Bryony Marseilles."

Philip Sydney: Male secondary character in Louisa May Alcott's 1869 novel "An Old-Fashioned Girl." Appears in literary form in "Before The Blood: Bryony Marseilles."

Talbert: A domestic in Abbot Simons home, John's post-Wesley valet. Appears in "Before The Blood: John Simons."

Tartars: Sometimes called "Tatars." A broad name for various Turkic ethnic groups. Mentioned in "Bryony."

Pyotr Ilyich Tchaikovsky: Real nineteenth century Russian composer, most famous for the ballets "Swan Lake" and "The Nutcracker." Mentioned in "Bryony" and "Before The Blood: Bryony Simons."

Mr. Teabody: World-traveler uncle of supernatural super sleuth Sherman Homes. Mentioned in "Cornell Dyer and the Howls of Basketville."

Miss English Teacher: Works at Sunnystorm School in "Cornell Dyer and the Calcium-Deficient Bones."

Mr. History Teacher: Works at Sunnystorm School in "Cornell Dyer and the Calcium-Deficient Bones."

Mr. Math Teacher: Works at Sunnystorm School in "Cornell Dyer and the Calcium-Deficient Bones."

Thomas Thackery: Owned a large parcel of land that Kellen Wechsler wanted for himself. Has a favorite niece named Penelope. Lives in Merdeith Manor Hosted a Michaelmas celebration on his grounds. Appears in "Before The Blood: Kellen Wechsler." See also Squire of Levonshire.

Ed Thompson: Client of 1940s Kellen's at R.C. Waters advertising agency in "Before The Blood: Kellen Wechsler."

Henry David Thoreau: Nineteenth century American essayist and political activist, best known for "Walden," his book of eighteen essays of living in the natural world. Mentioned in "Bryony."

Dr. Alvin Thradgort: A doctor who practices in Munsonville and Jenson Memorial Hospital. Physician to Elizabeth Bathory. Strong knowledge of hematology (blood and blood disorders). Appears in "Before The Blood: John Simons," "Before The Blood: Kellen Wechsler," "Before The Blood: Bryony Marseilles," "Before The Blood: Henry Matthews," "Before The Blood: Bryony Simons," "The Phoenix," "Call of the Siren," "House on Top of the Hill," "Snowbell," "Bryony," "Visage," and "Staked!" See also Dr. Brandon Gradthorn, Dr. Arnold Hartgerd, Dr. Edwin Gothart, and Dr. Abner Rothgard.

General Tom Thumb: Real American circus performer under P.T. Barnum. Married Lavinia Warren on February 10, 1863, at Grace Episcopal Church in New York City. Mentioned in "Before The Blood: John Simons."

James Thurber: A twentieth century American cartoonist, humorist, and writer. Mentioned in "Bryony."

Mark Twain: Pen name of Samuel Langhorne Clemens, a real nineteenth century American writer and humorist. Best known for the novels "The Adventures of Tom Sawyer," and "Adventures of Huckleberry Finn." Mentioned in "Before The Blood: Bryony Marseilles."

Danny Tyler: One of the Never Robbers in "Cornel Dyer and the Never Robbers."

The crooked old man: Sells plush dogs at the zoo gate in a short story in "Lycanthropic summer."

The Clock Man: Owner of The Clock Shop in Shelby and source of nightmares for Caryn Rochelle in "Lycanthropic Summer." Also appears in "Call of the Siren."

The Garbage Men: Appear frequently in "Cornell Dyer and the Calcium-Deficient Bones."

The Man: A mysterious, all-known guide who give hints that he's Jesus in "Cornell Dyer and the Never Robbers."

Thoreau: A reference to Henry David Thoreau's book "Walden," of which a passage is read in "Before The Blood: Bryony Marseilles."

Tillie: Servant girl in the laundry room at Simons Mansion. Appears in "Before The Blood: Bryony Simons."

Tonjes: Fellow laborer in the fields with Kellen Wechsler. Was dismissed for falling asleep on the job. Mentioned in "Before The Blood: Kellen Wechsler."

Oscar Tschirky: Swiss-American restaurateur. Maître d'hôtel of Delmonico's Restaurant and (later) the Waldorf-Astoria Hotel in Manhattan, New York. Appears briefly in "Before The Blood: Bryony Simons."

Tuatha Dé Danann: Supernatural race in Irish mythology. Mentioned in "Bryony" and "Staked!"

Uncle Burke: Deceased uncle at a client's séance in "Cornell Dyer and the Flu."

Henry van Dyke Jr.: A nineteenth and twentieth century American author, clergyman, diplomat, educator, and chair of the committee that wrote The Book of Common Worship of 1906, which was the first Presbyterian printed liturgy. In 1907, he wrote the lyrics to "Joyful, Joyful We Adore Thee" (1907). The hymns melody is Beethoven's "Ode to Joy." Mentioned in "Bryony."

Vanderbilts: One of the real wealthiest and prestigious families in the United States during the nineteenth century, with many members living in mansions on Fifth Avenue, New York. Mentioned in "Before The Blood: John Simons," "Before The Blood: Kellen Wechsler," and "Before The Blood: Henry Matthews."

Mrs. Variola: Shopkeeper in Leland Hills, Illinois, who has a tender heart for Henry Matthews and his boyhood family. Appears in "Before The Blood: Henry Matthew."

Velter: Fellow laborer in the fields with Kellen Wechsler. Was dismissed for bringing home an extra load of manure. Mentioned in "Before The Blood: Kellen Wechsler."

Michel Verdun: Sixteenth century French werewolf. Mentioned in "Lycanthropic Summer."

Vivien: Wannabe friend of Caryn Rochelle inn "Lycanthropic Summer."

Voll-Bauer: Wealthy farmer on the outskirts of Grotekop, Germany during the 30 Years Way. Leases part of his land for Kellen Wechsler to farm. Kellen Wechsler is also infatuated with Voll-

Bauer's Scottish wife. Appears in "Before The Blood: Kellen Wechsler."

Margaret Vollbauer: Mistress and secretary of 1940s Kellen Wechsler. Resembles Voll-Bauer's Scottish wife from the seventeenth century. Appears in "Before The Blood: Kellen Wechsler."

Mr. Walczak: Retired scientist and science teacher at Munsonville School in "Bryony."

Betty Walker: Resident of Munsonville. Wife of Daniel Walker, a fisherman. Mother of Nancy "Nan" Walker." Appears briefly in "Before The Blood: Bryony Simons" and "Call of the Siren."

Danny Walker: Son of Nan Walker. Appears in "Call of the Siren" and "House on Top of the Hill."

Daniel Walker: Fisherman and resident of Munsonville. Husband of Betty Walker. Mentioned in "Before The Blood: Bryony Simons" and "Call of the Siren."

Nan Walker: Daughter of Daniel Walker and Betty Walker. Single mother of Daniel Walker. Works at Munsonville Inn and Sue's Diner. Loyal friend of Sue Bass. Appears in "Before The Blood: Bryony Marseilles," "Before The Blood: Bryony Simons," Call of the Siren," and "House on Top of the Hill."

Judy Warman: Journalist. Works for The Munsonville Times, which her parents Nick Warman and Lynne Warman own. Married to Russ Miller. Appears in "House on Top of the Hill" and "Katie and the Big Fear." Mentioned in "Karla Joins In."

Lynne Warman: Co-owner of The Munsonville Times with her husband Nick Warman. Father of Judy Warman. Appears in "House on Top of the Hill."

Nick Warman: Co-owner of The Munsonville Times with his wife Lynne Warman. Father of Judy Warman. Appears in "House on Top of the Hill."

Lavinia Warren: Married General Tom Thumb, an American circus performer under P.T. Barnum, at Grace Episcopal Church on February 10, 1863, in New York City. Mentioned in "Before The Blood: John Simons."

Baby Bonnie Watson: Youngest child of a too-good-to-be-true family of piano students of John Simons. Daughter of Pastor Milton Watson and Flora Watson. Sister of Garrett Watson, Benjamin Watson, and Eugenia Watson. Briefly appears in "Before The Blood: John Simons."

Benjamin Watson: Youngest son of a too-good-to-be-true family of piano students of John Simons. Son of Pastor Milton Watson and Flora Watson. Brother of Garrett Watson, Eugenia Watson, and Baby Bonnie Watson. Briefly appears in "Before The Blood: John Simons."

Dr. Lou "Doc" Wallace: Evansville doctor. Mentioned in "Before The Blood: Henry Matthews."

Eugenia Watson: Oldest daughter of a too-good-to-be-true family of piano students of John Simons. Daughter of Pastor Milton Watson and Flora Watson. Sister of Garrett Watson, Benjamin Watson, and Baby Bonnie Watson. Briefly appears in "Before The Blood: John Simons."

Flora Watson: Domestic queen of a too-good-to-be-true family of piano students of John Simons. Wife of Pastor Milton Watson. Mother of Garrett Watson, Benjamin Watson, Eugenia Watson, and Baby Bonnie Watson. Briefly appears in "Before The Blood: John Simons."

Garrett Watson: Oldest son of a too-good-to-be-true family of piano students of John Simons. Son of Pastor Milton Watson and Flora Watson. Brother of Benjamin Watson, Eugenia Watson, and Baby Bonnie Watson. Briefly appears in "Before The Blood: John Simons."

Pastor Milton Watson: Head of a too-good-to-be-true family of piano students of John Simons. Husband of Flora Watson. Father of Garrett Watson, Benjamin Watson, Eugenia Watson, and Baby Bonnie Watson. Briefly appears in "Before The Blood: John Simons."

Jean Antoine Watteau: Real eighteenth century French painter in the Baroque style (emphasis on detail, color, movement). "Before The Blood: Henry Matthew."

Bill Watts: North Lyons police officer and cousin of Shirley Marguerite Rochaminster Rochelle. Appears in "Lycanthropic Summer."

Alheit Wechsler: Daughter of Kellen Wechsler and Catarin Wechsler. Died in childbirth, age unknown. Mentioned once "Before The Blood: Kellen Wechsler."

Allecke Wechsler: Eldest son of Kellen Wechsler and Catarin Wechsler. Died either in early childhood or from the bubonic plague, age unknown. Mentioned once "Before The Blood: Kellen Wechsler."

Apolonia Wechsler: Son of Kellen Wechsler and Catarin Wechsler. Died in childhood, age unknown. Appears in "Before The Blood: Kellen Wechsler."

Bartold Wechsler: Son of Kellen Wechsler and Catarin Wechsler. Died from bubonic plague, age unknown. Appears in "Before The Blood: Kellen Wechsler."

Brandt Wechsler: Father of Kellen Wechsler. Lover of Metta, Kellen Wechsler's teen mother. War hero/deserter in the 30 Years War. Appears in "Before The Blood: Kellen Wechsler."

Carsten Wechsler: Son of Kellen Wechsler and Catarin Wechsler. Died from bubonic plague, age unknown. Appears in "Before The Blood: Kellen Wechsler."

Catarin Wechsler: Resident of Grotekop, Germany, during the 30 Years War. Wife of Kellen Wechsler. Mother of Allecke Wechsler, Marige Wechsler, Jurgen Wechsler, Otto Wechsler, Hilmar Wechsler (son), Eugell Wechsler, Alheit Wechsler, Leveke Wechsler, Ruprech Wechsler, Statius Wechsler, Ludolph Wechsler, Nolthe Wechsler, Maren Wechsler, Bartold Wechsler, Hilmar Wechsler (daughter), Peternella Wechsler, Apolonia Wechsler, Kungund Wechsler, Danchmer Wechsler, Carsten Wechsler, a daughter whose name was "known only to the angels" (along with others). Appears in "Before The Blood: Kellen Wechsler." See also Catarin Bohnhorst

Charlie Wechsler: Middle son of Kellen Wechsler in the 1940s of world of Kellen's dying brain. Appears in "Before The Blood: Kellen Wechsler."

Danchmer Wechsler: Son of Kellen Wechsler and Catarin Wechsler. Died from bubonic plague, age unknown. Appears in "Before The Blood: Kellen Wechsler."

Donna Wechsler: Wife of Kellen Wechsler in the 1940s of world of Kellen's dying brain. Resembles Darlene Marchellis. Appears in "Before The Blood: Kellen Wechsler."

Elmer Wechsler: Eldest son of Kellen Wechsler in the 1940s of world of Kellen's dying brain. Appears in "Before The Blood: Kellen Wechsler."

Eugell Wechsler: Daughter of Kellen Wechsler and Catarin Wechsler. Died in early childhood, age unknown. Mentioned once "Before The Blood: Kellen Wechsler."

Floyd Wechsler: Infant son of Kellen Wechsler in the 1940s of world of Kellen's dying brain. Appears in "Before The Blood: Kellen Wechsler."

Hilmar Wechsler: Son of Kellen Wechsler and Catarin Wechsler. Died either in early childhood or from bubonic plague, age unknown. Mentioned once "Before The Blood: Kellen Wechsler."

Hilmar Wechsler: Daughter of Kellen Wechsler and Catarin Wechsler. Died in childbirth, age unknown. Mentioned once "Before The Blood: Kellen Wechsler."

Jurgen Wechsler: Son Kellen Wechsler and Catarin Wechsler. Died either in early childhood or bubonic, age unknown. Mentioned in "Before The Blood: Kellen Wechsler."

Kellen Wechsler: Cottager in the fictional Grotekop, Germany, during the 30 Years War. Was turned into a vampire/ nachtzehrer while dying from the bubonic plague. Husband of Catarin Wechsler and Donna Wechsler. Father of Allecke Wechsler, Marige Wechsler, Jurgen Wechsler, Otto Wechsler, Hilmar Wechsler (son), Eugell Wechsler, Alheit Wechsler, Leveke Wechsler, Ruprech Wechsler, Statius Wechsler, Ludolph Wechsler, Nolthe Wechsler, Maren Wechsler, Bartold Wechsler, Hilmar Wechsler (daughter), Peternella Wechsler, Apolonia Wechsler, Kungund Wechsler, Danchmer Wechsler, Carsten Wechsler, a daughter whose name was "known only to the angels" (along with others), Elmer Wechsler, Ruth Wechsler, Charlie Wechsler, Pauline Wechsler, and Floyd Wechsler. Obsessed with renowned pianist Seymor Cassidy. Manager of pianist John Simons (with a contract sealed in regular sips of John's blood). Appears in "Bryony," "Visage," "Staked!," "Before The Blood: John Simons," "Before The Blood: Kellen Wechsler," "Before The Blood: Henry Matthews," "Before The Blood: Bryony Simons," "The Phoenix," and "Cornell Dyer and the 'Mistical' Being."

Kungund Wechsler: Daughter of Kellen Wechsler and Catarin Wechsler. Died from bubonic plague, age unknown. Appears in "Before The Blood: Kellen Wechsler."

Leveke Wechsler: Daughter of Kellen Wechsler and Catarin Wechsler. Died in childbirth, age unknown. Mentioned once "Before The Blood: Kellen Wechsler."

Ludolph Wechsler: Son Kellen Wechsler and Catarin Wechsler. Probably died from bubonic plague, age unknown. Appears in "Before The Blood: Kellen Wechsler."

Maren Wechsler: Daughter of Kellen Wechsler and Catarin Wechsler. Died from bubonic plague, age unknown. Appears in "Before The Blood: Kellen Wechsler."

Marige Wechsler: Eldest daughter of Kellen Wechsler and Catarin Wechsler. Died in early childhood, age unknown. Mentioned once in "Before The Blood: Kellen Wechsler."

Nolthe Wechsler: Son Kellen Wechsler and Catarin Wechsler. Died from bubonic plague, age unknown. Appears in "Before The Blood: Kellen Wechsler."

Otto Wechsler: Son of Kellen Wechsler and Catarin Wechsler. Died either in early childhood or from bubonic plague, age unknown. Mentioned once "Before The Blood: Kellen Wechsler."

Pauline Wechsler: Youngest daughter of Kellen Wechsler in the 1940s of world of Kellen's dying brain. Appears in "Before The Blood: Kellen Wechsler."

Peternella Wechsler: Daughter of Kellen Wechsler and Catarin Wechsler. Died in childhood, age unknown. Appears in "Before The Blood: Kellen Wechsler."

Ruprech Wechsler: Son Kellen Wechsler and Catarin Wechsler. Died from bubonic plague, age unknown. Appears in "Before The Blood: Kellen Wechsler."

Statius Wechsler: Son Kellen Wechsler and Catarin Wechsler. Died from bubonic plague, age unknown. Appears in "Before The Blood: Kellen Wechsler."

Ruth Wechsler: Eldest daughter of Kellen Wechsler in the 1940s of world of Kellen's dying brain. Appears in "Before The Blood: Kellen Wechsler."

Herr Franz Weitermann: Shrewd, softspoken councilman in the fictional Seulobitz, Germany. Appears in "Before The Blood: Kellen Wechsler."

H.G. Wells: Prolific English novelist and historian, known especially for "The time Machine" and "War of the Worlds." Mentioned in "Before The Blood: Kellen Wechsler."

Kevin Wellman: Librarian with a German accent in "Cornell Dyer and the 'Mistical' Being."

Wendy: Worked for Dr. Fred Rochelle's veterinarian office in Shelby. Appears in "Lycanthropic Summer."

Banneker Wheatley: Loyal, English friend of Henry Matthews at Jenson College. Appears in "Before The Blood: Henry Matthews."

Walt Whitman Jr.: Nineteenth century American essayist and poet. Known as the "father of free verse." Mentioned in "Bryony."

Kimberly Whitney: A friend of Melissa Marchellis from Grovers Park, Illinois. A blonde, blue-eyed girl with a propensity for getting into trouble. Appears in "Bryony" and "Snowbell."

John Greenleaf Whittier: A nineteenth century American, Quaker poet. Influenced by the Scottish poet Robert Burns. Author of "The

Pumpkin," which Boswell Pike recites in "Before The Blood: Bryony Marseilles." Mentioned ibn "Bryony" and "Call of the Siren."

Eleanor Wilson: Wife of Ralph Wilson. Daughter of Everett and Prudence Spencer. Sister of Lucetta Spencer Simons, Martha Spencer, and Christine Spencer. Eventual owner and operator of Spencer Inn, New Haven Connecticut. Appears in "Before The Blood: John Simons." See also Eleanor Spencer.

Wilhelm: Fellow laborer in the fields with Kellen Wechsler. Was dismissed for tardiness. Mentioned in "Before The Blood: Kellen Wechsler."

Ralph Wilson: Fiancé, later husband, of Eleanor Spencer Wilson, John Simons' oldest aunt. Appears in "Before The Blood: John Simons."

Kirk Winkler: Gas station clerk with stutter and German accent in "Cornell Dyer and the 'Mistical' Being."

Lady Petunia Winsler: Gossiping guest at Jacob King's spacious townhome overlooking Kensington Gardens in London England. Married to Lord Winsler. Appears briefly in "Before The Blood: Kellen Wechsler."

Lord Winsler: Guest at Jacob King's spacious townhome overlooking Kensington Gardens in London England. Married to Lady Petunia Winsler. Flirted with Lady Siron at a tea party. Appears briefly in "Before The Blood: Kellen Wechsler."

Dr. Jim Wipston: Dr. John Watson "Sherlock Holmes" parody character. Part of a trio of supernatural super sleuths that include

Cornell Dyer and Sherman Homes Appears in "Cornell Dyer and the Howls of Basketville."

Miss Bethany Ann Wonderbuilt: Twin sister of Miss Bethany Ann Wonderbuilt. Daughter of the Wonderbuilt family who donated the indoor swimming pool to Sunnystorm School. The school's missing science teacher and the reason supernatural super sleuth Cornell Dyer is asked to substitute teach in "Cornell Dyer and the Calcium-Deficient Bones."

Beverly Wonderbuilt: Twin sister of Miss Bethany Ann Wonderbuilt. Daughter of the Wonderbuilt family who donated the indoor swimming pool to Sunnystorm School. Appears in in "Cornell Dyer and the Calcium-Deficient Bones."

Charles Frederick Worth: English fashion designer, father of haute couture and founder of House of Worth fashion house in Paris, France.

Brigham Young: Second president of the Church of Jesus Christ of Latter-day Saints, also known as the Mormon Church, from 1847 until his death in 1877. Mentioned in "Before The Blood: John Simons."

Zerubbabel son of Shealtiel: Governor of Yehud province in the Bible. Mentioned in "Before The Blood: Henry Matthews."

Zeus: Greek god of sky and thunder. Henry Matthews gives this nickname to the doctor in Leland Hills, Illinois, because of his great height and deep booming voice. Appears briefly in "Before The Blood: Henry Matthews."

Viktor Zhuravlev: Fictional Russian immigrant who entered the United States through Castle Garden. Appears briefly in "Before The Blood: John Simons."

Henry Ziegler: Nephew of William Steinway, who became the eventual head of Steinway & Sons. Master piano designer. Appears in "Before The Blood: John Simons."

PART TWO: PLACES

311 Reed Street: A home in Sunnystorm, which school officials are pushing supernatural super sleuth Cornell Dyer to buy in "Cornell Dyer and the Calcium-Deficient Bones."

4 East 7th Street: Address for Dr. Alvin Thradgort's office in "Before The Blood: Kellen Wechsler."

666 Fifth Street: Home of Gordon James, president of First Bank of Shelby. Appears in "Lycanthropic Summer."

7ᵗʰ Avenue: More precisely, 881 Seventh Avenue, Manhattan, New York, where Carnegie Hall is located. Appears in "Before The Blood: Bryony Simons."

703 Foster Avenue, Unit C, Chicago: Home of William and Etta Markham, sister and brother-in-law of Henry Matthews. Appears in "Before The Blood: Henry Matthews."

709 Marketplace: Address for Jenson photographer Roger Masury. Appears in "Before The Blood: Henry Matthews."

Academy of Music: A nineteenth century opera house in New York. It was demolished in 1926. John Simons performed there in "Before The Blood: John Simons."

Admont Abbey Library in Austria: A place where vampire Kellen hangs out and reads in "Before The Blood: Kellen Wechsler."

Angel Quilt: Sue Bass' term for her quilt, handmade by the ministering spirits.

Arc de Triomphe: A huge commemorative arch in Paris, France, which stands at the western end of the Champs-Élysée and measures 164 feet high and 148 feet wide. Mentioned in "Before The Blood: Kellen Wechsler."

Arcadia: Lord Girard's respite chateau of "simplicity, peace, and happiness" deep in the woods between Evansville and Munsonville. Appears in "Before The Blood: Henry Matthews." Mentioned in "The Phoenix."

Archdiocese of Detroit: Roman Catholic diocese in Detroit, Michigan, established as a diocese in 1833 and elevated to archdiocese in 1937. Diocesan officials were seeking the Reverend Galien Marseilles, as Henry Matthews learns in "Before The Blood: Henry Matthews."

Ascot: A historic county Berkshire, England, which is known for its racecourse on Ascot Heath and its principal event, the Ascot Gold Cup, established in 1807. Mentioned in "Before The Blood: Henry."

Astor Place Opera House: Famous real nineteenth century opera house in New York City, New York. It opened in 1847 and was demolished in 1890 due to negative publicity. In 189, a riot broke out over the correct interpretation of "Macbeth" by William Shakespeare and twenty-two people were killed. Mentioned in "Before The Blood: Henry Matthews.:

Auditorium Theatre: A real performance venue inside the Auditorium Building at 50 Ida B. Wells Drive in Chicago. It opened in 1889 and is the former home of the Chicago Symphony Orchestra. While on her honeymoon with John Simons in early 1984, Bryony Simons heard lectures there by Robert Ingersoll (annexation of

Hawaii) and William E. Mason (international trade). Mentioned in "Before The Blood: Bryony Simons."

Austria: Real landlocked country in Central, Europe, where nineteenth century pianist and composer John Simons played twice. Mentioned in "Bryony," "Before The Blood: Kellen Wechsler," and "Before The Blood: Bryony Simons."

Avenue Theatre: The Avenue Theatre in London, England, opened in March 1882. The French operetta "Les Brigands" opened there Sept. 6, 1889. Henry Matthews invited John Simons to attend with him in "Before The Blood: Kellen Wechsler" and "Before The Blood: Henry Matthews." Also mentioned in "Before The Blood: Bryony Simons."

Bakery Drive: The street (122 Bakery Drive) where supernatural super sleuths Sherman Homes and Dr. Jim Wipston live in "Cornell Dyer and the Howls of Basketville."

Basketville: A rundown town in Michigan where mysterious howls occur, and things go missing. Appears in "Cornell Dyer and the Howls of Basketville"

Bass Street: One of three streets on the hill in Munsonville, where the neighborhoods reside. Named for Theodore "Teddy" Bass, a master carpenter and one of Munsonville's earliest residents.

Bass & Betts woodshop: The carpentry and furniture business of Teddy Bass and Sebastian Betts in Munsonville, Michigan. Appears in "Before The Blood: Bryony Marseilles.," "Before The Blood: Henry Matthews," "Before TH Blood: Bryony Simons," and "The Phoenix."

Beacon Hill Garden Club: A real nonprofit gardening club in Boston Massachusetts, founded in the late 1920s. The daughters of Leo and Alannah Hasset belong to the club. Mentioned in "Call of the Siren."

Beefy Burgers: Name of a burger venue supernatural super sleuth Cornell Dyer frequents on his way to Marbleheart, Ohio in "Cornell Dyer and the Eerie Lake."

Belmont and Holland: Intersection in Leland Hills, Illinois, where Henry Matthews and his father sold newspapers as independent contractors. Mentioned in "Before The Blood: Henry Matthews."

Berlin, Germany: The place where Kellen Wechsler first encountered the style of John Simons' music. It's also the place where the Schwechten, a style of piano made with burr oak, was created by Georg Schwechten. Both Warren Holloway and John Simons owned a Schwechten made of burr oak. Appears in "Bryony," "Before The Blood: John Simons," and "Before The Blood: Kellen Wechsler," and "Before The Blood: Bryony Simons."

Bergdorf Goodman: A real luxury department store, founded in 1899, on Fifth Avenue in Midtown Manhattan, New York. John Simons takes Bryony Simons shopping there in "Before The Blood: Bryony Simons."

Bermuda Triangle: A real area in the North Atlantic Ocean, bordered by Bermuda, Miami, Florida; and Puerto Rico, where some aircraft and ships have supposedly disappeared under inexplicable circumstances. Also known as Devil's Triangle. In "Before The Blood: Kellen Wechsler," Kellen heads there to celebrate a victory with human dessert.

Betts & Brown workshop: The carpentry and furniture business of Sebastian Betts and Benjy Brown in Munsonville, Michigan. Appears in "Call of the Siren."

Beulah County: A fictional county in Northern Michigan, that encompasses Thornton, Shelby, Jenson, and Munsonville. Mentioned in "House on Top of the Hill."

Beulah County Fire Department: A fictional fire department in Northern Michigan, that serves Munsonville and unincorporated Beulah County. Mentioned in "House on Top of the Hill" and "Karla Joins In."

Big Horn Road: A fictional road Kellen Wechsler and Margaret Vollbauer encounter when driving on a business trip. Mentioned in "Before The Blood: Kellen Wechsler."

Biltmore Estate: Historic house museum. Originally built between 1889 and 1895 for George Washington Vanderbuilt. Located in Asheville, North Carolina

Blue Gill Road: The middle of three streets on the hill in Munsonville, where the neighborhoods reside. Named for Gil Blurode, one of Munsonville's earliest residents, lumberjack, and fisherman.

Boston National Historic Park: Association of related historical sites showing Boston's role in the American. Designated a national park in 1974. Appears in "Cornell Dyer and the Necklace of Forgetfulness."

Bouquet Mary's and her five connected greenhouses: A place in Chicago where Henry Matthews takes his oldest sister, Etta Matthews Markham, for potted flowers. Am fairly certain this was based on a real place in Chicago in the =nineteenth century. But I can't find it in my notes. Appears in "Before The Blood: Henry Matthews."

Brand and Market: Intersection in Leland Hills, Illinois where Henry Matthews and his father sold newspapers as independent contractors. Appears in "Before The Blood: Henry Matthews.":

Brentano's on State Street: Actually 101 State St. in Chicago. Half of the precursor to the Kroch's and Brentano's bookstore chain (which closed in 1995). Opened in 1884 by Arthur Brentano as the Chicago branch of the family-owned bookstore in New York. Appears in "Before The Blood: Henry Matthews."

Broadway Street in New York: Appears in Before The Blood: Henry Matthews" and "Before The Blood: Bryony Simons."

Buckingham Palace: The royal residence in London, England. Mentioned in "Before The Blood: Kellen Wechsler."

Café de l'Enferr: Also known as the Cabaret de L'Enfer (or Cabaret of Hell). A real hell-themed café founded in 1892 in Montmartre, France. Demolished in 1950 due to expansion of a supermarket. Appears in "Before The Blood: Kellen Wechsler."

Cake Court: A cul-de-sac in Basketville, Michigan. Mentioned in "Cornell Dyer and the Howls of Basketville.:"

Calais: A port city in France. Appears in Before The Blood: Kellen Wechsler."

Cameron Hotel: Fictional hotel in Concord, New Hampshire, known for its succulent duck. Appears in "Before The Blood: John Simons."

Canada: A country in North America, where nineteenth century pianist and composer performed. Mentioned in "Bryony" and "Before The Blood: Bryony Simons."

Cape Crag: Fictional town in Maine. Setting for "Cornell Dyer and the Missing Tombstone."

Cape Crag Bible Church: Appears in for "Cornell Dyer and the Missing Tombstone."

Cape Crag Historical Society: Appears in for "Cornell Dyer and the Missing Tombstone."

Cape Crag Lighthouse: Appears in for "Cornell Dyer and the Missing Tombstone."

Cape May: New Jersey city and seaside resort, located at the southern tip of Cape May Peninsula, where the Delaware Bay and the Atlantic Ocean meet. Appears in "Cornell Dyer and the Necklace of Forgetfulness."

Carnegie Hall: A concert venue at 881 Seventh Avenue, in Midtown Manhattan in New York City. Built between 1889 and 1991. Russian composer Pyotr Ilyich Tchaikovsky co-conducted a concert for the official opening on May 5, 1891. John Simons performed there in 1894 in "Bryony" and "Before The Blood: Bryony Simons."

Castle Garden: Constructed as a fort for the U.S. Army 1808 and 1811. Released to New York City in 1821 and became an entertainment venue and restaurant. "Swedish Nightingale" Jenny Lind performed there on Sept. 11, 1850. Connected to Manhattan in 1855 and became the Emigrant Landing Depot, More than eight million immigrants came through Castle Garden between 1855 to

1890. Ellis Island began processing immigrants in 1892. Appears in "Before The Blood: John Simons."

Castle of Creepy Cocoons: One of the supernatural mysteries solved by supernatural super sleuth Cornell Dyer. Mentioned in "Cornell Dyer and the 'Mistical' Being."

Central Park: Large park in Manhattan, New York. Appears briefly in "Bryony," "Before The Blood: John Simons" and "Before The Blood: Bryony Simons."

Central Park Zoo: Originally opened as a menagerie in Central Park in 1864. Mentioned in "Before The Blood: Kellen Wechsler."

Central Station: An intercity passenger terminal in downtown Chicago. It replaced Grand Central Station when it opened in 1893. It closed in 1972 and was demolished in 1974. Appears briefly in "Before The Blood: Bryony Simons."

Champ de Mars: Public green space near the Eiffel Tower in Paris, France and the site of the Expositions Universelles (World's Fair) in 1867, 1878, 1889, 1900, and 1937. Appears in "Before The Blood: Kellen Wechsler." Mentioned in Before The Blood: Bryony Simons."

Champs-Élysées: Iconic and beautiful avenue in Paris, France> Apers in "Before The Blood: Kellen Wechsler.

Chemical Bank of New York: Large United States bank (headquarters in New York City) from 1824 until 1996. Mentioned in "Before The Blood: John Simons."

Chicago: A city on Lake Michigan, Illinois, and one of the largest cities in the United States. Appears in "Before The Blood: Henry Matthews" and "Before The Blood: Bryony Simons."

Chicago Opera House: Former theater complex in Chicago. It opened in August 1885, had a fire that damaged part of its roof in December 1888, and was demolished in 1915. Bryony Simons saw Herrmann The Great perform there in 1894 in "Before The Blood: Bryony Simons."

Chickering Hall in Boston: A real auditorium in Boston, Massachusetts, in the late nineteenth century. Kellen Wechsler booked a John Simons concert there in "Before The Blood: John Simons."

Cloud Nine Way: The main thoroughfare in Paradise Falls, "the most restful, relaxing place in the entire world!" Appears in "Cornell Dyer and the Old Folks Home."

Codrington Library of Oxford University: A place where vampire Kellen liked to read by night. Appears briefly in "Before the Blood: Kelen Wechsler."

Conrad Seipp Brewing Company: Real brewing company in Chicago. Founded in 1854, closed in 1933, and currently reopened by a descendant. Mentioned in "Before The blood: Henry Matthews."

Cookery Drive: Street in "Cornell Dyer and the Howls of Basketville."

Cooper Union for the Advancement of Science and Art: A real college in New York, founded in 1859. Mentioned in "Before The Blood: John Simons."

126

Cooperstown, New York: Where Andrew Helsby served as headmaster of a small school before working for Abbott Simons. Mentioned in "Before The Blood: John Simonis."

Cremmins Music Hall: The rebranded Hewes Music Hall in Lower Manhattan, New York. Appears in "Before The Blood: John Simons."

Crook & Duff': Real fine dining restaurant in New York from 1858 to 1906. Mentioned in "Before The Blood John Simons.:

Crystal Caves: Tourist location in Wisconsin. Mentioned in "Cornell Dyer and the Old Folks Home."

Crystal Place, London: A real huge modular glass, wood and iron exhibition building in Hyde Park, London, which housed the Great Exhibition of 1851, A fire destroyed the Crystal Palace in 1936. Mentioned in "Before The Blood: Henry Matthews."

Dalton's Dry Goods: Family-owned store carrying textiles, household goods, and gifts. Located on Main Street in Munsonville. Appears in "Bryony," "Visage," "Staked!," "Call of the Siren," "House on Top of the Hill," "Lycanthropic Summer," "Julie and the Too-Hard Homework," "Katie and the Big Fear," "Brainy Ann," and "Karla Joins In."

Danube River: Second longest river in Europe. Mentioned in "Bryony," "Before The Blood: Kellen Wechsler," and "Before The Blood: Bryony Simons."

Delavan: The main road near Henry's childhood hovel in the fictional Leland Hills, Illinois. Appears in "Before The Blood: Henry Matthews."

Delmonico's: Famous New York fine dining restaurant, owned and operated by the Delmonico family from 1827 to 1923, which popularized a particular thick-cut steak. Charles Ranhofer, named Chef de Cuisine in 1862, is credited with inventing Baked Alaska, Chicken A la Keene, Eggs Benedict, and Lobster Newburg. Delmonico's is still in business, just not under the original family. Appears in "Before The Blood: John Simons" and "Before The Blood: Henry Mathews."

Detroit, Michigan: The largest city in Michigan. Mentioned or appears in "Bryony," "Visage," #Staked!," "Before The Blood: Bryony Marseilles," "Before The Blood: Henry Matthews," "Before The Blood: Bryony Simons," "The Phoenix," "Call of the Siren," and "House on Top of the Hill."

Detroit Science Center: A real science center founded in 1970 as a storefront science museum at 52 E Forest Ave. in Detroit. Michigan. Moved and expanded in 1978 to 5020 John R St. Closed briefly in 1990, reopened in 1991 to 1999 and then closed again for expansion and renovation, closing for good in 2011. It reopened the following year as a new nonprofit: Michigan Science Center, which is still in existence in 2023. Mentioned in "Bryony."

Detroit Symphony Orchestra: American orchestra based in Detroit, Michigan. Mentioned in "Bryony."

Deutsche Karl-Ferdinands-Universität in Prague: A real German university in Prague from 1882 to 1945. Mentioned in "Before The Blood: Kellen Wechsler."

Devil's Island: An island in the Salvation Islands of French Guiana that France operated as a penal colony from 1852 to 1952 (closed 1953). It's currently off-limits to tourists and visitors. Nevertheless, supernatural super sleuth Cornell Dyer briefly contemplated a vacation there in "Cornell Dyer and the Old Folks Home."

Dover: A real town and ferry port in Kent, South East England. Mentioned in "Before The Blood: Kellen Wechsler."

Dover Castle: A real castle built in dover in the eleventh century, which rises above the English Channel's white cliffs. Appears briefly in "Before The Bood: Kellen Wechsler."

Straits of Dover: The narrowest part if the English Channel. Mentioned in "Before The Blood: Bryony Simons."

Drake's General Store: The first store in Munsonville. First appears in "Before The Blood: Bryony Marseilles" and is last mentioned in "House on Top of the Hill." Also appears in "Before The Blood: Henry Matthews," "Before The Blood: Bryony Simons," "The Phoenix," and Call of the Siren."

Drury Lane: Also known as Theatre Royal, Drury Lane. Located in Covent Garden, England. Mentioned in "Before The Blood: Kellen Wechsler" and "Before The Blood" Bryony Simons due to John Simons having performed there.

Edison and Co.: The United Edison Manufacturing Company, also known as the Edison Company. Mentioned in "Before The Blood: Bryony Simons" in terms of where certain light fixtures derived.

Eircheard's' Emporium: Pawn shop in Jenson, run by a leprechaun-like man simply known as Eircheard. Mentioned in "Bryony" and "Karla Joins In." Appears in "Staked!"

El Escorial in Spain: Historical home of the King of Spain and favorite reading spot for vampire Kellen in "Before The Blood: Kellen Wechsler."

Ellis Island: Federally owned island in New York Harbor, that served as an immigrant processing site from 1892 to 1954, Appears in "Cornell Dyer and the "Necklace of Forgetfulness."

Emmerich, Germany: Real historic city in Germany that was once a Roman colony. Mentioned in "Before The Blood: Kellen Wechsler."

Emmett Street: A street in Jenson. Appears in "Before The Blood: Henry Matthews."

Evansville: A former company town in Northern Michigan approximately fifty miles east of Munsonville. Mentioned in "Bryony," "Staked!," "Before The Blood: Bryony Marseilles," "Before The Blood: Bryony Simons," "Call of the Siren," "House on Top of the Hill," "Julie and the Too-Hard Homework," and (possibly) "Brainy Ann." Appears in "Before The Blood: Henry Matthews" and "The Phoenix."

Exposition Universelle: 1889 Paris Exposition or World's Fair in Parish. Appears in "Before The Blood: Kellen Wechsler." Mentioned in "Before The Blood: Bryony Simons."

F.A. Simons & Company: New York bank owned by Farlow (or Farrow) Abbott Simons, father of nineteenth century pianist and composer John Simons. Appears in "Before The Blood: John Simons." Mentioned in "Before The Blood: Henry Matthews."

Fifth Avenue: Major thoroughfare in Manhattan, New York. A section near Central Park was once called "Millionaire's Row" due to all its mansions. Appears in "Before The Blood: John Simons," "Before The Blood: Henry Matthews," and "Before The Blood: Bryony Simons."

First Methodist Church of Thornton: Mentioned in a Munsonville Times new story in "Before The Blood: Bryony Marseilles."

First Street: The first street in the neighborhoods in the tourist village of Shelby Michigan. Appears in "Lycanthropic Summer" and "Call of the Siren."

Fisher Farm: Family farm with two farmhouses northwest of Munsonville, founded by Clyde Fisher in the nineteenth century. Mentioned in "Bryony." Appears in "Before The Blood: Bryony Marseilles," "Before The Blood: Bryony Simons," and "Call of the Siren."

Five and Dime: Gathering place for checkers, conversation, and sweet treats in "Cornell Dyer and the Old Folks Home."

Flemings Steak and Crab: Upscale restaurant in North, Lyons Michigan. "Mentioned in "Lycanthropic Summer."

Flynn's Fresh Fast Food: The name of the diner Flynn owns. Supernatural super sleuth Cornell Dyer eats there in "Cornell Dyer and the Old Folks Home."

Focaccia Avenue: A street in Basketville, Michigan, in "Cornell Dyer and the Howls of Basketville."

Fourth Street: Location of Mrs. Howell's Shelby boarding house in "Call of the Siren."

F.P Rogers: A fourteen-floor store in North Lyons that sells upscale merchandise. Mentioned in "Lycanthropic Summer."

Frick Coke Company: A real large coal-based fuel producing center from 1883 to 1931. Mentioned in "Before The Blood: John Simons."

Front Street: Main Street in the tourist village of Shelby. Appears in "Lycanthropic Summer" and "Call of the Siren."

Geisendorf: A real, former settlement in the region of Brandenburg, Germany. A place where Kellen traveled in "Before The Blood: Kellen Wechsler."

General Library of the University of Coimbra in Switzerland: A place where vampire Kellen liked to read by night in "Before The Blood: Kellen Wechsler."

Gevaudan: Real historical area of Southern France and location of the famous Beast of Gévaudan. Appears in "Before The Blood: Henry Matthews," "The Phoenix," "Lycanthropic Summer," and "House on Top of the Hill."

Ghoul Garage in Nebraska: A garage that had spied on supernatural super sleuth Cornell Dyer. Mentioned in "Cornell Dyer and the 'Mistical' Being."

Golden Egg Café: Restaurant in the tourist town of Shelby. Appears in "Lycanthropic Summer."

Grace Episcopal Church in New York City: The place where General Tom Thumb and Lavinia were married on "Tuesday, February 10, 1863. The real historic church, initially organized in 1808, is still in existence in 2023.

Grand Pacific: A real six-story upscale hotel in Chicago from 1873 to 192, when it was demolished to make room for the Continental Illinois Bank building. Incidentally, Continental was founded in

1910 and declared defunct in 1994. The Grand Pacific was one of the Big Four post-fire hotels. The other three are the Grand Pacific, the Palmer House, the Sherman House and the Tremont. The Grand Pacific is mentioned in "Before The Blood; Henry Matthews."

Great Griddle Cakes and More: A restaurant in Paradise Falls in "Cornell Dyer and the Old Folks Home."

Great Lakes: Five large interconnected freshwater lakes near the Canada–United States border: Huron, Ontario, Michigan, Erie, and Superior. Mentioned in "Before The Blood: Henry Matthews." Superior, Michigan, Huron, Erie, and Ontario and they are in general on or

Grendel: The name Mrs. Peabody gave to her old, dented truck in "Cornell Dyer and the Whispering Wardrobe."

Grotekop, Germany: A fictional region in seventeenth century Germany and home to Kellen and his family in "Before The Blood: Kellen Wechsler."

Grover's Park: A fictional suburb of Chicago and home to the Marchellis family and some of Melissa's friends. Appears in "Bryony," "Visage," "Staked!," House on Top of the Hill," "Melissa and the Hidden Treasure," Changes for Shelly." And "A Room for Laura."

Gullbringa: Means "gold breast." The name of the Viking ship upon which Gruff and Bumpy sailed in "Cornell Dyer and the Missing Tombstone."

Hal's Drive-In Restaurant: A place supernatural super sleuth Cornell Dyer stops for food in "Cornell Dyer and the 'Mistica' Being."

Happiness Hotel: The place where supernatural super sleuth Christine Lucille BeckmanShire stayed at Paradise Falls in "Cornell Dyer and the Old Folks Home."

Happy Hunting Grounds: The name of Kellen's chain of funeral homes, with the headquarters in Thornton. Michigan. Appears in "Staked!" and "Karla Joins In."

Harvard Law School: Founded in 1817 as part of Harvard University in Cambridge, Massachusetts. The United States' oldest continuously operating law school and one of the most eminent law schools internationally. Henry's cousin Archer Markham aspires to Harvard in "Before The Blood: Henry Matthews."

Heigh Ho: A town on top of a hill that appears in a short werewolf story in "Lycanthropic Summer."

Henrici's: A real, former white tablecloth restaurant in Chicago. Founded by Phillip Henrici in 1868 at the age of 23 as a small coffee and pastry shop near Madison and Wells. The most notable location was on Randolph Street between Dearborn and Clark streets, which was demolished in 1962 (it closed that year) to make room for the Daley Civic Center. Henry dines there in "Before The Blood: Henry Matthews."

Hewes Music Hall: A fictional music hall and opium den owned and operated by English businessman Dana Hewes in Lower Manhattan, New York.

His Majesty's Row: The main thoroughfare in Jenson. The street is lined with mansions, which once housed the area's notable merchants, entrepreneurs, attorneys, and physicians. Appears in "Visage," "Before The Blood: Henry Matthews," "Before The Blood: Bryony Simons," "Lycanthropic Summer," and "Call of the Siren."

Hitchcrook Lane: A street in Sunnystorm, Pennsylvania in "Cornell Dyer and the Calcium-Deficient Bones."

Holloway Farm: Retirement home of railroad magnate and robber baron Warren Holloway and his wife Savannah Hollway. Former home of Wyndham Franklin, who raised morgan horses there. Appears in "Before The Blood: John Simons" and "The Phoenix."

Hotel Dessiers: Famous fictional hotel in Paris, France, where and John Simons and Kellen Wechsler lived for a time. Mentioned in "Before The Blood: Kellen Wechsler" and "Before The Blood: Bryony Simons."

House of Worth: Real, former exclusive fashion house in Paris, France, and the beginning of haute couture. Founded by English fashion designer Charles Frederick Worth, the father of haute couture, in 1858, and operated by his descendants until 1952. House of Worth closed in 1956.

Mrs. Howell: Owner and operator of a boarding house in Shelby. Longtime friend of the Hasset family. Appears in "Call of the Siren."

Hudson Poor Farm: Also known as Hudson Almshouse. Built as charity housing 1818 and expanded in the 1880s, this real almshouse later became a mental health asylum, an academy for women, a private home, and (from 1959 to 2016) a private library. Mentioned in "Before The Blood: John Simons."

Hudson River: A river in Eastern New York that flows from north to south. Mentioned in "Before The Blood: Bryony Simons."

Hurttemberg: A fictional locale in the Austria-Germany region, where Kelln travels in pursuit of Seymour Cassidy in "Before The Blood: Kellen Wechsler."

Independence Hall: Historic building Philadelphia, Pennsylvania, where the United States' Founding Fathers debated and then adopted the Declaration of Independence and the U.S. Constitution. Appears in "Cornell Dyer and the Necklace of Forgetfulness."

Irish cake: Most likely a fruitcake. Served on Christmas Eve in "Before the Blood: John Simons."

Jenson: A town, initially built around Jenson College of the Liberal Arts, in Jenson, Michigan, approximately fifteen miles west of Munsonville.

Jenson College of Liberal Arts: A six-story, castle-like liberal arts college in Jenson, Michigan. The college was established in 1801 and banned all discrimination based on sex, race or religion, quite progressive for its time. Henry in "Before The Blood: Henry Matthews" audits several classes there and attends various events. Melissa Marchellis received a full scholarship in "Visage." Jenson College also appears in "Before The Blood: Bryony Simons" and "Call of the Siren" and is mentioned in "Before The Blood: Bryony Marseilles," "Julie and the Too-Hard Homework," and possibly "House on Top of the Hill."

Jenson Elementary School: Pete Miller taught there in "Karla Joins In."

Jenson Family Restaurant: Reasonably priced restaurant with a wide variety of menu items in Jenson. The Marchellis family orders hot chocolate there in "Bryony" and enjoys breakfast together there in "Visage." Julie Drake enjoys lunch there with her father and friends in "Julie and the Too-Hard Homework." The restaurant is mentioned in "Katie and the Big Fear."

Jenson High School: Al Miller served as an educator there in "Katie and the Big Fear," "Karla Joins In" and "Visage."

Jenson Junior High School: Ben Miller served as an educator there in "Katie and the Big Fear," "Karla Joins In" and "Visage."

Jenson Mall: An indoor shopping mall in the fictional town of Jenson, Michigan. Appears in "Visage." Mentioned in "Karla Joins In.

Jenson Nursing Home: The place that cared for Grandma Marchellis in "Bryony," "Visage" and "Staked!" and Carol Simotes in "Staked!"

J. H. Lloyd & Sons steam mill: A fictional steam mill located in the fictional Jenson in the nineteenth century. The steam mill was actually outside of Jenson since Jenson was mainly a college town. Referenced in "Before The Blood: Bryony Marseilles." It's located across the street from "Eircheard's Emporium."

Joe's General Store: Located on Main Street in Munsonville. Appears in "Bryony," "Staked!," "House on Top of the Hill," Julie and the Too-Hard Homework," "Katie and the Big Fear," and "Brainy Ann."

Johns Hopkins Hospital: Incorrectly cited as "John Hopkins" in some editions of BryonySeries books. Johns Hopkins University opened in 1876 and its hospital opened in 1889. Mentioned in "Before The Blood: Bryony Simons" and "The Phoenix."

Kenneth Electric: Fictional client of R.C. Walters advertising, where 1940s Kellen is a senior executive. Mentioned in "Before The Blood: Kellen Wechsler."

Kensington Gardens: One of London's eight royal parks. Mentioned in "Before The Blood: Kellen Wechsler" and "Before The Blood: Bryony Simons."

Klever Cuts: A hair salon in the fictional town of Jenson, Michigan, where Katie Dyer works. Mentioned in "Staked!" and "Karla Joins In."

Khust Castle: A real abandoned castle in Khust, Western Ukraine. Henry tells its history in "Bryony."

Kingsley's: A fictional Chicago restaurant inspired by a fine dining restaurant Chicago restaurateur Herbert M. Kinsley opened around 1880. Henry took his niece Adelaide Markham there in "Before The Blood: Henry Matthews."

Kurd Mountain: Real mountain located in northwestern Syria and southeastern Turkey and home to the fictional St. Romanos Monastery. Mentioned in "Before The Blood: Kellen."

Ladies Mile: A real historic shopping district in late nineteenth century Manhattan, New York City. John Simons takes Bryony Simons shopping there in "Before The Blood: Bryony Simons."

Lake Bliss: The beach hub at Paradise Falls in "Cornell Dyer and the Old Folks Home."

Lancaster, Pennsylvania: Former home of the Dominican Nuns of the Perpetual Rosary. Agnes King is cloistered there. Appears in "Before The Blood: Bryony Simons" and "The Phoenix." Mentioned in "Before The Blood: Henry Matthews."

Leland Hills: A fictional city in Illinois. Henry grew up in the poor part of town in "Before The Blood: Henry Matthews."

Leningrad, Russia: Part of Kellen's crows split away from him and head to this port city (now called St. Petersburg) in "Before The Blood: Kellen Wechsler."

Lesenkotz: A fictional locale in Germany where Kelln travels in pursuit of the vampire that turned him in "Before The Blood: Kellen Wechsler."

Little Arcadia: the name of Henry's greenhouse at Arcadia in "Before The Blood: Henry Matthews."

Livingston County: A fictional county in Northern Michigan. The company town of Evansville is located in Livingston County. Appears in "Before The Blood: Henry Matthews."

London Asylum for Orphans: In reality, the London Orphan Asylum. A real London orphanage from 1831 to 1901, where two cargo ship boys once lived. Mentioned in "Before The Blood: Kellen Wechsler.:"

Loring's Fine Foods: Grocery on Delavan in Leland Hills, Illinois, in "Before The Blood: Henry Matthews."

M. Harrington & Sons: Fictional international investment firm of the nineteenth century. Mentioned in "Before The Blood: John Simons" and "Before The Blood: Henry Matthews."

Madeline effect: Named for a little girl who vanished, which altered memories of groups of people in "Cornell Dyer and the Never Robbers."

Madison Square Theater: A real former Broadway theater, built in 1863 in Manhattan New York near Fifth Avenue. It operated as a theater from 1865 to 1908, when it was demolished to put an office building on that space.

Main Street: The primary street that runs through Munsonville, a fictional remote fishing village in Northern Michigan. Appears in "Bryony," "Visage," "Staked!," "Before The Blood: Bryony Marseilles," "Before The Blood: Henry Matthews," "Before The Blood: Bryony Simons," "The Phoenix," "Call of the Siren," "House on Top of the Hill," "Lycanthropic Summer," "Julie and the Too-Hard Homework," "Katie and the Big Fear," "Brainy Ann," and Karla Joins In."

Manhattan, Lower: The area of Manhattan in "Before The Blood: John Simons" and "Before The Blood: Kellen Wechsler" that's filled with over-population, crime, disease, and poverty/.

Marbleheart: A fictional, lakeside village in Ohio, the setting of "Cornell Dyer and the Eerie Lake."

Marennes-Oléron Bay: This real bay in Southwest France is known for its oyster production. Mentioned in "Before The Blood: Herny Matthews.

Marshall Field & Co. Five-story, upscale department store at the corner of State and Washington in Chicago. Founded in 1852 as a dry goods store known as P. Palmer and company, eventually becoming Marshall Field & Co. in 1881. The business was declared defunct in 2006. Appears in "Before The Blood: Henry Matthews."

Mary Our Holy Mother: Fictional parish school in Chicago where Henry Matthews' niece Emma Markham teachers. Mentioned in "Before The Blood: Henry Matthews."

McSorley's Old Ale House: A real Irish saloon in lower Manhattan and the oldest Irish saloon in New York. It opened in the mid-nineteenth century (accounts differ on the exact date), and it's still open today. McSorley's was a "men only" bar until it was forced to admit women in the 1970s. The floor is still sawdust; the bar area has no stools or cash register. Then and now: a plate of cheese, raw onions, and soda crackers is a favorite of patrons. Dusty wishbones hang above the bar. Legend says McSorley's gave a free turkey dinner to every soldier leaving to fight in World War I. The soldiers hung their wishbones before they left, so they could retrieve them when they returned. Presumably, the ones remaining are the soldiers who died in the war. Original memorabilia includes a "wanted" poster for Abraham Lincoln's assassination. Appears n "Before The Blood: John Simons" and "Before The Blood: Kellen Wechsler."

McVicker's Theatre: A real former Chicago playhouse (later movie house) from 1857 to 1984; it was demolished in 1985. Before that, it survived two fires (including the Great Chicago Fire). Five buildings, all McVicker's Theatre, stood on the same site at 25 W. Madison St. in Chicago, between State and Dearborn. Abraham Lincoln attended plays there in his younger years. Ironically, John Wilkes Booth performed there three years before he assassinated Lincoln. Dion Boucicault's play "Robert Emmet" really did open McVicker's on November 5, 1884, and closed after just three days. Both the theater and the play appear in "Bryony" and "Before The Blood: Henry Matthews."

Mercy Hospital: A real hospital established in 1852 by the Sisters of Mercy. First chartered hospital in Chicago. Now called Insight Hospital & Medical Center Chicago (2023). Mentioned in "Before The Blood: Henry Matthews."

Meredith Manor: Fictional home of Thomas Thackery, the Squire of Levonshire. Appears in "Before The Blood: Kellen Wechsler."

Methodist Episcopal Church: Also known as Eleventh Street Methodist Episcopal Chapel. This real church was built from 1868 to 1869 in a Gothic Revival style but was altered to a Colonial Revival style between 1900 to 1901. In 2011, the church was listed on the National Register of Historic Places. Appears in "Before The Blood: John Simons."

Metropolitan Opera House: This real opera house opened in 1883 at 1411 Broadway in Manhattan, New York City and was demolished in 1967. The current Metropolitan Opera House opened in 1966 at 30 Lincoln Center Plaza, New York. Appears in "Before The Blood: John Simons." Mentioned in "Before The Blood: Kellen Wechsler."

Metropolitan Theatre: This real theater opened in 1825 at 270 Tremont St. in Boston, Massachusetts. Designated a Boston Landmark in 1990. Now called the Wang Theatre. The daughters of Leo and Alannah Hasset attended performances at this theater. Mentioned in "Call of the Siren."

Milton Hotel: Supernatural super sleuth stayed at this hotel courtesy of the Sunnystorm School board while he taught science as a substitute teacher in "Cornell Dyer and the Calcium-Deficient Bones."

Mistenfeld: A fictional locale in Germany where Kelln travels in pursuit of the vampire that turned him in "Before The Blood: Kellen Wechsler."

Molly Blake School of Beauty: A trade school Katie Miller attended for a short time before dropping out. Mentioned in "Visage," "Staked!," and "Karla Joins In."

Monsieur Pierre: Upscale restaurant in North Lyons, Michigan. Appears in "Lycanthropic Summer."

Montmartre: A real district in Paris known for its artistic, village-like atmosphere. Appears in "Before The Blood: Kellen Wechsler."

Thomas C. Morretti's Restaurant and Bakery: A restaurant in Jenson that serves Jenson "the freshest fish, as well as boned and jellied meats, rissoles, and a variety of ice creams, meringues, and delicate pastries.'" Advertisement appears in "Before the Blood: Bryony Marseilles."

Muffin Lane: A street in Basketville, Michigan in "Cornell Dyer and the Howls of Basketville."

New Eden: Nickname early residents gave to Munsonville. Used in "Before The Blood: Bryony Marseilles."

New Haven, Connecticut: Location of Spencer Inn (owned by John Simons' maternal family) and the retirement farm of railroad mogul and robber baron Warren Holloway and his wife Savannah Holloway. Appears in "Before The Blood: John Simons" and "The Phoenix." Mentioned in "Before The Blood: Henry Matthews."

New York: Several BryonySeries characters either live in or travel to this state. Appears in "Bryony," Before The Blood: John Simons," "Before The Blood: Kellen Wechsler," "Before The Blood: Henry Matthews," "Before The Blood: Bryony Simons," and "The Phoenix." Mentioned in "Before The Blood: Bryony

Marseilles," "Call of the Siren," and possibly "House on Top of the Hill" and "Melissa and the Hidden Treasure."

New York Gazette: Prestigious, fictional New York publication. A favorite of Abbott Simons. Owned by Lord Girard. Published by Albert Brumfeldt. Not to be confused with the New-York Gazette, which was a real newspaper from 1725–1744. Appears in "Before The Blood: John Simons," "Before The Blood: Kellen Wechsler," "Before The Blood: Bryony Marseilles," "Before The Blood: Henry Matthews," "Before The Blood: Bryony Simons," and "The Phoenix."

Niagara Falls State Park: Built in 1885. Oldest state park in the United States. Mentioned in "Before The Blood: Herny Matthews.:

Notre-Dame de Paris: A real Catholic cathedral in France. Established in 1163. Closed for renovation in 2019 after a devastating fire. Appears in "Before The Blood: Kellen Wechsler."

Nottingen: A fictional locale in the Austria-Germany region, where Kelln travels in pursuit of Seymour Cassidy in "Before The Blood: Kellen Wechsler."

Oceanus Germanicus: The real name for the North Sea until World War I. Appears in "Before The Blood: Kellen Wechsler."

Odic force: A real belief in the nineteenth century that all objects emitted an energy or life force. Appears in "Call of the Siren."

Oakridge Cemetery: Cemetery in Thornton, Michigan. Mentioned in "Before The Blood: Bryony Marseilles."

Queens: A real district in New York City, New York. Mentioned in "Before The Blood: John Simons."

Palmer House: Potter Palmer built the first Palmer House at State and Quincy in Chiago, a real hotel that opened on September 26, 1870, and burned on October 9, 1871, during the Great Chicago Fire. A second Palmer House – seven stories tall – opened in 1875 on State and Monroe. The Palmer House was one of the Big Four post-fire hotels. The other three are the Grand Pacific, the Sherman House and the Tremont. The Palmer House is mentioned in "Before The Blood: Henry Matthews" and briefly appears in "Before The Blood: Bryony Simons."

Paradise Falls: The fictional tourist town in "Cornell Dyer and the Old Folks Home."

Paris of the West: The real nineteenth century nickname for Detroit, Michigan, most likely because of its French roots. The city was founded by French explorer and trader Antoine de la mothe Cadillac on July 24, 1701. Expression used in "Before The Blood: Bryony Marseilles."

Perkins School for the Blind: A real school and first school for the blind in the United States. Founded in 1829 in Watertown, Massachusetts. A blind character in "Before The Blood: Bryony Marseilles" attends the school.

Pike Street: One of three streets on the hill in Munsonville, where the neighborhoods reside. Named for Boswell Pike, an early Munsonville resident and first mayor (appointed by Munsonville founder Owen Munson).

Pilgrim Park: More correctly Pilgrim Hill in Central Park, New York. Bryony Simons toboggans down that hill in "Before The Blood: Bryony Simons."

Pinecrest Retirement Community for the Delicately Aged: A gated home deep in the woods in "Cornell Dyer and the Old Folks Home."

Pink Moravian goblin: A mischievous supernatural creature mentioned in "Cornell Dyer and the Old Folkes Home."

Pizza Express: A pizza parlor in Grovers Park, Illinois. Appears in "Bryony" and possibly "Melissa and the Hidden Treasure," "Changes for Shelly," and "A Room for Laura." Mentioned in "Visage."

Pleasant Street: A street in Jenson. Appears in "Before The Blood: Henry Matthews."

Potel et Chabot: A real Parisian caterer since 1820. Mentioned in "Before The Blood: Kellen Wechsler" and "Before The Blood: Bryony Simons."

Poussin Hall: A section inside Jacob King's primary mansion on Fifth Avenue in New York. Appears in "Before The Blood: Henry Matthews."

Prospect, Indiana: A fictional American town featured in "Cornell Dyer and the Never Robbers" and mentioned in "Karla Joins In."

P.T. Barnum circus: Its full name was the "P.T. Barnum's Great Traveling Museum, Menagerie, Caravan, and Hippodrome," which was founded in 1871.It merged with the Cooper and Bailey Circus in 1881 and became the Ringling Bros. and Barnum & Bailey Circus. Mentioned in "Before The Blood: John Simons."

Quebec: A province of Canada. Mentioned in "Before The Blood: Bryony Simons."

Race Brothers New England Oyster House: A real, former restaurant in the nineteenth century at 114 W. Madison St., Chicago. Appears in "Before The Blood: Henry Matthews."

Range Road: A road in Basketville, Michigan, in Cornell Dyer and the Howls of Basketville.

Rat Portage: A real city on the Lake of the Woods in Ontario, Canada. Now named Kenora. Mentioned in "Before The Blood: Bryony Marseilles."

Rees Trading Company: Fictional trading company in eighteenth century England. Appears in "Before The Blood: Kellen Wechsler."

Relief and Aid Society: The real Chicago Relief and Aid Society provided aid to poverty-stricken families living in the late nineteenth century. Henry's cousin Emma Markham was involved in "Before The Blood: Henry Matthews."

Rhode Island: A United States state in New England, known for its coastal towns. The hometown of Andrew Helsby, John Simons' tutor. Mentioned in "Before The Blood: John Simons."

Room 27: A second-floor room in Munsonville Inn, where key events occur. Appears in "The Phoenix," "House at the Top of the Hill," and possibly "Lycanthropic Summer."

Royal Albert Hall: A real, iconic concert hall in London, England, opened by Queen Victoria in 1871. Mentioned in "Before The Blood: Kellen Wechsler" because John Simons played there.

Route Nanoc Elyod: A road in Basketville, Michigan. Appears on "Cornell Dyer and the Howls of Basketville." The name is also an anagram in homage to Conan Doyle, the author of the Sherlock Holmes series since "Howls" is a Sherlock Holmes parody.

Ruisch Family Bakery: A bakery in the tourist village Shelby, Michigan. Mentioned in Call of the Siren."

Saints Peter and Paul: The name of the fictional church Reverence Galien Marseilles once pastored in Detroit, Michigan. Mentioned in "Before The Blood: Bryony Marseilles."

Salon Carré: An iconic room inside the Louvre Palace, Paris, France, that showcases art. Appear sin "Before The Blood: Kellen Wechsler."

Savannah Historic District: Gen. James E. Oglethorpe, founder of the British colony of Georgia, planned the district's grid-like layout in 1733. The district features 22 park squares. Highlights include boutiques, cobblestones streets, restored eighteenth century homes, monuments, museums and more than 100 restaurants. Appears in "Cornell Dyer and the Necklace of forgetfulness."

Savoy Hotel: A real luxury hotel in London, England, which opened in August 1889. Appears in "Before The Blood: Kellen Wechsler" and mentioned in "Before The Blood: Bryony Simons."

Schogl's on Wells Street: A real Chicago saloon and restaurant that opened in 1879 near the Chicago Daily News building,

Seulobitz: Fictional town in Germany and the location where Kellen closed his first blood deal and (temporarily) found a hometown. Appears in "Before The Blood: Kellen Wechsler."

Seventh Heaven: The name of the inn where supernatural super sleuth Cornell Dyer stays while vacationing at Paradise Falls in "Cornell Dyer and the Old Folks Home."

Shelby: A fictional tourist village in northern Michigan. Appears in "Visage," "Staked!," "Before The Blood: Bryony Simons," "Call of the Siren," "Lycanthropic Summer," and possibly "House on Top of the Hill." Mentioned in "Before The Blood: Bryony Marseilles."

Shelby Motel: Two-story, L-shaped motel in the tourist village of Shelby. Has tennis courts and a huge swimming pool. Appears in "Lycanthropic Summer."

Sherman House: The Sherman House was one of the Big Four post-fire hotels. The other three are the Grand Pacific, the Palmer House and the Tremont. The Sherman House is mentioned in "Before The Blood: Henry Matthews.:

Simons Estate: The property that includes Simons Mansion, the stables, the servant's cottage, the orchards, and the gardens. Appears in "Bryony," "Visage," "Staked!," "Snowbell," "Before The Blood: Bryony Simons," "The Phoenix," "Call of the Siren," "House on Top of the Hill," and Karla Joins In." Mentioned in "Julie and the Too-Hard Homework," "Katie and the Big Fear," and Brainy Ann."

Simons Mansion: The home John Simons built for his bride in the woods just beyond the developed part of Munsonville, a fictional fishing village in Northern Michigan, and used as the couple's primary residence. Appears in "Bryony," "Staked!" (as flashback), "Snowbell," "Before The Blood: Bryony Sions," "The Phoenix," "Call of the Siren," and "House on Top of the Hill."

Simons Woods: The portion of land owned by John Simons beyond the house and estate, which forever bears his name. Appears in "Bryony," "Visage," "Staked!," "Snowbell," "Before The Blood: Bryony Marseilles" (before John owned that portion), "Before The Blood: Henry Matthews" (ditto), "The Phoenix," "Call of the Siren," "House on Top of the Hill," "Julie and the Too-Hard Homework," "Katie and the Big Feat," "Brainy Ann," and "Karla Joins In."

Solenberg: A fictional locale in Germany where Kelln travels in pursuit of the vampire that turned him in "Before The Blood: Kellen Wechsler."

Spencer Inn: A fictional eighteenth and nineteenth century lodge in New Haven, Connecticut, owned and operated by John Simons' maternal grandparents. Appears in "Before The Blood: John Simons."

St. Adelbert's: Fictional Catholic church in Jenson, Northern Michigan. Appears in "Before The Blood: Henry Matthews."

St. James Hall: A concert hall in London, England, that opened in 1858 and was demolished in 1905. The Piccadilly Hotel was later built on its site. Appears in "Before The Blood: Kellen Wechsler" because John Simons played there. Mentioned in "Before The Blood: Bryony Simons."

Stanhoper's: The complete fictional title is Stanhoper Paper Mill. Mentioned "Before The Blood: Bryony Marseilles."

State Street: One of the real main streets in Chicago, Illinois. Lord Girard had a home off State Street. Appears in "Before The Blood: Henry Matthews" and "The Phoenix."

Steak Shack: Fictional eatery in North, Lyons, Michigan. Appears in "Lycanthropic Summer."

Steinway Hall: William Steinway, nineteenth century owner of Steinway & Sonds pianos, built the first Steinway Hall, a real concert hall with 2,000 seats and a large stage to hold a 100-piece orchestra. Steinway Hall opened in 1866 behind the showrooms on 14th Street, Manhattan, New York. John Simons played in this hall. and was one of the first concert halls for wider audiences in New York City. In addition to its current location on at 1133 Avenue of the Americas in New York, Steinway Halls also exist in London, England; Berlin, Germany; Vienna, Austria; and formerly Chicago, Illinois. Appears in "Before The Blood: John Simons." Mentioned in "Before The Blood: Kellen Wechsler."

St. Athanasius Church: Fictional Eastern Orthodox Church in Detroit, Michigan. Appears in "Bryony" and "House on Top of the Hill."

St. John's Cemetery: Fictional cemetery in Grotekop, Germany. Appears in "Before The Blood: Kellen Wechsler."

St. Joseph Orphanage for Boys: A fictional orphanage in Hartford, Connecticut, found and operated by the Sisters of Mercy. Mentioned in "Before The Blood: John Simons"

St. Margaret's Church: A 12th-century church next to Westminster Abbey, London, England. Appears in "Before The Blood: Kellen Wechsler" and mentioned in "Before The Blood: Bryony Simons" (where she mistakenly calls the church a cathedral).

St. Patrick's Cathedral, New: A real large, full city block-sized parish church and current seat of the Archbishop of New York in New York City, New York. Construction to replace Old St. Patrick's Cathedral began in 1858, stopped during the Civil War, was completed in 1878 and dedicated on May 25, 1879. Abbott Simons refused to recognize the new cathedral, even though it was partly on Fifth Avenue, and stubbornly continued attending Old St. Patrick's Cathedral, a mystery since he loathes Lower Manhattan. Appears in "Before The Blood: John Simons."

St. Patrick's Cathedral, Old: The real former seat of the Archdiocese of New York until 1879., located in Lower Manhattan, New York City. Built between 1809 and 1815.designated a New York City landmark in 1966, added to the National Register of Historic Places in 1977, and declared a minor basilica by Pope Benedict XVI on Saint Patrick's Day, March 17, 2010.

St. Romanos monastery: Fictional monastery in Syria. Mentioned in "Before The Blood: Kellen Wechsler."

State Emigrant Hospital: A real hospital that opened in 1847 on Ward's Island, New York City, New York, for poor, sick immigrants coming into Castle Garden immigration center. Was the largest hospital in the world in the 1850s. Mentioned in "Before The Blood: John Simons."

Sturtevant House: Popular hotel on Broadway and 29th Street, New York City, New York. Opened in 1871 and was demolished 1903, is on the left. Mentioned in "Before The Blood: John Simons."

Sue's Diner: THE place to eat in Munsonville, a fictional remote fishing village in Northern Michigan. Opened October 29, 1926, and has never closed. Appears in "Bryony," "Staked!," "Call of the

Siren," "House on Top of the Hill," "Katie and the Big Fear," and "Brainy Ann." Mentioned in "Julie and the Too-Hard Homework," and "Karla Joins In."

Sumner Tunnel: The first real traffic tunnel in Massachusetts. Located in Boston. The daughters of Leo and Alannah Hasset mentioned it in "Call of the Siren."

Sunnystorm: A fictional town in Pennsylvania and the setting for "Cornell Dyer and the Calcium-Deficient Bones."

The Big City: Appears by name in a short story in "Lycanthropic Summer."

The chapel: A tiny, out-of-the-way chapel for wayfarers to stop and pray or meditate. Appears in "Call of the Siren."

The Clock Shoppe: A shop that sells and repairs clocks in the tourist village of Shelby. Appears in "Lycanthropic Summer" and "Call of the Siren."

The Fair Store at the corner of State and Adams: A real discount department store in Chicago, Illinois. Founded in 1874, expanded to numerous locations. Through the years was owned by the company that owned K-Mart and, later, Montgomery Ward. The State Street location was closed and demolished in 1984. Appears in "Before The Blood: Henry Matthews."

The First Bank of Prospect: A bank that comes and goes in the fictional Prospect, Indiana. Appears (and disappears) in "Cornell Dyer and the Never Robbers."

The Good Egg: A restaurant in Paradise Falls, where supernatural super sleuth Cornell Dyer vacations in "Cornell Dyer and the Old Folks Home."

The Home Insurance Building: A ten-story skyscraper that stood on the corner of Adams and Lasalle in Chicago. Built in1885 and demolished in 1931. Appears in "Before The Blood: Henry Matthews."

The School of St. Savina Petrilli for Young Ladies: Fictional, all-girls exclusive school in North, Lyons, Michigan. Mentioned in "Lycanthropic Summer."

The White House: The official residence and workplace of the United States president ever since John Adams in 1800. Mentioned in "Before The Blood: Bryony Simon" since John Simons played there.

The Wisten Hotel: A prestigious, fictional hotel in Jenson, Michigan. Appears in "Before The Blood: Henry Matthews" and "Call of the Siren."

Theatre de la Fleur: Fictional outdoor theater in nineteenth century France. Appears in "Before The Blood: Kellen Wechsler" because John Simons plays there.

Thornton: Fictional city in Northern Michigan. Appears in "Visage," "Staked!," "Before The Blood: Henry Matthews," "Before The Blood: Bryony Simons," and possibly "House on Top of the Hill" and "Brainy Ann." Mentioned in "Bryony," "Before The Blood: Bryony Marseilles," "The Phoenix," "Call of the Siren," "Lycanthropic Summer," "Karla Joins In," and "Katie and the Big Fear."

154

Thornton Hotel: A fictional straight three-story building with a restaurant in Thornton, Michigan. Mentioned in "Before The Blood: Henry Matthews." Appears in "Before The Blood: Bryony Simons."

Tim's Quick Lunch: A fictional short order restaurant on Delavan Street in fictional city of Leland Hills, Illinois in the place where the fictional Ye Olde Gote tavern once stood. Appeared in "Before The Bood: Henry Matthews."

Toronto: The capital city of Ontario, one of the provinces of Canada. Mentioned in "Before The Blood: Bryony Simons."

Tremont: The Tremont was one of the Big Four post-fire hotels. The other three are the Grand Pacific, the Palmer House, and the Sherman House. The Tremont is mentioned in "Before The Blood: Henry Matthews."

Turtle Tree, Nebraska: The fictional home of Charlie Charleston, supernatural super sleuth Cornell Dyer's guide in "Cornell Dyer and the Flu."

Unicorn: A fictional wild beast and source of nutrition for werewolves. Appears in "Lycanthropic Summer."

University of Michigan: Founded in 1817, twenty years before Michigan became a state. Mentioned in "Before The Blood: Bryony Marseilles" because a Munsonville resident graduated with honors from the University of Michigan.

Utopia: The concept of a perfect or nearly perfect community. Used sarcastically as a pseudonym for Munsonville in "Before The Blood: Bryony Marseilles."

Villa Helsby: The nickname John Simons' tutor Andrew Helsby gives to his shabby apartment in Lower Manhattan, New York. Appears in "Before The Blood: John Simons."

Village Hall: The public center of Munsonville, a fictional remote fishing village in Northern Michigan. Appears in "Bryony," "Staked!," "Snowbell," "Before The Blood: Bryony Marseilles," "Before The Blood: Henry Matthews," "Before The Blood: Bryony Simons," "The Phoenix," Call of the Siren," "House on Top of the Hill," Julie and the Too-Hard Homework," Katie and the Big Fear," and "Brainy Ann."

Village Nègre: A human zoo where 400 indigenous people were exhibited at the Exposition Universelle in 1889 in Paris, France. Mentioned in "Before The Blood: Kellen Wechsler" and "Before The Blood: Bryony Simons."

Voravia: A fictional locale in the Austria-Germany region, where Kelln travels in pursuit of Seymour Cassidy in "Before The Blood: Kellen Wechsler."

Waldorf-Astoria: The Waldorf-Astoria was two real hotels on Fifth Avenue in New York, New York. They were built in 1893, expanded in 1897, and demolished 1929in order to construct the Empire State Building on that site. The Waldorf Astoria New York currently on Park Avenue was built in 1931. John and Bryony Simons stayed there in 1894 a few months after their marriage. Appears in "Before The Blood: Bryony Simons."

Walker's Apothecary: A fictional drug store in Munsonville, a fictional remote fishing village in Northern Michigan. Appears in "Bryony," "Staked!," "House on Top of the Hill," "Lycanthropic Summer," "Katie and the Big Fear," and "Brainy Ann."

Wards Island Asylum: New York City Asylum for the Insane, a real institution that opened in 1863. It became the 4,400-bed Manhattan State Hospital in 1899, the largest psychiatric hospital in the world. Currently the Manhattan Psychiatric Center, a New York-state psychiatric hospital on Wards Island in New York City. Mentioned in "Before The Blood: John Simons."

Wards Island: An island in New York City, New York. Mentioned in "Before The Blood: John Simons."

Washington D.C. The capital city of the United States. Mentioned in "Before The Blood: Bryony Simons" because John Simons played at the White House.

Wesley Music Conservatory: Fictional college of music in Concord, New Hampshire. Includes Aubrey Hall (Latin, geography, grammar and rhetoric, algebra, geometry), McKenzie Hall (conservatory reserved afternoons and evenings for endless music instruction), and Collicott Hall (dining room), Appears in "Before The Blood: John Sions." Mentioned in "Before The Blood: Bryony Simons."

Westgalia: A fictional locale in the Austria-Germany region, where Kelln travels in pursuit of Seymour Cassidy in "Before The Blood: Kellen Wechsler."

Western and Clark: Intersection in Leland Hills, Illinois, where Henry and his father sold newspapers. Appears in "Before The Blood: Henry Matthews."

Wild Unicorn National Park: A tourist attraction mentioned in "Cornell Dyer and the Old Folks Home."

Williamsburg: An independent city Williamsburg noted for its American colony roots. Appears in "Cornell Dyer and the Necklace of Forgetfulness."

Windy City: Real nickname for Chicago, Illinois. Used in "Before The Blood: Bryony Simons."

Wisten Hotel: See The Wisten Hotel.

Woman's Hospital Medical College: Also referred to as Women's Medical College in Chicago, Illinois, a real, former medical college. Established in 1870 and purchased a building in 1877. Allied with Northwestern University in 1892. Closed in 1902. Mentioned in "Before The Blood: Henry

Yale: A real private Ivy League university in New Haven, Connecticut. Founded in 1701. Mentioned in "Before The Blood: Bryony Simons."

Ye Olde Antique Shop: The place where supernatural super sleuth Cornell Dyer begins and ends his investigation in "Cornell Dyer and the Necklace of Forgetfulness."

Ye Olde Gote: "Gote" means watercourse, so tongue-in-cheek name for a cheap bar on Delavan Street in the fictional city of Leland Hill, Illinois. Appears on "Before The Blood: Henry Matthews.." See also Tim's Quick Lunch

PART THREE: THINGS

1 Timothy 5:8: "But if anyone does not provide for his relatives, and especially for members of his household, he has denied the faith and is worse than an unbeliever. First Timothy, five, eight." Appears in "Before The Blood: Bryony Simons."

1240 "Sifridus" chalice from Germany's Osnabrück Cathedral: This is a real ceremonial chalice most likely from St. Peter's Cathedral in Osnabrück, Germany, the cathedral of the Roman Catholic Diocese of Osnabrück. King Charlemagne founded the diocese in 700; the church, built in 785, was destroyed by the Normans in 885. The current church was built after 1100. Legend says the chalice was stolen during the Thirty Years War. Appears in "Before The Blood: John Simons" and "Call of the Siren."

1477 atlas: Henry Matthews browsed through one at Jenson College, noting its errors, in "Before The Blood: Henry Matthews."

1808 bottle of Denis Mounie: A very rare bottle of cognac, considering the company that produced it was not founded until 1838 by winemakers, Justin Denis and Henri Mounié. This cognac is no longer produced. Kellen enjoys a bottle of it when breaking the fourth wall in "Before The Blood: Kellen Wechsler."

2 Corinthians 4:18: "We fix our eyes not on what is seen, but on what is unseen." Appears in "Before The Blood: Bryony Simons."

" A chipmunk and a rabbit. Say, I wonder how this comes out?": Quote from the real 1932 film "Red Dust" starring Clark Gable and Jean Harlow. Appears in "Before The Blood: Kellen Wechsler."

"A discourse Concerning God's Judgements; Resolving many weighty questions and cases Relating to them: A just narrative or account of the man whose hands and legs rotted off:" A real book by Simon Ford published in 1678. Appears in "Before The Blood: Bryony Simons."

"A general system of gardening and botany, Volume 3," by George Don: Real book published in 1834. Appears in "Before The Blood: Bryony Simons."

A Dog of Flanders: A real 1872 novel by English author Marie Louise de la Ramée published under her pseudonym "Ouida. About a Flemish boy named Nello and his dog, Patrasche, and is set in Antwerp. "Before The Blood: Bryony Marseilles."

"A Doll's House" by Henrik Ibsen: A real three-act play, which premiered December 21, 1878, in Denmark, about the restricted role of women at the time and the imbalance of power between men and women. Appears in "Before The Blood: Henry Matthew."

"A Psalm of Life" by Henry Wadsworth Longfellow: A real poem Longfellow wrote after the death of his wife. Initially published anonymously in 1838. English teacher Harold Masters recites the poem in class at Munsonville School in "Bryony."

"A Visit from St. Nicholas" by Clement C. Moore: Also known as "'Twas the Night Before Christmas." Was published anonymously in 1823. Moore claimed authorship in 1837. Mentioned in "Before The Blood: Bryony Marseilles."

Aconitum napellus: See "wolfsbane."

Adler & Sullivan: A real nineteenth century architectural firm in Chicago that remodeled McVicker's Theatre in 1885. Mentioned in "Before The Blood: Henry Matthews."

"An Old Fashioned Girl" by Louisa May Alcott: A real 1869 novel by Alcott, telling the story of a country girl who retains her values when visiting her rich city friends. Excerpts appear in "Summer Sisters" and "Before The Blood: Bryony Marseilles," since this is one book the Fisher girls read together.

Adeste Fideles: Latin for the Christmas hymn "O Come, All Ye Faithful," which has origins in the seventeenth century. Abbott Simons is walking back from midnight Mass with John Simons in "Before The Blood: John Simons," and John Simons sings it while walking back from midnight Mass with Kellen Wechsler in "Before The Blood: Kellen Wechsler."

"And the fishermen will lament, and all those who cast a line into the Nile will mourn, and those who spread nets on the waters will pine away." Isaiah 19:8: One of the earliest Bible verses Bryony Marseilles heard her father read. Appears in "Before The Blood: Bryony Marseilles."

Albrecht Altdorfer Danube landscapes: Real paintings by the Altdorfer that appear in "Before The Blood: Kellen Wechsler."

Algernon Charles Swinburne's Poems and Ballads: A real book that Galien Marseilles bought for him and Adele Belanger before they left Detroit, Michigan for the fictional Munsonville. Mentioned in "Before The Blood: Bryony Marseilles."

"All Things Bright and Beautiful" by Cecil Frances Alexander: Bryony hums this real nature hymn, first published in 1848, while strolling toward Main Street in "Before The Blood: Bryony Marseilles."

Amazing Grace: Popular Christian hymn with lyrics by English Anglican clergyman and poet John Newton. First published in 1779. John Simons piano student learned to play it in "Before The Blood: John Simons." Mrs. Parks hummed it while scrubbing pots in "Before The Blood: Bryony Marseilles."

Amazonian skill: Having the strength and prowess of Amazons, a group of female warriors in Greek mythology. Henry gives his sister Lizzie that compliment while battling cockroaches in "Before The Blood: Henry Matthews."

Ambrosia: Drink of the gods. Used sarcastically in "Before The Blood: Henry Mathews."

American Express: Began offering pensions in 1875, perhaps the first private company to do so. Mentioned in "Before The Blood: Henry Matthews."

"Ancient Law" by Henry James Sumner Maine: Areal book based on a series of lectures the author gave. First published in 1861. Henry's cousin Archer Markham owns an edition in "Before The Blood: Henry Matthews."

"And I heard a voice from heaven saying unto me, 'Write, Blessed are the dead which die in the Lord from henceforth: Yea, saith the Spirit, that they may rest from their labors; and their works do follow them." Henry hears these words from Revelation 14:13 in the Bible at a gravesite in "Before The Blood: Henry Matthews."

Anise: A flowering herb in the parsley family with a taste resembling licorice. Appears briefly in "Karla Joins In."

Antitoxin: A injectable medication of antibodies to treat diphtheria. Formerly used as prevention of diphtheria. Bryony recalled how Dr. Gothart saved many of the villagers with the antitoxin in "Before The Blood: Bryony Simons."

Apoplexy: Rupture and hemorrhage of an internal organ. Former synonym for a hemorrhagic stroke. Used in "Before The Blood: Bryony Simons."

Apple butter: Super concentrated applesauce, often topped on pancakes or muffins. Served at Fisher Farm in "Before The Blood: Bryony Simons."

Applejack: A strong alcoholic beverage made from hard cider. Served at a communal Thanksgiving potluck dinner in "Before The Blood: Bryony Marseilles."

Apple turnover: Pastry filled with sweetened apples. Served on Christmas Eve at the fictional Spencer Inn in New Haven, Connecticut in "Before The Blood: John Simons."

Aquiline nose: A nose curved like a beak. Seymour Cassidy's nose was described thus in "Before The Blood: Kellen Wechsler."

Arabian horses: A real ancient horse breed with distinctive head noted for their beauty, courage, gentleness, intelligence, loyalty, stamina, and speed. The Turkish government introduced the horses to the United States at the 1893 Chicago World's Fair, which is how John Simons wound up buying some. Appears in "Bryony" and "Before The Blood: Bryony Simons."

Armagnac: A real complex and robust brandy produced in the Armagnac region in Gascony, France. Lord Girard serves and drinks it in "Before The Blood: Henry Matthews."

"Around the Wicket Gate" by Charles Spurgeon: A real faith commentary published in 1841. Reverend Galien Marseilles reads it in "Before The Blood: Bryony Marseilles."

Arthur Rackham illustration: Bryony compares a human to the dreamlike, distinctive style of this real British book illustrator in "Before The Blood: Bryony Simons."

Ashputtel: Another name for Cinderella. Mentioned in "Before The Blood: Bryony Marseilles," and "Before The Blood: Bryony Simons."

Aspic: Savory meat gelatin made from bone broth. Appears in "Before The Blood: Henry Matthews.

Asthma: Chronic lung disease where the airways tighten and narrow. Henry suffers from asthma in "Before The Blood: Henry Matthews."

Astral projection: An out-of-body experience where the soul travels to the astral plane (a place between life and death) but remains connected to the body by means of a silver cord. Discussed as a medical theory in "Call of the Siren."

Auld Lang Syne: A real old Scottish folk song. Robert Burns added the text in 1788. The traditional tune was added in 1799. Boswell Pike and Owen Munson sing a drunken version on New Year's Eve in "Before The Blood: Bryony Marseilles."

Aura Lee: A real sentimental, American song about a maiden. Published by the John Church Company in 1861. Owen Munson sings "Aura Lee" in "Before The Blood: Bryony Marseilles. "Mitch Cooper and Eugene Miller sang the song at Munson Day 1892 in "Before The Blood: Bryony Simons."

Auspratchaus: A pretend magical plant with fragrant violet-colored petals. Appears in "Karla Joins In."

Australian Shepherd: A real herding dog, popular with ranchers with origins in the Asturias (northwest of Spain). The breed was developed in California during the nineteenth century. Clyde Fisher owned Australian Shepherd in "Summer Sisters" and "Before The Blood: Bryony Marseilles."

Aynsley rose: A real pattern of Aynsley China. Aynsley was an eighteenth century British manufacture of bone China tableware. Mentioned in "Before The Blood: Henry Matthews."

Aztec calendar: Most likely a real Aztec calendar stone that was carved in the sixteenth century. Appears in "Before The Blood: John Simons" and "Call of the Siren."

Azureous sky: A bright blue sky Bryony sees in a dream in "Before The Blood: Bryony Simons."

B&O Railroad: The Baltimore and Ohio Railroad, a real United steam-operated railway that carried freight and passengers. It was chartered in 1827 and opened its first section in 1830. It also offered one of the first, if not the first, employer/worker financed pension plan. Mentioned in "Before The Blood: Henry Matthews."

Ballantine scotch: A real blended Scotch whiskey, first produced in 1827. Appears in "Before The Blood: Kellen Wechsler."

Baguettes: A long thin French bread with a crisp crust. Henry brings baguettes to his brother-in-law William Markham's workplace when he surprised him with lunch in "Before The Blood: Henry Matthews."

Baroque sculptures: An artistic style that developed in the seventeenth and early eighteen centuries. These lavish and ornate sculptures focused on the movement of the human body. Mentioned in "Before The Blood: John Simons" and "Call of the Siren."

Battle of Breitenfeld: One of the real battles in the Thirty Years War. The battle took place on November 2, 1642, in Germany. Mentioned in "Before The Blood: Kellen Wechsler."

Battle of Fort Sumter I during the Civil War: Major in "Before The Blood: Henry Matthews" said he fought during this war.

Baudot code: One of the real first telecommunication codes for telegraph machines. Émile Baudot invented it in the 1870s. Henry learns this code while living at Arcadia in "Before The Blood: Henry Matthews.:

Bay windows: Flanking windows with a large window in the middle and a smaller one on each side. A feature of Simons Mansion in "Bryony," "Before The Blood: Bryony Simons," and "Lycanthropic Summer." Mentioned in "Staked!"

Beast of Gévaudan: Name given to a real mysterious creature that killed more than 100 people between 1765 and 1767 in rural Southern Frances. Appears in "Before The Blood: Henry Matthews," "The Phoenix," "Lycanthropic Summer," and "House on Top of the Hill."

Beaux Arts structure: Real architecture is both symmetrical and grandiose. John Simons' childhood home on Fifth Avenue was a Beaux Arts structure. Appears in "Before The Blood: John Simons," "Before The Blood: Henry Matthews," and "Before The Blood: Bryony Simons."

Bedford Limestone: A real, highly uninformed limestone (sedimentary rock) from Indiana. Bedford Limestone was used in the construction of Simons Mansion. Mentioned in "Before The Blood: Bryony Simons."

Bella: One of Savannha Holloway's thoroughbred horses. Appears in "Before The Blood: John Simons."

Belladonna: Also known as atropa belladonna or deadly nightshade. Belladonna alkaloids were used to treat asthma through at least 1950 due to its bronchodilation effects. Henry briefly uses this medicine in "Before The Blood: Henry Matthews."

Bemis Company: The Bemis company was a real company that made packaging products. The Bemis Brothers Bag Company was founded in 1858. The mascot on its printed cotton bags was a cat named Biddy. Mrs. Parks made a quilt for Bryony from these bags. Appears in "Before The Blood: Bryony Simons."

Ben-Hur: "Ben-Hur: A Tale of the Christ" by Lew Wallace, was a real bestselling novel in 1852. Professor Astor G. Clarke at Jenson College mentions the book to Henry in "Before The Blood: Henry Matthews."

Benjamin Franklin's autobiography: The real unfinished memoir of Benjamin Franklin. A copy appears at the bedside of Henry's cousin Adelaide Markham in "Before The Blood: Henry Matthews."

Beowulf: A real Old English epic poem. A contestant at a Jenson College recitation contest at Jenson College recited part of this poem in "Before The Blood: Henry Matthews."

Bergamot: A real citrus fruit from Italy. Caryn Rochelle smells in it in cologne in "Lycanthropic Summer" and John Simons uses it in a tea he makes Bryony in "Before The Blood: Bryony Simons."

Bergère wing chairs: Real French chairs from the seventeenth century with gilded wood (such as mahogany) frames, tailored seat cushion, and backs and arms upholstered with fine silk or velvet.

Bertrand the Mouse: An attic mouse John-Peter Simotes rescues in "Staked!" The protagonist in a set of stories Bryony tells Anna in "Before The Blood: Bryony Simons." The mouse who helped free the lion in "Cornell Dyer and the Whispering Wardrobe." The main character in the Bertrand The Mouse picture books for young children.

Betude: A pretend magical plant with long red grassy stalks. Appears in "Karla Joins In."

Biddy: The real trademark cat printed on The Bemis Brothers Bag Company, which was founded in 1858. Appears on a handmade quilt in "Before The Blood: Bryony Simons."

Bicycle craze in Boston: The love of bicycling really skyrocketed in 1877 in Boston, Massachusetts, which led to the formation of The Boston Bicycle Club, the first such club in the United States. Mentioned in "Before The Blood: Henry Matthews."

Bienenstich: Also known as German bee sting cake, so called because its topped with honey. A real cake that appears in "Before The Blood: Kellen Wechsler."

Bikavér: Real nineteenth century Hungarian wine. A favorite of Dr. Edwin Gothart. Mentioned in "Call of the Siren."

Billo-Cream: A fictional hair cream worn by Mr. History Teacher in "Cornell Dyer and the Calcium-Deficient Bones."

Birds of America: A real book published by John James Audubon in 1827. It contains prints of 435 species of American birds, which are based on Audubon's paintings. Bryony has a copy, which she loves perusing, in "Before The Blood: Bryony Marseilles."

Bisque: A real type of porcelain. John and Bryony Simons bought dolls made of bisque for the nursery of their baby. Appears in "Before The Blood: Bryony Simons."

Blackberry crumble: A baked dessert made with fruit and a topping of butter cut into flour and sugar. Spencer Inn served blackberry crumble in "Before The Blood: John Simons."

Black-Eyed Susan: A real wildflower that attracts pollinators. It has yellow petals and a black center, which inspired its name. Appears in "Lycanthropic Summer."

Black Jack gum: A real licorice-flavored gum first manufactured in 1884. It was the first flavored gum in the United States and the first gum sold in sticks. Priscilla Cummings chews it during Bible study at Jenson College in "Before The Blood: Henry Matthews."

"Black's Law Dictionary" by Henry Campbell Black: Although this real book was not published in 1891, Henry's cousin Archer Markham has a copy at his bedside in "Before The Blood: Henry Matthews."

Blutwurst: A rea; German sausage made of pig blood and barley. Appears in "Before The Blood: Kellen Wechsler."

Bonnat Chocolates: A real type of cubed-shaped chocolate, which Félix Bonnat first produced in 1884. Henry sent a box of these to Victoria Rush in "Before The Blood: Henry Matthews.

Bordeaux: A real dry, full-bodied red wine from Bordeaux, France. Appears in "Before The Blood: Kellen Wechsler," "Before The Blood: Herny Matthews," and "The Phoenix."

Botanist: Someone who studies plant life. Mentioned in reference to Henry Matthews in "Before The Blood: Bryony Simons."

Brazilian rosewood: A real luxurious wood used to make furniture, cabinets, and musical instruments. The Steinway grand piano that John plays in his father's Fifth Avenue home in "Before The Blood: John Simons" is made from Brazilian rosewood.

Bowler: A real hard black felt hat with a narrow brim and rounded top. London hat-makers Thomas and William Bowler created the hat in 1849. Appears in "Bryony" and "Before The Blood: Henry Matthews."

Broadcloth: A real plain-woven cloth, originally made with wool. First produced in Flanders, Belgium, in the eleventh century. Henry tries on a broadcloth coat in a haberdashery in "Before The Blood: Henry Matthews."

Brocade: A real shuttle-woven fabric with an embossed design made with silk threads (colored, gold, or silver), which is created during the actual weaving. The fabric is not reversible, due to the design. They are often used for draperies and upholstery. Melissa wakes up in Henry's study in "Bryony" wearing a brocade dress.

170

The fabric also shows up in "Before The Blood: John Simons" (to French brocade drapery and upholstery at Savannah Holloway's farmhouse), "Before The Blood: Kellen Wechsler" (the curtains in Dr. Thradgort's office), "Before The Blood: Bryony Marseilles" (curtains in Mayor Pike's colonial), and "Before The Blood: Bryony Simons" (napkins in Simons Mansion).

Brooch: A real decorative pin, often worn near the neck. Melissa wears one when she meetings Lisa Harding in "Bryony." Adele Marseilles wears one that belonged to her mother in "Before The Blood: Bryony Marseilles," which Bryony herself wears in "Before The Blood: Bryony Simons." Harold Matthews gifts one (most likely stolen) to his daughter Maggie in "Before The Blood: Henry Matthews," and

Brownstone: Real multistory rowhouses made of brown sandstone. Henry's sister Etta and her family live on the third floor of a brownstone in Chicago in "Before The Blood: Henry Matthews."

Bryony: A real poisonous weed with predator-type qualities. Can grow up to 6 inches a day, quickly cover the sides and tops of trees, and block all light to the host plant. A pretend variety was specially bred for Simons Mansion in Munsonville. Mentioned or appears in nearly every BryonySeries book since this plant is its theme.

Bryony, Bryony Quite Contrary: A parody nursery rhyme of "Mary, Mary Quite Contrary," which Kellen Wechsler spontaneously recites to Bryony in "Before The Blood: Bryony Simons."

Bungalow: A real, small, single-story house with sloped roofs and wide front porches with overhanging eaves. Fr. Alexis Panchuk, pastor at the fictional St. Athanasius Church in Detroit, Michigan, lives in one in "Bryony" and "House on Top of the Hill." John buys one in Jenson for him and Melissa in "Visage." Henry noticed the bungalows in Jenson in "Before The Blood: Henry Matthews," and Caryn Rochelle placed them in a short werewolf story in "Lycanthropic Summer." Sherman Homes and Dr. Jim Wipston lives in a bungalow in the fictional Basketville, Michigan, in "Cornell Dyer and the Howls of Basketville."

Bury Me Not on the Lone Prairie: A real cowboy folk song that Owen Munson sings in "Before The Blood: Bryony Marseilles."

Calceolarias: A real annual, showy, orchid-like flower. Henry notices golden yellow ones when he takes his sister Etta to Bouquet Mary's in "Before The Blood: Henry Matthews."

Calvados: A real French apple brandy. Lord Girard and Albert Brumfeldt enjoyed glasses of it while opening Christmas cards at Arcadia in "Before The Blood: Henry Matthews.:

Canvasback duck: A real species of diving duck found in North America. Colin and Elaine Greene served it up with a runny version at a music salon they hosted at their Jenson home in "Before The Blood: Henry Matthews."

Capisci: Italian word for "understand." Owen Munson uses it when speaking to Bryony in "Before The Blood: Bryony Marseilles."

Carbolic acid: Also known as phenol, a real derivative of coal tar. Scottish doctor Joseph Lister started using carbolic acid in 1867 as an antiseptic and disinfectant. Dr. Edwin Gothart also uses it for similar reasons in "Before The Blood: Bryony Marseilles."

Carter Jones and the Sunset Ghost: Short story by Henry Matthews that ran in serial form in the Evansville Courrier in "Before The Blood: Henry Matthews."

Cat and Mouse: A real party game. One person is the cat. Another person is the mouse. The rest of the players stand in a circle with their hands held. The object is to not let the cat catch the mouse in a preset time period. "Before The Blood: Bryony Marseilles."

Cat heads: Real nineteenth century vulgar slang for women's breast. Henry uses it in "Before The Blood: Bryony Simons."

Catacombs: A real underground cemetery with recesses for tombs. Old St. Patrick's Cathedral in New York has catacombs. John walks Bryony through them in "Before The Blood: Bryony Simons."

Cattelimons: Pretend plant with luminous orange buds and magical properties. Appears in "Karla Joins In."

Caudle: Warm wine mixed with oats. Neta Ashmore prepares it for Dr. Martin Parks in "Call of the Siren."

Chamomile tea: A real tea made from hot water and the dried flowers of this daisy-like plant. Helps promote sleep, soothe stomach upsets, and reduce anxiety. May boost the immune system. Lucetta stuffed dried chamomile into a dream pillow for her sister Eleanor in "Before The Blood: John Simons." Adele Marseilles enjoyed a cup of chamomile tea when visiting with the other women in "Before The Blood: Bryony Marseilles." Henry enjoyed a cup of chamomile tea when relaxing with Lord Girard at Arcadia in "Before The Blood: Henry Matthews." John prepared it for Bryony in "Before The Blood: Bryony Simons." Kellen stocked his limousines with bottled iced chamomile tea in "Staked!" Also in

"Staked!," John-Peter played the tin whistle to delicate flower fairies reposing across the corn chamomile. Caryn Rochelle bought a number of sleep-inducing herbs, including chamomile, from a shoppe in Shelby in "Lycanthropic Summer."

Châtelaine: A real set of ornamental chains on a dress to carry purses, keys, watches, and other items. Bryony Simons wears one to carry her mother of pearl fan at a reception for John at Brumfeldt's home in "Before The Blood: Bryony Simons."

Chantilly Cheese: A real type of cheese made from beaten cheese, such as goat, that also has cream beaten into it. Herbert and Della Rutherford served theirs with brandied fruit at the twenty-fifth wedding anniversary in "Before The Blood: John Simons."

Charon: The ferryman of Hades in Greek mythology. Appears in "Cornell Dyer and the Eerie Lake." Mentioned in "Call of the Siren."

Charter oaks: Fictional white oaks that grow in the woods near Spencer Inn in "Before The Blood: John Simons." The original Charter oak was a real white oak tree that grew on Wyllys Hyll in Hartford, Connecticut, from approximately the twelfth century until it fell in 1856 during a storm.

Chateau: A large French, castle-like house in the country or, in Lord Girard's case, so deeply located in the woods between Munsonville and Evansville that few ever know of its existence. The chateau in "Before The Blood: Henry Matthews" is called Arcadia.

Chateaubriand: A real steak roast from the center cut of the beef tenderloin. Henry eats it at rather uneasy meal with Lord Girard,

Brumfeldt, and Carlton and Elizabeth Mandeville when they latter two visit Arcadia in "Before The Blood: Henry Matthews."

Cheshire cat: A fictional cat with a wide, mischievous grin that appears in "Alice's Adventures in Wonderland" by Lewis Carroll. John compares Kellen to the Chesire cat in "Before The Blood: John Simons."

Chevron: A mustache, shaped like a chevron (inverted V) that covers the upper lip and extends downward. Marshall Harrington wears a black in "Before The Blood: Bryony Simons."

Chicago Express: A real newspaper in the mid-nineteenth century that Henry hawked on the streets with his father Harold in "Before The Blood: Henry Matthews."

Chicago Sun: A fictional newspaper in the mid-nineteenth century that Henry hawked on the streets with his father Harold in "Before The Blood: Henry Matthews."

Chicago Times: A real newspaper in the mid-nineteenth century that Henry hawked on the streets with his father Harold in "Before The Blood: Henry Matthews."

Chicago Tribune: A real newspaper in the mid-nineteenth century (and still in print in 2023) that Henry hawked on the streets with his father Harold in "Before The Blood: Henry Matthews." A newspaper Bryony reads with John over black tea flavored with bergamot and treacle scones served with marmalade in "Before The Blood: Bryony Simons."

Chicken fricassee and dumplings: A French chicken stew where the meat is first sauteed (but not browned) in butter. The chicken is then simmered in broth, which is thickened with cream and egg.

Savannah Holloway prepares it for John in "Before The Blood: John Simons."

Chicken Marengo: A French dish. Chicken, tomato, and garlic are sautéed in oil and *when done) garnished with fried eggs and crayfish. Lord Girard served it at Arcadia for Henry's fourteenth birthday in "Before The Blood: Henry Matthews" because it was a favorite of piano master Seymour Cassidy, who also attended.

Chicken Primavera: A 1970s American dish consisting of pasta, chicken, and fresh vegetables in a cream sauce. Can substitute shrimp for pasta. Katie serves it to Cornell in "Visage." Karla recalls the memory in "Karla Joins In."

"Child Life: A Collection of Poems" by Whittier, John Greenleaf: A real book, first published in 1871. Sue Bass discovers this book at Munsonville School in "Call of the Siren."

Chinese primroses: Also called primula sinensis. A real perennial houseplant with pink or lilac flowers. Henry pots one as a gift for his sister Etta in "Before The Blood: Henry Matthews."

Chinook: The name of Henry's Siberian husky. The name means "warm wind." Appears in "Bryony," "Before The Blood: Henry Matthews," "Before The Blood: Bryony Simons," and "The Phoenix."

Chippendales: A real type of furniture designed in the eighteenth century by London cabinet maker Thomas Chippendale. Dr. Hiram and Amelia Rush own "a jumble of pieces" in their Jenson mansion in "Before The Blood: Henry Matthews."

Chivas scotch: A real blended Scotch whiskey, first produced in the eighteenth century. Appears in "Before The Blood: Kellen Wechsler."

Chloroform: A real, powerful anesthetic that is typically inhaled. First used in the mid-nineteenth century. Mentioned in "Before The Blood: Bryony Simons."

Chlorosis: A real archaic term for what was most likely iron-deficiency anemia in adolescent girls and young women in the nineteenth century. The disease disappeared by the 1930s. The diagnosis Dr. Gothart gives Bryony in "Before The Blood: Bryony Simons."

Chocolate tortes: A rich, egg-heavy chocolate dessert with nuts or breadcrumbs instead of flour. Agnes King feeds some to Henry in "Before The Blood: Henry Matthews."

Chronometer: A real, extremely accurate, mechanical, portable timepiece, originally designed for ships. Henry compares the actions of Babbie to one in "Before The Blood: Henry Matthews."

Ciphering: A real archaic term for arithmetic. Used in "Before The Blood: Kellen Wechsler," "Before The Blood: Bryony Marseilles," "Before The Blood: Henry Matthews," and "Summer Sisters."

Cider wine: A signature beverage at Spencer Inn in "Before The Blood: John Simons."

Cinerarias: A real hybrid flowering plant in the sunflower family. Henry notices some when he takes his older sister Etta to Bouquet Mary's in "Before The Blood: Henry Matthews."

Cloistered Dominican Nuns of the Perpetual Rosary: Based on real order of the same name, originating in France, that never actually moved to Lancaster until the 1950s. The Lancaster monastery closed in 2021, its school in 2023, and the graves were moved in 2022. Appears in "Before The Blood: Bryony Simons" and "The Phoenix." Mentioned in "Before The Blood: Henry Matthews."

Clothes wringer: A wringer washer. Appears in "Before The Blood: Bryony Marseilles" and "Katie and the Big Fear." Mentioned in "Karla Joins In."

Cobbler: A dessert with fruit in syrup covered by a dough topping and baked in "Before The Blood: Bryony Marseilles" or a person who makes and sells shoes in "Before The Blood: Henry Matthews."

Codger: An elderly eccentric man. Appears in "Before The Blood: Henry Matthews."

Columbine: A real perennial plant with pendant flowers that can be blue, pink, purple or white. Appears at Mama Prudie's wake in "Before The Blood: John Simons" to mask the smell of death. Grows on Fisher Farm in "Before The Blood: Bryony Marseilles." Arranged in vases at the Hasset home in "The Phoenix" and also in Simons Mansion (to mask the smell of death."

"Come loving and soothing death. Undulate 'round the world, serenely arriving, arriving. In the day, in the night, to all, to each, sooner or later, delicate death." Henry quotes this line from Walt Whitman's poem "When Lilacs Last in the Dooryard Bloom'd" in "Bryony."

"Commentaries on American Law" by Chancellor James Kent:
A real book first published in 1826 Henry's cousin Archer Markham
has a copy at his bedside in "Before The Blood: Henry Matthews."

**"Commentaries on the Laws of England" by Sir William
Blackstone:** Henry buys a copy of this real book for his cousin
Archer Markham in "Before The Blood: Henry Matthews

Coney dogs: The favorite hot dog of Sam Barnes, who insisted
Sue's Diner serve it in "Call of the Siren." The Coney dog is a real,
natural casing hot dog in a steamed bun topped with a chili meat
sauce, chopped raw onions, and a drizzle of mustard. One bite and
Sue Bass was a believer.

Confiteor Deo: "I confess to Almighty God, to blessed Mary Ever-
Virgin, to blessed Michael the Archangel, to blessed John the
Baptist, to the holy Apostles Peter and Paul, and to all the Saints that
I have sinned exceedingly in thought, word, and deed, through my
fault, through my fault, through my most grievous fault. Therefore,
I ask blessed Mary Ever-Virgin, blessed Michael the Archangel,
blessed John the Baptist, the holy Apostles Peter and Paul, and all
the Saints, to pray for me to the Lord our God. Amen." Prayed in
some Roman Catholic, Lutheran, and Anglo-Catholic Masses.
Appears in Latin in "Before The Blood: Kellen Wechsler."

Cornish pasties: Peppery beef and vegetables tucked inside pastry.
Dana Hewes wife served this to John in "Before The Blood: John
Simons."

Cordgrass: A tall, brackish marsh grass that's really found on the
coasts of certain U.S. states including Connecticut. Appears in
"Before The Blood: John Simons."

Cornell's Concise Crystallomancy: A fictional guide to crystal gazing by supernatural super sleuth Cornell Dyer that is anything but concise. Appears in "Staked!" and "Karla Joins In."

Coterie: A real French word for a group of people with a shared interest. Used in "Before The Blood: Henry Matthews."

Creatures of the Night: Witches, Werewolves, and Vampires: Fictional reference book on witches, werewolves, and vampires. Appears (so far) in "Bryony," "Visage," and "Cornell Dyer and the Old Folks Home."

Crèche: A model representing Jesus' birth. Appears in "Before The Blood: Henry Matthews."

Creamed sweetbreads: The thymus gland and pancreas in calves, lambs, and pigs, which is boiled and served in a creamed sauce. Appears in "Before The Blood: John Simons" and "Before The Blood: Kellen Wechsler."

Cremsol shaving cream: Fictional shaving cream of which 1940s Kellen wrote a successful advertising campaign. Appears in "Before The Blood: Kellen Wechsler."

Critique of Pure Reason: A real book by German philosopher Immanuel Kant. Boswell Pike reads it while eating lunch with the other lumberjacks in "Before The Blood: Bryony Marseilles."

Croque-en-bouche: Also spelled croquembouche. A real French dessert dating back to at least 1806. It's made of choux pastry puffs stacked into a tower and bound together with caramel threads. Henry enjoyed it as part of a private Christmas Eve dinner at Arcadia with Lord Girard and Brumfeldt in "Before The Blood: Henry Matthews."

Croquets of Fowl with Piquant Sauce: Chopped fowl (maybe chicken, maybe not) seasoned, shaped into bites, rolled into bread crumbs and then fried and served with a spicy tomato-based sauce. Bryony was eating this dinner with John at Simons Mansion when he received the invitation to play at Carnegie Hall. Appears in "Before The Blood: Bryony Simons."

Croquet: A real sport played on grass where people hit wooden balls with wooden mallets through wire hoops or wickets. Origins of the game date back to the seventeenth century. Played in "Bryony" and "Before The Blood: Bryony Simons."

Crudités: A real French appetizer where raw whole or sliced vegetables are dipped in a vinaigrette. This was served with tapenade at Arcadia when Carlton and Elizabeth Mandeville came to visit in "Before The Blood: Henry Matthews."

Crullers: A real deep-fried doughnut-like pastry. Mrs. Parks fries them in "Before The Blood: Bryony Marseilles." Mary Singler insists Henry take a few when he leaves dinner to cover a story in "Before The Blood: Henry Matthews." Sue Bass and Luther Hasset enjoyed some together hear the little chapel outside Shelby in "Call of the Siren." Lucille DuBois serves them to Cornell Dyer as part of a hearty breakfast in "Cornell Dyer and the Missing Tombstone."

Crumpet: A real small unsweetened griddle bread similar to an English muffin. It's one of the first items Henry eats at Arcadia in "Before The Blood: Henry Matthews."

Cumulus clouds: Cottony, cauliflower-shaped clouds typically seen in the sky during fair weather. They appear in one of Bryony's dreams in "Before The Blood: Bryony Simons."

Cupid's arrows: A reference to Greek and Roman mythology. Cupid (eros) plays with emotions by shooting golden arrows. Mr. Parks refers to them when talking about the volatile relationship between Teddy and Sally Bass in "Before The Blood: Bryony Marseilles."

"Cymbeline" by Shakespeare: A student at Jenson College read a passage from this tragedy during an orator's contest in "Before The Blood: Henry Matthews."

Daily News: Full name of this real newspaper was the Chicago Daily News. Founded in 1875 and published for the last time in 1978. Mentioned in "Before The Blood: Henry Matthews."

Daphnis and Chloe: A ancient Greek romance novel written in the Roman Empire by second-century AD by Longus, his only known work. Henry quotes from this when seducing Anges King, who seduces him in return in "Before The Blood: Henry Matthews."

Davenport China: A real high quality English porcelain tableware produced by the Davenport family, between 1794 and 1887. Even the Prince of Wales (later King George IV) owned it. Appears in "Before The Blood: John Simons."

"Death comes in its own time, in its own way. Death is as unique as the individual experiencing it." Henry quotes this poem, often attributed to Henry van Dyke Jr., in "Bryony."

Declaration of Independence: The founding document of the United States. Read at an 1892 Independence Day celebration in Munsonville in "Before The Blood: Bryony Simons."

Dendera lamp: A fictional lamp lit by the mythical Egyptian form of lighting technology. Appears in "Before The Blood: John Simons" and "Call of the Siren."

Detroit Sun: A fictional newspaper of which the real Alan Pinkerton produces a clipping in "Before The Blood: Henry Matthews. However, a similarly named publication, The Detroit Sun, was published, beginning in 1944.

Deuteronomy 12:21–23: "Then thou shalt kill of thy herd and of thy flock, which the Lord hath given thee, as I have commanded thee, and thou shalt eat in thy gates whatsoever thy soul lusteth. The unclean and the clean shall eat of them alike. Only be sure that thou eat not the blood. For the blood is the life." Appears in "Staked!," "Before The Blood: Bryony Marseilles," and "Before The Blood: Henry Matthews."

Deutsche Messe und Ordnung des Gottesdiensts: "German Mass and Order of Worship" published by Martin Luther in 1526. Appears in "Before The Blood: Kellen Wechsler."

Dewberries: Similar to blackberries but with a smaller fruit and trailing (as opposed to upright) stems with red hairs on their slender thorns. Grows in Michigan, particularly the fictional Munsonville. Appears in "Before The Blood: Bryony Marseilles" and "Before The Blood: Bryony Simons."

Dickens' "Mugby Junction:" A real book of short stories published in 1866. Authors include Charles Dickens and collaborators Charles Collins, Amelia B. Edwards, Andrew Halliday, and Hesba Stretton. Bryony quotes from it when standing at the train station in Thornton for the first time in "Before The Blood: Bryony Simons."

Diapheromera femoratas: A real stick-like insect found in North America. Mentioned in "Before The Blood: Henry Matthews."

'Die Ersten werden die Letzten sein.'": In English, this means, "The first is the last and the last is the first." Matthew 20:16. Voll-Bauers wife delivers this message to Kellen in "Before The Blood: Kellen Wechsler."

Diphtheria: A real serious bacterial infection of the nose and throat that's now preventable by vaccine and treated with an antitoxin. The infection grows characteristic grey membrane over the back of the throat, which impedes breathing. Bryony recalls how the disease killed several of her friends in "Before The Blood: Bryony Simons."

Dogberry tree: See "rowan."

Dream-Ghouls: The name of the fictional movie that Julie Drake and her friends weren't allowed to see in "Julie and the Too-Hard Homework."

Duvet: A real type of French comforters. Its interchangeable covers are typically filled with down. Henry sleeps beneath them at Arcadia in "Before The Blood: Henry Matthews."

Eastern Europe's eighteenth century vampire hysteria: A real phenomena where various diseases were attributed to vampires. Mentioned in "Before The Blood: Bryony Marseilles."

Ecclesiastes 12:14: "For God will bring every deed into judgment, with every secret thing, whether good or evil," John's grandfather quotes this passage when sharing a family secret in "Before The Blood: John Simons."

Ecole des Beaux-Arts: A real French art school. Mentioned with scorn in "Before The Blood: Kellen Wechsler" and offhandedly in "Before The Blood: Bryony Simons."

Edith Fox bonnet: A style of luxury bonnet from the nineteenth century from a famous, upscale, fictional milliner. Edith Fox was to hats as House of Worth was to gowns. Louise Girard was wearing one the last time Lord Girard ever saw her in "Before The Blood: Heny Matthews."

Eight-day longcase clock: A real grandfather clock that needed winding just once a week. Appears in the parsonage in "Before The Blood: Bryony Marseilles."

Eighteenth century oriental porcelain flask: A valuable Chinese antique. Appears in "Before The Blood: John Simons" and "Call of the Siren."

Eleventh century Olyphant: A real large ivory hunting horn, mentioned in "Song of Roland." Appears in "Before The Blood: John Simons" and "Call of the Siren."

Elsie Dinsmore: A real Christian book series written by Martha Finley between 1867 and 1905. Mentioned in "Before The Blood: Bryony Marseilles."

El Station Rodic 73 watch: A fictional, supernaturalish timepiece used by supernatural super sleuth Cornell Dyer in "Cornell Dyer and the 'Mistical' Being."

"Emmerson's Essays," by Ralph Waldo Emmerson: Melissa tries to amuse herself by reading this real book of essays while being ignored by the vampires in Simons Mansion in "Bryony."

Emerson's "Self-Reliance": Reverend Galien Marseilles reads a passage from this real book by Ralph Waldo Emmerson while riding a train with Adele Belanger in "Before The Blood: Bryony Marseilles."

Empire chair: A real French chair with legs curved like the letter "C" The Empire style originated in the French court of Napoleon I and was most popular from 1800 to 1815. Henry sees an oil painting of his mother sitting on the edge of an Empire chair in Lord Girard's office in "Before The Blood: Henry Matthews."

Ene, tene, mone, mei: German for eeney, meeny, miny, moe. Kellen plays the children's game trying to decide which vein on the Burgermeister of Seulobitz's neck to lance with his fangs in "Before The Blood: Kellen Wechsler."

Enkelsohn: German word for grandson. Appears in "Before The Blood: Kellen Wechsler."

Erben pipe organ: A real, 1868 Henry Erben organ with 2,500 pipes that is still being used in side Old St. Patrick's Cathedral in New York. Appears in "Before The Blood: John Simons."

Escargot Beignet: Snail fritters. Henry packs these as part of the lunch he brings to his brother-in-law William Markham in "Before The Blood: Henry Matthews."

Etymology: Study of origin of words. More precisely, this study was the "entomological etymology" or the origin of insect names. Appears in "Before The Blood: Henry Matthews" when Henry shares afternoon with a nephew who adores this hobby,

"Evangeline, A Tale of Acadie," by Henry Wadsworth Longfellow: Sue Bass Barnes quotes a passage from this real epic poem of two separated lovers in "Call of the Siren."

Evansville Courier: A fictional newspaper in the fictional company town of Evansville, Michigan. Mentioned in "Before The Blood: Bryony Marseilles" and "The Phoenix." Appears in "Before The Blood: Henry Matthews."

EW Transcontinental railway: A fictional railway owned by Lord Girard in "Before The Blood: Henry Matthews."

Exodus: Algernon Demars discussed this book during his Bible study at Jenson College in "Before The Blood: Henry Matthews."

Ezekiel's Valley of Dry Bones: Dr. Martin Parks sees a vision of this Biblical scene in "Call of the Siren."

Faber-Castell pens: Real high quality art tools. Founded in 1761 in Germany. Appears in "Before The Blood: Henry Matthews."

Fadette: The main character in "La Petite Fadette," a real 1849 novel by French novelist George Sand. Mentioned in "Before The Blood: Bryony Marseilles."

Faith: A skittish calico cat that is afraid of ghosts in "Cornell Dryer and the Missing Tombstone." Based on my real calico named Faith.

Federal-style architecture: Real architecture that is square or rectangular, two to three stories high, two octangular rooms deep, hipped roof (all sides gently slope to the ground), and with more ornamentation than a colonial. John mistakenly refers to Old St. Patrick's Cathedral having Federal-style architecture, but it's actually Gothic Revival style. St. Patrick's Old Cathedral School across the street, which was built from 1825 to 1826 is the Federal-style building. While Old St. Patrick's is still open, the school closed in 2011 for low enrollment. The school itself became a New York City landmark in 1966 and was added to the National Register of Historic Places in 1977.

Fenny Snake: An item that goes into Macbeth's witch's brew. It could mean a snake from the wetlands (fens), or it could refer to the Jack-in-the-pulpit flower (arisaema triphyllum), also known as "snake's meat." Appears in "Karla Joins In."

Fenny Snake, Inc.: A fictional manufacturer of wooden snake banks. Appears in "Karla Joins In."

Fenny Snake Prison: Karla and John-Peter's terms for Karla's grounding until she solves the mystery of the Fenny Snake in "Karla Joins In."

Ferdinand XGE: Fictional luxury car. Mentioned in "Lycanthropic Summer."

Figaro: A fictional expensive cigar brand. Henry tries one in "Before The Blood: Henry Matthews."

Filagree: Real ornamental metalwork from fine gold or silver wire, often used in making jewelry. Henry gives Victoria Rush a silver filigree brooch with a single pearl in "Before The Blood: Henry Matthews."

Filet Mignon ala Bordelaise: Tender beef steak served with a sauce made from Bordeaux wine, shallots, veal broth, butter and flavored with thyme. Henry packs this in the lunch he brings to his brother-in-law William Markham in "Before The Blood: Henry Matthews."

188

Foie gras: A real delicate French food made from forcibly fattening the liver of a duck or goose. Henry enjoys it at a meal with Arcadia with Lord Girard, Brumfeldt, and Carlton and Elizabeth Mandeville in "Before The Blood: Hemry Matthews."

Fop: A real derogatory term for a man who over-emphasizes his dress. Henry calls the man flirting with Bess at a party in "Before The Blood: Henry Matthews" a fop.

"For in the hand of the Lord there is a cup, and the wine is red; it is full of mixture; and he poureth out of the same: but the dregs thereof, all the wicked of the earth shall wring them out and drink them." Psalm 75: 8: Reverend Galien Marseilles cruelly quotes this Bible verse as a means of intensifying the distress a friend is experiencing following a tragedy in "Before The Blood: Bryony Simons."

"For the good that I would I do not: but the evil which I would not, that I do." This verse, Romans 7:17, in the Christian Bible, is the first line in "Before The Blood: Bryony Simons" and the only one marked in heavy underlining in Reverend Galien Marseilles' personal Bible.

For the wages of sin is death: Verse Romans 6:23 in the Bible. Reverend Galien Marseilles reminds himself of this verse as self-blame in "Before The Blood: Bryony Marseilles."

For this is the chalice of my blood: The words spoken during the consecration of wine in a Roman Catholic Mass. Appears in "Before The Blood: Henry Matthews."

Forensic graphology: Using science-based methods to study the pattern of handwriting. Appears in "Karla Joins In."

Fortnight: A period of two weeks. Henry spends a fortnight in Jenson with Brumfeldt in "Before The Blood: Henry Matthews."

Fox in the Hole: A real traditional children's game involving hopping on one leg. One of the children's games Felicity Helsby organizes for the garden party at Simons Mansion in "Before The Blood: Bryony Simons."

Franc: A basic unit of currency in France and several other countries until the introduction of the euro in 1999. Kellen refers to the franc in terms of a John Simons' performance in "Before The Blood: Kellen Wechsler."

Frances: A wise tabby cat that appears in "Bertrand and the Lucky Clover," "Bertrand and the Christmas Surprise," and "Before The Blood: Bryony Simons." Based on my real tabby named Frances.

François-Henri Clicquot's organ at Notre-Dame de Paris: John admires this organ made by the eighteenth century organ-builder for this twelfth century Roman Catholic cathedral in "Before The Blood: Kellen Wechsler."

Franklin P. Lumpen: A friend of Bertrand The Mouse in "Bertrand Spends the Night."

Freemasonry: A real fraternal organization dating back to the fourteenth century. Mentioned during a meeting of the Munsonville Society for the Humanities in "Before The Blood: Henry Matthews."

Freesia: A real light and sweetly fragrant flower from Africa. Mentioned as wedding flower in "Before The blood: Herny Matthews."

French cuisine: A blanket term for customs and cooking practices of France, from the fourteenth century to the present. Mentioned in "Before The Blood: Henry Matthews."

French gothic chateau: A real architectural style in France from the twelfth century to the sixteenth century. New York Jacob King lives in a French gothic chateau on Fifth Avenue.

French Renaissance architecture: Homes made of brick or stone with arched entranceways, sloping roofs, towers, and turrets. Henry notes a number of mansions in this style on Fifth Avenue in New York in "Before The Blood: Henry Mathews."

French Renaissance paneling: Real ornamental embossed oak paneling from the sixteenth century. A parlor and salon (reception room) in Jacob King's Fifth Avenue home was overed in these in "Before The Blood: Henry Matthews."

French Revolution: A decade of political and societal upheaval from 1789 to 1799, which included the storming of the Bastille on July 14, 1789, and the rise of Napoleon to power. Mentioned in "Before The Blood: Kellen Wechsler." Mentioned in "Before The Blood: Kellen Wechsler."

Frisky: The pet cat in Kellen's 1940 family.

Frizzled eggs: A real type of fried egg, crispy on the outside and soft on the inside. Kellen develops a taste for them in "Before The Blood: Kellen Wechsler."

"From All That Dwell Belong the Skies: Hymn by Isaac Watts: A real hymn from 1719. Referenced in "Before The Blood: Bryony Marseilles.'

Frumenty: A thick-grained porridge of hulled wheat boiled in milk and flavored with cinnamon and sugar. Kellen overheard people on the streets talking about as Christmas approached in "Before The Blood: Kellen Wechsler."

Fuchsias: A real flowering plant or small bush featuring pink, purple, or white flowers. Henry passes some when he takes his sister Etta to Bouquet Mary's in "Before The Blood: Henry Matthews."

Fun Fact: The term "Fun, Facts, and Fancies" extends back to the mid-nineteenth century, while "Fun Fact" goes back to at least the mid-1940s. Kellen uses the term when he drops his mean secret in "Before The Blood: Bryony Simons."

Gallicas: Real French roses, one of the first rose species to be cultivated in Western Europe. Henry grows them inside Little Arcadia in "Before The Blood: Henry Matthews" and sends them as a gift to Victoria Rush in Jenson.

Gardenias: A real flowering plant in the coffee family with wonderfully fragrant white flowers and shiny green leaves. John Simons sends gardenias to Helsby's wedding in "Before The Blood: Johnm Simons." Mentioned as wedding flower in "Before The blood: Herny Matthews."

Gastritis: In 2023, it refers to inflammation of the soft lining in the stomach. In the nineteenth century in the BryonySeries world, "gastritis" was a layman's, catch-all phrase for any inflammation or disease in the gastrointestinal tract. Appears in "Before The Blood: John Simons" and alluded to in "The Phoenix."

Gates of Horn and Ivy: A literary image from the Greek language to discern between fact and fancy. Appears as a method for discernment in "Call of the Siren."

Gazebo: An open structure with a rood, often used for entertaining guests or relaxing. The gazebo at Simons Mansion in mentioned in "Bryony," "Visage," "Staked!," "Snowbell," and "Before The Blood: Bryony Simons." A gazebo also appears in "Cornell Dyer and the Never Robbers."

Genesis 1:27: "So God created man in his own image, in the image of God created he him; male and female created he them:" Reverend Marseilles reads this passage at a meeting of the Munsonville Society for the Humanities" to refute misogyny in "Before The Blood: Bryony Marseilles."

Geraniums: A real type of flowering plant with more than four hundred annual, biennial, and perennial species. They are popular for hanging in baskets. Henry passes by some when he takes his sister Etta to Bouquet Mary's in "Before The Blood: Henry Matthews."

German lace curtains: A real machine-made lace developed in Plauen, Germany, in the mid-nineteenth century. The lace is stitched on chemically treated fabric in such a way to create a continuous motif. When the design is completed, the remaining fabric disintegrates. Adele Marseilles orders curtains made with German lace for the parsonage in "Before The Blood: Bryony Marseilles."

German mercury glass: Real glass that was "silvered" in a solution of grape sugar and silver nitrate. Manufactured in Germany from approximately 1840 to 1930. Bohemia and England also made mercury glass at different time frames. One use for mercury glass was Christmas ornaments. John mocks his father for ordering yet another shipment of the ornaments in "Before The Blood: John Simons."

Germain Royal silver tureen: A real French silversmith designed this thirty-pound silver tureen in the early eighteenth century for Louis XV. Appears in "Before The Blood: John Simons" and "Call of the Siren."

"Getting Married:" A real compilation of twelve short stories that depicted various stances of marital life by Swedish writer Swedish August Strindberg. Discussed by the Munsonville Society for the Humanities in "Before The Blood: Bryony Marseilles."

Ghost detector: A cannister apparatus with a hose that can detect ghosts in any situation. Appears in "Cornell Dyer and the Missing Tombstone" and "Karla Joins In."

Ghost flashlight: A powerful, high-beamed flashlight that is invisible to mortals. Used (so far) in "Cornell Dyer and the Calcium-Deficient Bones" and "The Howls of Basketville."

Ginger snaps: A small, crisp, spicy cookie made with molasses and ginger. Referenced in "Before The Blood: Bryony Marseilles."

Giuseppe Garibaldi's funeral march: The nineteenth century Italian composer, conductor, and pianist Timoteo Pasini composed this real funeral march for the Italian flautist and composer Giuseppe Garibaldi. Pasini's death is mentioned in "Before The Blood: John Simons."

Glee Club: Henry hears this diverse club at Jenson College sing in "Before The Blood: Henry Matthews."

Gloria, in excelsis Deo: Latin for "Glory to God in the Highest" and sun as part of the Great Doxology in the Roman Catholic Mass. The phrase lingers in John's mind after midnight Christmas Mass in "Before The Blood: John Simons."

"God is our God for ever and ever: he will be our guide even unto death." Psalm 48:14: Kate Miller quotes this Bible verse as comfort and encouragement to Bryony in "Before The Blood: Bryony Simons."

God Rest Ye Merry Gentlemen: Real sixteenth century English Christmas carol. Bryony hears Owen Munson singing the song at night as he staggers by her window in "Before The Blood: Bryony Marseilles."

Godey's Lady's Book: A real monthly magazine for women, published from 1830 to 1896. Mentioned of appears in "Before The Blood: John Simons," "Before The Blood: Bryony Marseilles," and "Before The Blood: Herny Matthews."

Golden cords: A fictional golden cord attaching body to soul. Appears in "Cornell Dyer and the Flu" and "Call of the Siren."

Goldilocks and the Three Bears: Henry dreams of a macabre version of this real, nineteenth century fairy tale by the English poet Robert Southey during an asthma attack in "Before The Blood: Henry Matthews."

Going to Jerusalem: A real party game. Also known as musical chairs. A number of chairs (one less than the partygoers) are arranged in a circle and music is played or sung. When the music stops, everyone scrambles for a chair. The chairless one is out of the game and another chair is removed. The game continues until the last two people sits in the lone chair. Played at Iris Pike's birthday party on Valentine's Day in "Before The Blood: Bryony Marseilles."

Golgotha: The real site outside Jerusalem where Jesus was crucified and died. Mentioned in "Before The Blood: Bryony Marseilles."

"Gone From My Sight" by Henry van Dyke Jr: : Henry lauds death by quoting a line from this poem in "Bryony."

Good Book: Technically the humanist Bible. In the BryonySeries, the expression "the good book" is used as a synonym for the Holy Bible. Used in "Before The Blood: Henry Matthews," "Before The Blood: Bryony Simons," and "Call of the Siren."

Gossip: A real party game. Also known as Telephone or Chinese Whispers. The first person whispers a message to a person and so forth until the last person receives the message. The final message is usually profoundly different than the original due to human error and interpretation. Played at Iris Pike's birthday party on Valentine's Day in "Before The Blood: Bryony Marseilles." Mentioned in "Before The Blood: Bryony Simons."

Grandmother clock: A free-standing clock, smaller than a grandfather clock. Lord Girard has at least one ivory grandmother clock in "Before The Blood: Henry Matthews."

Gelatin bromide dry plates: Plates preceded film in photography. Dry plates, which were dipped in a gelatin silver bromide salutation, could be mass produced and stored until use. Wet plates were dipped into a solution of silver nitrate and were prepared before each use. Mentioned in "Before The Blood: Henry Matthews."

Great and Holy Book: Synonym for the Christian Bible in "Before The Blood: Bryony Marseilles."

The Great New York City Fire of 1845: A real fire in a candle factory in Lower Manhattan on July 19, 1945, that spread to a saltpeter warehouse. Owen Munson alludes to this fire in his watermelon story in "Before The Blood: Bryony Marseilles."

Great Upheaval: A real series of railroad strikes in the late 1870s. Police, the National Guard and the U.S. Army came out to address the angry mobs. Mentioned in "Before The Blood: Henry Matthews."

Gregorian chant: A real ancient chant in Latin used in Roman Catholic churches. Mentioned in "Before The Blood: John Simons."

Grimm's Fairy Tales: A real German collection of fairy tales by the Brothers Grimm. Bryony owns a copy in "Before The Blood: Bryony Marseilles," and she hid her birthday fortune among its pages.

Grippe: Synonym for influenza. Mentioned in "Before The Blood: John Simons" and "Before The Blood: Bryony Marseilles."

Goocrux.: Pretend magical maize-colored weed with magical properties. Appears in "Karla Joins In."

Gustave Doré demon: Bryony refers to the image conceived by the French artist Gustave Doré in "Before The Blood: Bryony Simons."

Guastavino tiles: A real type of terracotta, self-supporting arch system that Spanish architect and builder Rafael Guastavino introduced to the United States in 1885 and patented in 1892.

Guten Morgan: "Good morning" in the German language. Used in "Before The Blood: Kellen Wechsler."

Haberdashery: A men's clothing and accessory store. Henry visits one in Jenson in "Before The Blood: Henry Matthews."

Hamburgers: A common dinner food in "Lycanthropic Summer" and a favorite food overall for supernatural super sleuth Cornell Dyer.

Handel's Messiah: A real English-language oratorio composed by George Frideric Handel in 1741. It was originally intended for the Easter season and is now associated with Christmas. A chorus of several hundred voices presents a full performance on Christmas Eve at Arcadia in "Before The Blood: Henry Matthews."

Hand-gallop: Real vintage slang for masturbation. Kellen uses the term once in "Before The Blood: Bryony Simons."

Hanoverians: A real strong, sleek, elegant horse breed from Germany. Boswell Pike owns quite a few in "Before The Blood: Bryony Marseilles."

Ham bone and giblets: Real nineteenth century vulgar slang for male genitals. Used by Henry in "Before The Blood: Henry Matthews."

Hansom cab: A real horse-drawn carriage that New York architect Joseph Hansom designed and patented in 1834. Appear in "Before The Blood: John Simons" and "Before The Blood: Kellen Wechsler."

Harrigan and Hart Broadway musical: Musical by Edward Harrigan and Tony Hart, fathers of musical theater and musical

198

comedy. Known for their realistic plays, more than twenty of which appeared on Broadway in New York. Mentioned in "Before The Blood: John Simons."

Hark the Herald Angels Sing: An English Christmas carol from 1739. "Before The Blood: Bryony Marseilles."

Harvey's Elementary Grammar and Composition: Thomas W. Harvey (Thomas Wadleigh) published his real grammar books in the late nineteenth century. Appears in "Before The Blood: John Simons."

Hay & Lyall thermometer: A real, mercury-filled outdoor thermometer from the nineteenth century. Dr. Edwin Gothart has one outside his colonial house in "The Phoenix" and "Call of the Siren."

"He saw two boats lying at the edge of the lake; but the fishermen had gotten out of them and were washing their nets." Luke 5:2: One of the earliest Bible verse Bryony Marseilles heard her father read. Appears in "Before The Blood: Bryony Marseilles."

Hecate: Hecate, goddess of magic and the underworld, who is often depicted waiting at a crossroad with a large dog. Moonstone (hecatolite) is named for Hecate. She appears in "Lycanthropic Summer."

Hecatolite: A real gem named for Hecate. Appears in "Lycanthropic Summer." See also "moonstone."

Heidi by Johanna Spyri: Bestselling children's fiction and Swiss literature published between1880 and 1881 about a young girl growing up in the Alps with her grandfather the Alm-Uncle. Bryony daydreams about the book during church services in "Before The Blood: Bryony Marseilles."

Hematophagist: Hematophagy is the practice of animals feeding blood. John calls Kellen "a rather extreme hematophagist" in "Before The Blood: Kellen Wechsler."

Hemoglobin: The protein in red blood cells that delivers oxygen from the lungs to the tissues. Mentioned in "Before The Blood: Kellen Wechsler."

Hemp: A plant grown for a number of uses, including ropemaking. John mentions how Lucetta grew hemp in her room in "Before The Blood: Bryony Simons."

Henry's wedding toast: Henry cobbled together his toast for John and Bryony Simons' wedding from a number of Shakespeare plays. "May a flock of blessings light upon thy back" Romeoville and Juliet) and "Fair thought and happy hours attend you" (Merchant of Venice) "Look down, ye gods, and on this couple drop a blessed crown." (The Tempest). "I wish you all the joy you can wish." (Merchant of Venice) "The best of happiness, honor, and fortunes keeps with you." (Timon of Athens). "Combine your hearts in one." (The Life of King Henry V). "Recited in "Before The Blood: Bryony Simons."

"Hero and Leander" by Christopher Marlowe: "She ware no gloves; for neither sun nor wind, would burn or parch her hands, but to her mind, or warm or cool them, for they took delight to play upon those hands, they were so white." Henry quotes this passage from Christopher Marlowe's poem to Agnes King in "Before The Blood: Henry Matthews.

"Here We Come A-wassailing" (or Here We Come A-Caroling): Traditional English carol at least as old as the mid-nineteenth century. Bryony overhears two inebriated men – Owen Munson and Bowell Pike – singing this carol shortly after midnight on New Year's Day 1886 as they ambled past her window in "Before The Blood: Bryony Marseilles."

Hero and Leander: The main characters in a tragic love story in Greek Mythology in the sixteenth century narrative poem by Christopher Marlowe. Henry quotes part of the poem to Agnes King in "Before The Blood: Henry Matthews."

Himenelac tree: A tall pretend tree where the lowest branches are about at least feet from the ground in "Cornell Dyer and the Old Folks Home."

History of the Persian Wars: A gallant Henry removes a copy of this book from a high shelf in the Jenson College library and then hands it to Victoria Rush in "Before The Blood: Henry Matthews."

Hoberdy's lantern: The name for an Irish jack-o-lantern. Rows of them appear at a harvest party on Fisher Farm in "Before The Blood: Bryony Marseilles." Mentioned in "Before The Blood: Bryony Simons."

Hohenheim: A soft, round German cheese. Voll-Bauer's wife serves it to Kellen on a tray, along with a roasted egg, a soft round of Hohenheim, toast, marmalade, and Leberwurst in "Before The Blood: Kellen Wechsler."

Holsteins: Holstein Friesian. Breed of cow in dairy farming, Appear in "Before The Blood: Bryony Marseilles."

Holy God, We Praise Thy Name: The lyrics were written by German Catholic priest Ignaz Franz in 1771, paraphrasing the fourth century Latin hymn "Te Deum." Appear in "Before The Blood: Bryony Marseilles."

Homberg hat: A semi formal hat of felt fur, first popularized in the late nineteenth century. A Homberg has a dent in the crown, a wide silk or satin hatband, and a curled-up brim. Henry tries on several at a haberdashery in Jenson in "Before The Blood: Henry Matthews."

Honeysuckle: Fragrant, coloring flowering vines. Honeysuckle is cultivated on the Simons Estate in "Before The Blood: Bryony Simons."

Hornpipe: Bryony is referring to the "Sailor's Hornpipe," a lively melody from the late eighteen century. Miles hums it in "Before The Blood: Bryony Simons."

Hortobágyi palacsinta: Dr. Gothart offers this savory Hungarian crepe, filled with veal, onions, mushrooms, paprika, sour cream, to Kellen to see if his "treatments" are working in "Before The **Blood: Kellen Wechsler.**"

Hoyden: Tomboy. Mrs. Parks uses this term to describe Daisy Fisher in "Before The Blood: Bryony Marseilles."

Hudson River Valley's abundant grape crop: Reported by Felix Coates for the New York Gazette in "Before The Blood: Henry Matthews."

Hunchback of Lower Manhattan: Kellen parodies the phrase "Hunchback of Notre Dame" in describing Dr. Edwin Gothart's appearance in "Before The Blood: Kellen Wechsler."

Hunt the Thimble: A party game. Someone hides a thimble or other small object for people to find. Played at Iris Pike's birthday party on Valentine's Day in "Before The Blood: Bryony Marseilles."

Hyderphobia: Mispronunciation of hydrophobia by Owen Munson, as well as Polly Mendel. Hydrophobia means a fear of water. It's a symptom of rabies. Appears in "Before The Blood: Bryony Marseilles" and "Before The Blood: Henry Matthews."

Hypertrichosis: Excessive hair growth. Appears in "Lycanthropic Summer."

"I know a place where the wild thyme grows": John-Peter quotes this line from William Shakespeare's "A Midsummer's Night Dream," that becomes a hidden theme in "Karla Joins In."

"I Ride an Old Paint:" Begins with "O when I die, take my saddle from the wall." A traditional cowboy song. Owen Munson sings it in "Before The Blood: Bryony Marseilles." Mitch Cooper and Eugene Miller sang the song at Munson Day 1892 in "Before The Blood: Bryony Simons."

Imperial Diamond: Displayed at the Exposition Universelle in 1889 in France, the largest in the world at the time. Mentioned in "Before The Blood: Kellen Wechsler" and "Before The Blood: Bryony Simons."

Impressionism: A nineteenth century French artistic practice of painting spontaneously outside. Debated in "Before The Blood: Kelen Wechsler."

Incy Wincy Spider: An old nursery rhyme Kellen sings as he works his way up John's arm to his jugular in "Before The Blood: Kellen Wechsler."

Incubus: Male demon. The term Seymour Cassidy uses in Kellen's direction in "Before The Blood: Kellen Wechsler."

"In quo omnes thesauri sapientiae et scientiae," or "In which are stored all treasures of knowledge and science.": The inscription at the entrance of The Wiblingen Monastery in Germany, an eleventh century library, of which Kellen visits in "Before The Blood: Kellen Wechsler."

Indian hemp: Henry's nickname for cannabis in "Before The Blood: Henry Matthews."

Iron horse: A nineteenth century term for steam locomotives. Appears in "Before The Blood: Bryony Marseilles" and "Before The Blood: Bryony Simons."

Inverness coat: A loosely belted outercoat with a capelet reaching the length of the sleeves. John wears a sepia Inverness in "Before The Blood: Bryony Simons."

"It happened in Jacksboro, boys, in the year of seventy-three:" See "The Buffalo Skinners."

Jacob's Ladder: A visual illusion toy with wooden blocks held together with ribbon, as it appears in "Before The Blood: Bryony Marseilles" or the Biblical Jacob's dream of a ladder leading to heaven. Henry uses this term to describe the majestic, primary staircase at Arcadia in "Before The Blood: Herny Matthews."

Jasmine: climbing shrubs or vines in the olive or lilac family with white or yellow star-shaped, sweet-smelling flowers. Appears in "Karla Joins In."

Java sparrows: One of the birds the American Acclimatization Society introduced to Central Park, New York in 1864. Mentioned in "Before The Blood: John Simons."

Javanese gamelan music: A traditional ensemble of the Javanese people, typically consisting of percussion instruments. Mentioned in "Before The Blood: Kellen Wechsler" and "Before The Blood: Bryony Simons."

Je t'aime de tout mon coeur, tout mon ame, tout mon etre: Translates to "I love you with all my heart, all my soul, all my strength." The inscription Lord Girard had carved into Louise Girard's headstone. Appears in "Before The Blood: Henry Matthews."

Jelly tart: An open pastry filled with jam or jelly. Appears in "Before The Blood: John Simons" and "Before The Blood: Henry Matthews" (as lemon tarts).

Jenson Reporter: The primary newspaper in Jenson, a fictional town in Northern Michigan. Mentioned in "Visage," "Staked!," "Before The Blood: Henry Matthews." "Before The Blood: Bryony Simons,"

Jeremiah 16:16: "Behold, I am going to send for many fishermen," declares the Lord, "and they will fish for them." One of the earliest Bible verses Bryony Marseilles heard her father read. Appears in "Before The Blood: Bryony Marseilles."

John Tenniel's Queen of Hearts: John Tenniel created the first and perhaps the most enduring illustrations for Lewis Carroll's books "Alice's Adventures in Wonderland" and "Through the Looking-Glass." Henry describes Mrs. Variola, a shopkeeper, neighbor, and caretaker of his family, as looking like Tenniel's rendition of the Queen of Hearts in "Before The Blood: Henry Matthews."

Joie de vivre: An exuberant joy in life. That was Lord Girard's estimation of Louise Girard when talking about her to Henry in "Before The Blood: Henry Matthews."

Jumbo: A real zoo elephant that P.T. Barnum purchased and then brought to the United States to exhibit in 1882. Mentioned at the Smythe's dinner party in "Before The Blood: Bryony Simons."

Kabanos: A real, long, thin, dry Eastern European sausage. Originated in Poland in the Middle Ages. Appears in "Call of the Siren."

Kachelofen: A real, German tiled stove that first originated five hundred years ago. Appears in "Before The Blood: Kellen Wechsler."

Kaleidoscope: A real, optical instrument with titled mirrors and color glass that create unlimited views of geographic shapes. Bryony owned one in "Before The Blood: Bryony Marseilles."

Karneval: The real "fifth season" in Germany, from November 11 through Ash Wednesday. Its main celebration, shortly before Lent, resembles Mardi Gras. Mentioned in "Before The Blood: Kellen Wechsler."

Katydid: More specifically, a real long-tailed meadow katydid, which are found in Northern Michigan. Katydids are related to grasshoppers and crickets. The long-tailed meadow katydid sings with ticks and then with whirring buzzes. Bryony hears them on Fisher Farm in "Before The Blood: Bryony Marseilles" and "Before The Blood: Bryony Simons."

Kenneth Electric: A fictional account belonging to 1940s Kellen, a senior partner in the fictional R.C. Walter advertising agency in "Before The Blood: Kellen Wechsler."

Kick the Can: A real, outdoor, vintage, strategy game of unknown origins related to "Capture The Flag." Appears in "Before The Blood: Henry Matthews."

King of the Hill: A real, outdoor, vintage, game of unknown origins, where one person dominates a small hill, and the other plays try to remove him. Appears in "Before The Blood: Henry Matthews."

Kippers: A herring that has been split open, gutted and cleaned, salted or picked, and then smoked. Brumfeldt complains his are cold when he and Henry stay at The Wisten in Jenson in "Before The Blood: Henry Matthews."

Körözött: A real Hungarian cheese spread. Appears in "Call of the Siren."

Kyrie eleison: A rea; Greek phrase for "Lord have mercy." A phrase Reverend Marseilles reproaches himself for using in "Before The Blood: Bryony Marseilles."

L. Prang and Company cards: Real greeting cards produced in the late nineteenth century by Louis Prang's company. Prang was a Polish American lithographer and printer and immigrant from Germany and was also known as the "Father of the American Christmas Card." Appears in "Before The Blood: John Simons."

Labskaus: A real type of German hash. Its simplest variation is salted meat, potatoes and onions. Mentioned in "Before The Blood: Kellen Wechsler."

Lacey Cosmetics: A fictional account belonging to 1940s Kellen, a senior partner in the fictional R.C. Walter advertising agency in "Before The Blood: Kellen Wechsler."

"Lady Adcock's Murder:" Short story by Henry Matthews that ran in serial form in the Evansville Courrier. Mentioned in "Before The Blood: Henry Matthews."

"La Belle Sauvage:" Also known as "The Indian Princess," a real play about Pocahontas by James Nelson Barker, first produced in 1808. Appears in "Before The Blood: Henry Matthews."

"La Petite Fadette:" A real 1849 novel about love and social class by French novelist George Sand. Mentioned in "Before The Blood: Bryony Marseilles."

La pompe: Real acoustic movements for playing gypsy jazz. Appear in "Before The Blood: Henry Matthews."

Little Bo Peep: The protagonist in a real children's nursery rhyme dating back to the early nineteenth century. Bryony refers to her countries self as Little Bo Peep in "Before The Blood: Bryony Simons."

Larry the Llama: A recurring character in the BryonySeries subseries The Adventures of Cornell Dyer. Appears (so far) in "Cornell Dyer and the Eerie Like" and "Cornell Dyer and the Flu."

Lavendar: A real flowering plant in the mint family with a light floral scene and light violet color. A sick Ruprech fell asleep near the lavender in "Before The Blood: Kellen Weschler" and Karla's spirit disguises itself with lavender in "Staked!"

Leberwurst: A real German liver sausage. Voll-Bauer's wife serves it to Kellen on a tray, along with a roasted egg, a soft round of Hohenheim, toast, and marmalade.

Lebkuchen: A real type of German gingerbread, sweetened with honey and with a consistency between a cake and a cookie. The fictional Burgomeister of Seulobitz, Germany, serves it at a party in "Before The Blood: Kellen Wechsler."

Lecher: Someone, usually a man, who consistently acts inappropriately in regard to sexual advances. A table of Jenson College students referred to some of their professors in that manner in "Before The Blood: Hery Matthews."

Leeks: A real vegetable resembling large scallions. In the same family as onions and garlic. John-Peter enjoys them in a one-dish meal in "Staked!" Bryony enjoys them in soup in "Before The Blood: Bryony Simons." Kellen compares them to stale blood in "Before The Blood: Kellen Wechsler."

Lemon tarts: See jelly tarts.

"Les Brigands:" A real French operetta that opened at the Avenue Theatre in London. England, on Sept. 6, 1889. Henry Matthews invited John Simons to attend with him in "Before The Blood: Kellen Wechsler" and in "Before The Blood: Henry Matthews." Also mentioned in "Before The Blood: Bryony Simons."

Les enfants: A real French phrase meaning "the children." Caroline Matthews uses it in "Before The Blood: Henry Matthews."

Lewis Carroll's mock turtle: A fictional turtle (purportedly the main ingredient in the Victorian mock turtle soup) that appears in Lewis Carroll's real 1865 book "Alice's Adventures in

Wonderland." Henry uses the analogy to call Kellen Wechsler a sham of a manager in "Before The Blood: Henry Matthews."

"Life on the Mississippi" by Mark Twain: One of the real books discussed at the Munsonville Society for the Humanities in "Before The Blood: Bryony Marseilles."

Lilith: A primordial she-demon with many folklore variations built around her. Henry mentally calls Millicent Gothart "Lilith" the first time he encounters her in "Before The Blood: Henry Matthews."

Little Jack Horner: A real eighteenth century English nursery rhyme that Boswell Pike Junior blurts out at his sister's birthday party in "Before The Blood: Bryony Marseilles."

London Guardian: Founded in 1821 and now known as simple The Guardian. Agnes reads aloud to Henry from this real publication in "Before The Blood: Herny Matthews."

"Long, Long Ago": A real song about nostalgia. Written by English composer Thomas Haynes Bayly in 1833. Owen Munson sings it in "Before The Blood: Bryony Marseilles." Mitch Cooper and Eugene Miller sang the song at Munson Day 1892 in "Before The Blood: Bryony Simons."

Longfellow: One of Savannha Holloway's thoroughbred horses. Appears in "Before The Blood: John Simons."

Longfellow's "Voices of the Night.": Book of poetry by Henry Wadsworth Longfellow. See also "Psalm of Life." Henry owned an old musty copy of the book in "Before The Blood: Henry Matthews."

Lord Byron's The Giaour: Henry recalls the verses about the vampire and mentally applies them to Edwina Smythe when he first meets her in "Before The Blood: Henry Matthews."

Lycanthropy: In folklore, the belief that a person can shapeshift into a werewolf. In psychiatry, the delusion that a person can shapeshift into a werewolf. Both themes are present in "Lycanthropic Summer."

Ma Cherie: French for "My dear." Lord Girard's term of endearment for his sister Louise Girard in "Before The Blood: Henry Matthews."

Mack: The name of the Collie at Fisher Farm in "Before The Blood: Bryony Simons."

Magic Chocolate Milk: A fictional type of chocolate milk that never spoils or requires refrigeration. Appears in "Cornell Dyer and the 'Mistical' Being."

Májkrém: A real Hungarian liver paste. Appears in "Call of the Siren."

Man in the Moon face: The face that people may see in the moon. Numerous stories in mythology to explain it. Teddy Bass is said to look like the Man in the Moon in "Before The Blood: Bryony Marseilles," "Before The Blood: Bryony Simons," and "Call of the Siren."

Map Magnifer 589T: A type of gadget supernatural super sleuth Cornell Dyer uses in "Cornell Dyer and the Calcium-Deficient Bones."

Marcel iron: More specifically, a Marcel curling iron. A real set of tongs that are heated to curl the hair. Invented by French hairdresser named Marcel Grateau in 1872. Henry's cousin Giselle used a Marcel iron in "Before The Blood: Henry Matthews."

Marennes-Oléron oysters: Oysters bred in the real Marennes-Oléron Bay in Southwest France. A project of Henry's in "Before The Blood: Henry Matthews."

Marigolds: The name means "Mary's gold." A plant in the daisy family with bright yellow or orange buds. Mentioned briefly in "Karla Joins In."

Marjoram: An herb in the mint family with a taste similar to oregano or thyme. Appears briefly in "Karla Joins In."

Marmalade: A real type of jam using citrus fruit. Dick Dougherty, mayor of the fictional Evansville, wants Henry to publish his wife's pear marmalade (most likely a pear-orange marmalade) in the town's newspaper, The Courrier in "Before The Blood: Henry Matthews." Bryony enjoys treacle scones with marmalade with John in "Before The Blood: Bryony Simons."

Mary, Mary, Quite Contrary: A nursery rhyme. which Kellen Wechsler parodies and spontaneously recites to Bryony in "Before The Blood: Bryony Simons."

Matthew 18: 1 to 3: At the same time came the disciples unto Jesus, saying, "Who is the greatest in the kingdom of heaven?" And Jesus called a little child unto him, and set him in the midst of them, and said, "Verily I say unto you, Except ye be converted, and become as little children, ye shall not enter into the kingdom of heaven. Whosoever therefore shall humble himself as this little child, the same is greatest in the kingdom of heaven." Referenced in "Before The Blood: Bryony Marseilles."

Matthew 26:49: And forthwith he came to Jesus, and said, "Hail, master," and kissed him. One of the verses that comes to mind when Reverend Galien Marseilles muses on Boswell Pike's betrayal of Owen Munson in "Before The Blood: Bryony Marseilles."

Mazurka: A real lively dance from Poland. Victoria Rush teaches the dance to Henry at a party in "Before The Blood: Henry Matthews."

McGuffey Eclectic Primer: A real, illustrated textbook for beginning readers by William Holmes McGuffey. Used widely in the United States from the mid-nineteenth century to the early twentieth century. Regained popularity among home-schooling families. Used in Munsonville School in "Call of the Siren."

McGuffey's First Eclectic Reader: A real illustrated textbook for young readers by William Holmes McGuffey. Used widely in the United States from the mid-nineteenth century to the early twentieth century. Regained popularity among home-schooling families. Used in Munsonville School in "Call of the Siren" and on Fisher Farm in "Before The Blood: Bryony Marseilles."

McGuffey's Eclectic Spelling Book: Areal, illustrated textbook with all the spelling rules and children and adults will need by William Holmes McGuffey. Used widely in the United States from the mid-nineteenth century to the early twentieth century. Regained popularity among home-schooling families. Used in "Before The Blood: Bryony Marseilles" during the Thanksgiving potluck adult spelling bee.

Measles: Also known as rubeola. A real, highly contagious, respiratory virus with flu-like symptoms and rash. It causes blindness in Iris Pike in "Before The Blood: Bryony Marseilles" and Bryony mistakenly thinks she has measles (when she really has something far worse) in "Before The Blood: Bryony Simons."

Meowing nuns: Mass hysteria that supposedly gripped the nuns in a fifteenth century French convent and referenced in "Before The Blood: Henry Matthews."

Melina: The name of Henry's well-behaved horse, breed unknown, in "Before The Blood: Henry Matthews."

Mephistopheles: The comparison of Boswell Pike's facial features to Eugène Delacroix' real lithograph of the Mephistopheles, a demon featured in German folklore, most notably the "Faust" series. Analogy appears in "Before The Blood: Bryony Marseilles" and "Before The Blood: Henry Matthews."

Merck's Medical Manual: A real copy sits on the nightstand of Henry's cousin Adelaide Markham in "Before The Blood: Henry Matthews." How it got there is a mystery since the manual wasn't published until 1899 and is still in print as of 2023.

Merryboy: The "scraggly fur wad" belonging to Oscar Briggs, the rail master in the fictional town of Evansville, Michigan, in "Before The Blood: Henry Matthews."

Merv: Another mutt belonging to Oscar Briggs, the rail master in the fictional town of Evansville, Michigan, in "Before The Blood: Henry Matthews."

Michaelmas: A real Christian feast day honoring the Archangel Michael. Western Christians celebrate it on September 29. Easter

Christians celebrate it on November 8. Kellen attends a huge Western celebrate on the estate of the Squire of Levonshire in "Before The Blood: Kellen Wechsler."

Michelangelo's David: The real Renaissance artist created this marble statue of David from the Bible between 1501 to 1504. The statute is standing and nude. Kellen compare s the naked Seymour Cassidy to this statue in "Before The Blood" Kellen Wechsler."

Midas touch: Carlton Mandeville said the railroad mogul Warren Holloway had the "Midas touch" because of his successes. The phrase is named after the real Greek myth of King Midas, who turned everything he touched into gold. Phrase appears in "Before The Blood: Henry Matthews."

Mignardises: A real bite-sized dessert, served at the end of a meal. Henry includes these in the lunch he brought to his brother-in-law William Markham at his workplace in "Before The Blood: Henry Matthews."

Mille-feuille: A real French dessert dating back to at least the eighteenth century. Traditionally comprised of three layers of ultra-light puff pastry with two alternating layers of pastry cream. The top layer might be dusted with cocoa or chocolate, iced, or topped with whipped cream. Was the favorite dessert of Seymour Cassidy. Lord Girard serves it at Arcadia in honor of Henry's fourteenth birthday in "Before The Blood: Henry Matthews."

Milliner: A person who makes and sells hats typically for women. Mentioned in "Before The Blood: Kellen Wechsler" and "Before The Blood: Henry Matthews."

Middle Ages: A real period of time in European history from the last fifth century to the late fifteenth century. According to Brumfeldt in "Before The Blood: Henry Matthews," "The Girard family practically ruled France in the Middle Ages."

Mist: A very thin fog. Appears in a macabre way in "Bryony," "Visage," "Before The Blood: Bryony Simons," "The Phoenix," "Call of the Siren," and House on Top of the Hill."

Mitchell's map book: A real atlas in the nineteenth century. Appears in "Call of the Siren."

Mittens: The name of one of Julie Drake's cats in "Julie and the Too-Hard Homework," and possibly "Brainy Ann,"

Mode 9: Fictional economy car. Appears in "Lycanthropic Summer."

"Modern botany, or, A popular introduction to the natural system of plants: According to the classification of De Candolle," by Mrs. Jane Loudon: A real book published in 1842 that Bryony said in "Before The Blood: Bryony Simons" that she read as a child.

Mon Dieu: French for "My God." Used by Lord Girard in "Before The Blood: Henry Matthews."

Monkshood: See wolfsbane.

Monocle: A single corrective lens for just one eye, costly to produce because of the need for custom-fitting. Brumfeldt wears one in "Bryony," "Before The Blood: Henry Matthews," and "The Phoenix."

Monster Support Group: A support group for ex-monsters that Kellen started and oversees at Happy Hunting Grounds. Appears in "Staked!" Mentioned in "Karla Joins In."

Montgomery Ward catalogue: Montgomery Ward was a nineteenth U.S. merchant who pioneered mail-ordering in 1872. The brand later also became a department store chain until 2001. Montgomery Ward Inc. relaunched in 2004 under a new owner and is now a U.S. online-only retailer. In "Before The Blood: Bryony Marseilles," Adele Marseilles ordered a number of items for the parsonage from a Montgomery Ward catalogue obtained from Drake's General Store. Those items actually appeared in a Montgomery Ward catalogue for the time.

Monty Rogers Dance Band: Fictional band that appears in name only in a short story in "Lycanthropic Summer."

Moonstone: Also known as hecatolite. A real stone in the feldspar group with a blue to white sheen reminiscent of moonlight. Appears in "Lycanthropic Summer."

Moorish castle: Name of a medieval fortress in Gibraltar. The design element was incorporated into part of Kingsley's, a fictional restaurant in Chicago in "Before The Blood: Henry Matthews" inspired by a real restaurant called Kinsley's, which was open from 1884 to 1905.

Morality in the Modern World: The name of a fictional class Reverand Galien Marseilles once taught when Algernon Demars was his student. Mentioned in "Before The Blood: John Simons."

Morgans: One of the earliest developed horse breeds really developed in the United States, known for being compact and refined. Wyndham Franklin raised morgans on his farm in "Before The Blood: John Simons."

Morning Glory: A species of flowering plant with tendrils and heart-shaped leaves, whose flowers fully open in the morning. Flower colors include magenta, pink, purple-blue, and white. Appears in "Karla Joins In."

Morphine: A real narcotic derived from opium. Used in "The Phoenix" and "Call of the Siren."

Morse code: A real method of dots and dashes used in telecommunication. Named for Samuel Morse, who developed it in the mid-nineteenth century. Henry learns it at Arcadia in "Before The Blood: Henry Matthews."

Motorized olausopeller: A pretend gadget to add speed to a board. Supernatural super sleuth Cornell Dyer uses one in "Cornell Dyer and the Eerie Lake."

Mouillette: Fingers of toasted, buttered bread for dipping into soft-boiled eggs. Appears on the breakfast table at Arcadia in "Before The Blood: Henry Matthews."

Mountain ash: See "rowan."

Mr. Sneed: Marionette belonging to Cuddy Lane, performer at Hewes Music Hall in Lower Manhattan, New York. Appears in "Before The Blood: Kellen Wechsler."

Mudroom: An entranceway and possible storage area at the back of the house, to prevent mud from being tracked into the house. Appears in "Before The Blood: Bryony Marseilles" and "Katie and the Big Fear."

Muffy: One of Julie Drake's two cats in "Julie and the Too-Hard Homework" and possibly "Brainy Ann."

Mugwort: A real, invasive flowering plant in the daisy family. Appears in "Karla Joins In."

Mumps: A realm respiratory virus that may cause fever and inflammation in the salivary glands, testicles, ovaries, and breasts. Appears or mentioned in "Before The Blood: John Simons" and "Before The Blood: Bryony Simons."

Münchner Weißwurst: Real, short grey sausage made from minced veal and pork back bacon and flavored with cardamom, ginger, lemon, mace. onions, and parsley. Kellen attempts to sway Seymour Cassidy by the mention of this sausage in "Before The Blood: Kellen Wechsler."

Munson Day: A day to honor Munsonville's founder Owen Munson. Celebrated for several years on June 28, the holiday fell into disuse long before the twentieth century. Appears in "Before The Blood: Bryony Simons."

Munsonville Society for the Humanities: A group of men who gathered in Munsonville's parsonage to drink, smoke, and talk. The group was led by the Reverend Galien Marseilles. Appears in "Bryony," "Staked!," "Before The Blood: Bryony Marseilles," "Before The Blood: Henry Matthews," and "Before The Blood: Bryony Simons."

Mustangs: Real feral horses of the Western United States. Owen Munson and Clyde Fisher bring batches of the horses to Fisher Farm, gentle them, and then sell them in "Before The Blood: Bryony Marseilles." Mentioned in "Before The Blood: Bryony Simons."

Mutton: Real meat of a mature sheep, approximately two to three years old. Served in "Before The Blood: John Simons," "Before The Blood: Kellen Wechsler," "Before The Blood: Henry Matthews," Before The Blood: Bryony Simons," and "The Phoenix."

Mutton chops: Meat cut from a sheep's rib. See "mutton" above. Also, sideburns that grow into the area of a man's cheek, to resemble a mutton meat chop. Dr. Edwin Gothart has mutton chops in "Before The Blood: Kellen Wechsler," "Before The Blood: Henry Matthews," Before The Blood: Bryony Simons," and "The Phoenix."

"My Bonnie lies over the ocean:" Real, traditional Scottish folk song with roots in the mid-eighteenth century. Owen Munson sings it in "Before The Blood: Bryony Marseilles."

Nachtzehrer: A type of German vampire that typically consumes its own family members first. Term used for Kellen in "Before The Blood: Kellen Wechsler."

Napoleon III love seat: A love seat is a small sofa for two people. Napoleon III (Second Empire) furniture is the period between 1848 to 1880. This real furniture was lavishly upholstered with expensive damask, satin, velvet, or other fabric, with the possible addition of fringes, motifs, and/or tassels. Tassels. The actual woods was ornately carved with paw feet. Henry takes a nap in one of these love seats in Algernon Demars' office in "Before The Blood: Henry Matthews."

Napoleonic Wars: A real series of wars between France and other European powers between 1799 to 1815. Mentioned in "Before The Blood: Kellen Wechsler."

New England vampire panics: The real supernatural attribution of tuberculosis outbreaks in the New England states between 1793 and 1892. Mentioned in "Before The Blood: Bryony Marseilles" and "The Phoenix."

New Haven blue spruce: A real conifer tree with blue-green needles that is native to the Rocky Mountains area. At some point the tree was introduced to New England. Whether that was before or after the time of "Before The Blood: John Simons" (where the trees are mentioned as being cultivate in New Haven, Connecticut) is unknown to the author. So for the sake of literacy license, we will assume that is true in the BryonySeries world,.

New Woman: Real nineteenth century term for women who challenged the societal norms in terms of education, employment, image, equality of the sexes, image, lifestyle, and sexuality. Mentioned by the Munsonville Society for the Humanities attendees in "Before The Blood: Bryony Simons." Henry sarcastically gives that assessment to his niece Giselle in "Before The Blood: Henry Matthews." Clarissa Betts in "Before The Blood: Bryony Simons" was also considered one, due to her reading choices, artificially curled hair, and use of cosmetics.

New York Philharmonic Orchestra: Real orchestra, founded in 1842. Housed in Steinway Hall from 1866 to 1867. Mentioned in "Before The Blood: John Simons."

Newsboys strike in New York: A real, youth-led strike in 1899 that halted circulation of two prominent newspapers for several days and inspired the 1992 musical "Newsies." Henry Matthews said he covered that story for the fictional New York Gazette in "Call of the Siren."

Newfoundland: A real, large, affectionate, gentle working dog developed on Newfoundland island. A stray develops a fleeting attachment to Melissa in "Bryony."

Niagara Falls: A series of three waterfalls in the Canada and New York areas. Bryony uses the term as a euphemism when she sees a horse urinate in the road for the first time in "Before The Blood: Bryony Simons."

Nickel brass: Clyde Fisher packs his brew in barrels with nickel-plated brass metals in "Before The Blood: Bryony Simons" due to its rest-resistant properties.

"No, No Nanette:" A real. popular, farcical musical comedy from the 1920s about three couples sharing a cottage together in Atlantic City with themes of love, money, and blackmail. The 1940s Kellen attends this musical in "Before The Blood: Kellen Wechsler."

Nocturnal Lore: The Collected Tales of Henry Matthews: A fictional book of short horror stories. Appears in "Bryony."

Nom de plume: Literal French translation: pen name. A brief conversation about Lord Girard's assumed name occurs in "Before The Blood: Henry Matthews."

North Lyons High School: The fictional high school Caryn Rochelle attended in "Lycanthropic Summer" after she was kicked out of boarding school."

Norway Pine: A red pine tree, native to Connecticut. Christmas tree in Spencer Inn. Mentioned in "Before the Blood: John Simons."

"Now as Jesus was walking by the Sea of Galilee, He saw two brothers, Simon who was called Peter, and Andrew his brother,

casting a net into the sea; for they were fishermen. And He said to them, 'Follow Me, and I will make you fishers of men.'" Matthew 4:18-22: One of the earliest Bible verses Bryony Marseilles heard her father read. Appears in "Before The Blood: Bryony Marseilles."

October 29, 1926: Opening day of Sue's Diner and birthday of Sue Barnes. Appears in "Call of the Siren."

"Of all the creatures living in the water of the seas and the streams, you may eat any that have fins and scales." Leviticus 11:10: One of the earliest Bible verses Bryony Marseilles heard her father read. Appears in "Before The Blood: Bryony Marseilles."

Old Drew: The name of Orville Parks' old draft horse. Appears in "Before The Blood: Bryony Marseilles."

Old Puss: The name of Bertha Parks' old tabby. Appears in "Before The Blood: Bryony Marseilles."

Old Vieux Cognac: "Vieux" is French for "old." However, when Kellen swipes a bottle of Old Vieux Cognac in "Before The Blood: Kellen Wechsler," the term applies to a fictional brand.

Omelette au Rhum: A real, two-egg omelet topped with caramelized sugar and flambeed rum. John and Bryony eat this as part of their breakfast on the train to Detroit, Michigan in "Before The Blood: Bryony Simons."

"One concert on Saturday night, sells pianos on Monday morning:" A real quote attributed to William Steinway, owner of the piano manufacturing company Steinway & Sons and the reason why concerts in Steinway Hall were so valuable. Appears in "Before The Blood: John Simons." Della Rutherford also alludes to this quote to her husband Herbert Rutherford, owner of a fictional piano manufacturing company in "Before The Blood: Bryony Simons."

One Hundred and One Sandwich Variations Sandwich Café: Sandwich shop in "Cornell Dyer and the Old Folks Home."

One-Eye Blue: Clyde Fisher's Australian shepherd. Appears in "Before The Blood: Bryony Marseilles." Mentioned in "Before The Blood: Bryony Simons."

"One Thousand and One Nights:" A real collection of Middle Eastern folktales as fictionally told by the wife of a king who habitually executes his wives. So to delay her own execution, she tells him part of a story each night. The following night, she finishes the story and starts another partial story. Mentioned in "Before The Blood: Henry Matthews."

"One Touch of Venus:" A real 1948 romantic musical comedy about a man who falls in love with a mannequin in shop window, which comes to life after he kisses it. Mentioned in "Before The Blood: Kellen Wechsler."

Opéra Comique: A real French opera with arias and spoken dialogue. John and Kellen saw a performance at the Exposition Universelle of 1889 in "Before The Blood: Kellen Wechsler." Also mentioned in "Before The Blood: Bryony Simons."

Opium: A real narcotic derived from the juice of the opium poppy. Dana Hewes ran an opium den as a side business in "Before The Blood: John Simons" as Henry discovered in "Before The Blood: Henry Matthews." Also in "Before the Blood: Henry Matthews," the doctor in Leland Hills treats Henry's severe asthma attacks with opium to relax his airways.

Orange blossoms: A real, fragrant flower of the orange tree and considered by some to be an aphrodisiac. Mentioned as a possible wedding flower in "Before The Blood: Henry Matthews."

Orange crushie deluxe: A favorite drink of supernatural super sleuth Cornell Dyer in "Cornell Dyer and the Old Folks Home."

Organdy: A real, fine cotton fabric for girls' and women's dresses. Rose Fisher and Lilac Fisher wore organdy dresses to Iris Pike's birthday party in "Before The Blood: Bryony Marseilles."

Oriental rugs: Real, hand-knotted rugs with intricate designs made in oriental countries with high quality materials. Appears in the dining rooms at Simons Mansion in "Bryony," "Before The Blood: Bryony Simons" and "The Phoenix," as well as in the Jenson College library in "Visage."

Ossau-Iraty: A real type of French cheese made from sheep's milk. Henry enjoys it at Arcadia in "Before The Blood: Henry Matthews."

Ottoman-Hungarian wars: A real series of battles between the Ottoman Empire and medieval Hungary, which particularly fascinated Dr. Edwin Gothart in "Call of the Siren."

Palinka: A real Carpathian fruit spirit. Dr. Edwin Gothart serves it at Millicent Gothart's engagement party in "Before The Blood: Bryony Simons" and Bryony decides it resembles urine.

Pandora's box: A box owned by Pandora, the first woman I Greek mythology. She was forbidden to open it. But when she did, all the troubles of the world flew out. Caryn Rochelle's father in "Lycanthropic Summer" compares her muse to "Pandora's Box. Bryony compares the evil let loose in "Before The Blood: Bryony Simons" to Pandora's box.

Paper mache: A real composite material of paper pulp and glue, which were used to make dolls in "Before The Blood: Bryony Marseilles" and "Before The Blood: Bryony Simons."

Parable of the Sower: A real parable Jesus told in the Bible to explain how different people received his teachings. In "Before The Blood: Bryony Simons," Bryony mentally misinterprets this parable to illustrate how unbridled curiosity can lead to a negative outcome.

Pea coat: A real double-breasted wool coat. Henry tries pea coats on at Jenson's haberdashery in "Before The Blood: Henry Matthews."

Peach dahlia: Real, bushy tuberous plants native to Central America and Mexico. A relative to the daisy, chrysanthemum, sunflower, and zinnia. Henry seduced Agnes King in her father's greenhouse when she reached for a peach dahlia in "Before The Blood: Henry Matthews."

"Penny Whistles:" The original name of the real poetry book for children in "A Child's Garden of Verses" by Robert Lewis Stevenson in 1885, which would have made it a brand new book for Bryony Marseilles when it appears in "Before The Blood: Bryony Marseilles."

Perambulators: Archaic term for baby buggy or baby stroller. Used in "Before The Blood: Bryony Simons."

Peters Soap Powder: A fictional product for which 1940s Kellen writes an advertising campaign in "Before The Blood: Kellen Wechsler."

Pewter: A real, malleable metal alloy made of antimony (formerly lead), bismuth, copper, silver (sometimes) and tin. The metal used in flatware in "Before The Blood: Bryony Simons."

Phaistos disc: A real disc of fired clay with symbols on both sides from the island of Crete. Made 2000 to 1000 BC. Disco. Italian archaeologist Luigi Pernier discovered it in 1908 during the excavation of the Minoan palace of Phaistos. Ironically, both the fictional couple Warren and Savannah Holloway – and then the also fictional Bartholomew and Edwina Smyth – and this disc in their possessions in the nineteenth century in "Before The Blood: John Simons" and "Call of the Siren."

Pfennig: A real German penny, in use from the ninth century until the euro was introduced in 2002. Mentioned in terms of soul-selling in "Before The Blood: Kellen Wechsler."

Phenacetin: A real drug to reduce fever and pain. Introduced in 1887 and widely used for many decades. Canada withdrew it in 1973 and the U.S. Food and Drug Administration withdrew it in 1983. The drug may be carcinogenic and injurious to kidneys. Lord Girard stirred the powdered version into beverages in "Before The Blood: Henry Matthews," as a tonic, he said.

"Pictorial History of the World" by John Frost: A real book that Andrew Helsby longed to own in "Before The Blood: John Simons." As of 2023, a number of the 1850 editions are circulating online. The University of Wisconsin-Eau Claire has a copy of the 1848 edition in its special collections. Some editions had more than five hundred engraved plates and cuts. Considering what Helsby did for John, we hope John gifted Helsby with a copy of this book.

Pilgrim's Progress: A real Christian allegory and theological work of fiction written in 1678 by John Bunyan. Mentioned in "Before The Blood: Bryony Marseilles." Further allegorized in "The Phoenix."

Pillbox: A real, small straight brimless hat with a flat crown, popular hat with women in the 1930s to the 1960s. Margaret wore a pillbox in "Before The Blood: Kellen Wechsler."

Pinafore: A real, sleeveless, apron-like garment that girls wore over their dresses. Susan Betts wore a clean one over her old dress to Iris Pike's in "Before The Blood: Bryony Marseilles."

Pinard horn: A real, hollow plastic, metal, or wooden horn-shaped stethoscope, similar to an ear trumpet, for listening to the fetal heart rate through the woman's abdomen during pregnancy. French obstetrician Dr. Adolphe Pinard, a French obstetrician invented it during the nineteenth century. It is still used in some parts of the world as of 2-23/ Briana Miller uses one during Sue Barnes' pregnancy in "Call of the Siren."

Pink oilcloth with geometric designs for the kitchen floor: Canvas covered in oil paint and used an inexpensive covering for floors, tables, shelves, and work spaces. Adele Marseilles orders some for the parsonage kitchen floor from the Montgomery Ward catalogue at Drake's General Store in "Before The Blood: Bryony Marseilles."

Pinner Qing Dynasty vase: A real, old sixteen-inch porcelain vase from China's Quing Dynasty (1644 to 1911) that a family found in 2010 in the Pinner, a suburb of the London Borough of Harrow, while cleaning out a deceased relative's home. The vase sold for $85.9 million, reports said. Ironically, both the fictional couple

Warren and Savannah Holloway – and then the also fictional Bartholomew and Edwina Smyth – and this disc in their possessions in the nineteenth century in "Before The Blood: John Simons" and "Call of the Siren."

Pinocchio: The protagonist in the real 1883 children's novel "The Adventures of Pinocchio," about a wooden puppet who wants to be a real boy. Dr. Sidney Stone uses the story as sarcasm when referring to Munsonville at a meeting of the Munsonville Society for the Humanities "Before The Blood: Bryony Marseilles."

Pistachio cream: A sweet cream. In the version often made in the eighteenth and nineteenth centuries, half is made with pulverized pistachio paste and the other half is cream, sugar, egg yolks, and a bit of brandy for flavoring. Pistachio cream is used as a topping for chocolate cake at a dinner party at Simons Mansion in "Before The Blood: Bryony Simons."

Pistou: A cold sauce from France made with basil, garlic cloves, and olive oil. Bryony eats potato topped with pistou at dinner with Henry orders up at Simons Mansion in "Before The Blood: Bryony Simons."

"Poems Of Passion" by Ella Wheeler Wilcox: A real book of poetry published in 1896. and now in the public domain, that Sue Bass finds while attending Munsonville School. She keeps the book and uses the select poems to give voice to certain emotions in "Call of the Siren."

Polychromatic Soup.: A versatile, fictional potion that doubles as lunch. Can prepare with any combination of magical herbs as long as garlic is added, too.

Pombec: Fictional currency created by Ed Calkins, Steward of Tara. Stands for "Proposal Of Marriage By Ed Calkins." Appears in "Ruthless" and "Cornell Dyer and the Howls of Basketville."

Pomegranate and Angostura bitters: A real, concentrated herbal alcoholic preparation. Henry was served a version with pomegranate at a party at Jacob King's Fifth Avenue Mansion in "Before The Blood: Henry Matthews."

Pompadour: A real hairstyle that originated in 1680 in France's royal court, with many variations. The basic idea is that hair is combed up and back over the head to add vertical volume. Savannah Holloway wore a "regal" version in "Before The Blood: John Simons." Janet Pike wore a "splendid" one in "Before The Blood: Bryony Marseilles." Mrs. Cady wore a gray one in "Before The Blood: Henry Matthews." Many of Munsonville's women wore the hairstyle in "Before The Blood: Bryony Simons." Lillian Hasset Pike wore a "soft brown" version in "The Phoenix."

Pork ragout: A real French stew made by simmering pork with spices, especially with scallions and cloves, the way Henry preferred eating it at Arcadia in "Before The Blood: Henry Mathews."

"Portrait of a Lady" by Henry James: A real story of love and betrayal, serialized in The Atlantic in 1880 and 1881 and published as a novel in 1881. Discussed by the Munsonville Society for the Humanities in "Bryony" and "Before The Blood: Bryony Marseilles."

Pounce: A real, fine white powder made from cuttlefish bones or resin from the sandarac tree (a cypress-like tree), used to prepare paper for ink or to dry ink after writing. Henry compares the color of Dr. Rush's white toes to pounce in "Before The Blood Heny Matthews."

Pounded cheese: Cheese whipped or "pounded" into a smooth, velvety texture that spreads as easily as butter. Pounded cheese was served at Christmas Eve at Spender Inn in "Before The Blood: John Simons." Mayor Dick Dougherty wants Henry to run his wife Meg's pounded cheese recipe in The Courrier in "Before The Blood: Henry Matthews."

Prairie style architecture: Architecture with a focus on horizontal buildings and not vertical buildings that Henry notices emerging in Chicago in "Before The Blood: Henry Matthews."

Prince of Darkness: Another name for Satan or the Christian devil. John-Peter's nickname for Kellen. Used in "Staked!" and "Karla Joins In."

Princess' pea: "The Princess and the Pea" is a real literary fairy tale by Hans Christian Andersen. A queen decides to test a woman's claim to being a princess by secretly placing a hard pea beneath twenty mattresses, which she covered with twenty eider-down beds. Henry compares the height and lavishness of the bed on which he sleeps at Arcadia in "Before The Blood: Henry Matthews" with this bed,

Privy: A real toilet in a small shed apart from a house. Appears in "Before The Blood: Henry Matthews."

Proclamation 261—Thanksgiving Day, 1884: This real proclamation by Chester A. Arthur, twenty-first president of the United States (1881 to 1885) appears in The Munsonville Times in "Before The Blood: Bryony Marseilles."

Protestant theology: The main beliefs of the Christian denomination of Protestantism and the favorite interest of Algernon Demars in "Before The Blood: Henry Matthews."

Proverbs 2:18–19: "Her course leads to the shades. All who go to her cannot return And find again the paths of life." Henry's estimation of Millicent Gothart the first time he encounters her in "Before The Blood: Henry Matthews."

Proverbs 10:19: "In the multitude of words there wanteth not sin." A Bible verse stitched on a sampler in Reverand Galien Marseilles' parsonage office in "Before The Blood: Bryony Marseilles" and "Before The Blood: Bryony Simons." It's also the only picture that hands in his office.

Proverbs 31: The final chapter of the Book of Proverbs in the Hebrew Bible or the Old Testament of the Christian Bible. Its final verses give the characteristics the ideal woman should possess. Mentioned in "Call of the Siren."

Psalm 37:2: Everett Spencer quotes this verse – "For they shall soon be cut down like the grass, and wither as the green herb." – while wandering the grounds of Spencer Inn with John and discussing sordid family history in "Before The Blood: John Simons."

Pumpkin chips: A sweet way to serve pumpkin. Sliced ripe pumpkin is covered with lemon juice and sugar and then boiled until translucent. The pumpkin is served in glasses topped with the strained syrup. Spencer Inn serves these chips on Christmas Eve in "Before The Blood: John Simons."

Punch: A real, weekly humorous and satirical British magazine, established in 1841 by Henry Mayhew and wood-engraver Ebenezer

Landells. Historically, it was most influential in the 1840s and 1850s, when it helped to coin the term "cartoon" in its modern sense as a humorous illustration. Sir John Tenniel was Punch's chief cartoon artist from 1850 to 1901. The magazine's popularity peaked and declined and had a few revivals before it stopped publishing for good in 2002. Brumfeldt refers to it in "Before The Blood: Henry Matthews."

Purgatory: A real Roman Catholic doctrine that imperfect souls destined for heaven first go to place of temporary suffering after death. Henry compares listening to his cousin Emma confess to her parents to purgatory in "Before The Blood: Henry Matthews."

Quadrille: A real type of dance for four couples that was popular int eh eighteenth and nineteenth centuries. Henry watched the guests at Hiram and Amelia Rush's party dance, which included this dance in "Before The Blood: Henry Matthews."

Queen Anne: Real, medieval-looking architecture that emerged in the United States from 1880 to 1910 and was prominent in the fictional town of Jenson, Michigan. Characteristics included an intersecting gable roof, dormers or turrets, and multi-paned windows. Appears in "Before The Blood: Henry" and "Visage." In "Visage," an old Queen Anne serves as Jenson College's library. Also in "Visage," Jenson College music professor John Simotes lives in an upstairs apartment in a converted Queen Anne.

Queen Anne's Lace: A real invasive species consisting of tiny white flowers in flat-topped lacy patterns. Appears in "Lycanthropic Summer" and "Before The Blood: Bryony Marseilles."

Quadrivium: The real study of the mathematical arts: arithmetic, astronomy, geometry, and music. Part of Henry's coursework in "Before The Blood: Henry Matthews."

QWERTY Keyboard: A real keyboard design for typing in English. Christopher Sholes designed and patented his QWERTY Keyboard in 1874 and then sold it to E. Remington and Sons that same year. Henry learns to use this keyboard on a new Remington typewriter in "Before The Blood: Henry Matthews."

Ralph Waldo Emerson, Philosopher and Seer: An Estimate of His Character and Genius in Prose and Verse: Commentary by Amos Bronson Alcott. This book was discussed at the Munsonville Society for the Humanities in "Before The Blood: Bryony Marseilles."

Ray's Primary Arithmetic: Covers counting, addition, subtraction, multiplication and division with word problems. First published in 1857 by Joseph Ray. A real textbook Sue Bass uses during her first year at Munsonville School in "Call of the Siren."

R.C. Walter's Company: A fictional advertising company somewhere in the United States during the 1940s. Kellen works there as a senior partner in "Before The Blood: Kellen Wechsler."

"Red River Valley:" A real folk song and cowboy song with unknown origins. Boswell Pike and Clyde Fisher laud Owen Munson in song with this piece in "Before The Blood: Bryony Marseilles."

Red Rover: A real outdoor children's game where one child tried to break through the clasped hands of children in the opposite team. Mentioned in "Before The Blood: Bryony Simons."

Remington typewriter: A real typewriter from the company E. Remington and Sons (1816–1896), which manufactured the for first commercial typewriter in 1873. Henry had two new ones at Arcadia in "Before The Blood: Henry Matthews."

Renaissance oils: Real oil paintings from the fifteenth and sixteenth centuries. The fictional couple Warren and Savannah Holloway – and then the also fictional Bartholomew and Edwina Smyth – own oil paintings from this era in "Before The Blood: John Simons" and "Call of the Siren."

Red-Breasted Robin: A friendly talking bird with an English accent that supernatural super sleuth Cornell Dyer encounters in the Land Not Quite Beyond the Wardrobe in "Cornell Dyer and the Whispering Wardrobe."

"Recipes for the Novice Potioner." Published by the League of Pookas: Fictional potion book in "Karla Joins In."

Réveillon: A French tradition of a long celebratory dinner of traditional foods late on Christmas Eve. Henry celebrates it with Lord Girard and Brumfeldt at their homes in Arcadia, and Chicago, Illinois, and with Jacob King and his family in New York City, New York, in "Before The Blood: Henry Matthews."

Rice jelly: A real nineteenth century recipe for people who are sick, made with a little rice boiled in a lot of water until it jells. Sally Bass cooks rice jelly and feeds it to Pearl Griffith in "Before The Blood: Bryony Marseilles."

Ringelringelreihen: German for "Ring Around the Rosie," a real nursery song. Kellen watches Catarin and the other children play in "Before The Blood: Kellen Wechsler."

Ring Around the Rosie: A real game where children join hands and walk in a circle singing the verses to the nursery thyme. They sit at the last line. The last to sit stands in the middle of the ring for the next round. Mentioned in "Before The Blood: Bryony Simons."

Riots at Astor Place Opera House: A real riot that broke out at the former opera house in New York City, New York, over the correct interpretation of Macbeth. More than twenty people were killed and more than 100 were injured. Mentioned in "Before The Blood: Henry Matthews."

Robber Baron: A real derogatory term for wealthy nineteenth century businessmen who presumably gained their wealth through unscrupulous practices. Used in "Before The Blood: Henry Matthews."

Robert Emmet: A real Irish rebel leader who died in 1801 at the age of 25. The Irish playwright Dion Boucicault wrote a four-act drama about his life, also titled "Robert Emmet," which appears in "Bryony" and "Before The Blood: Henry Matthews" during its opening night on November 5, 1884, at the former McVicker's Theatre in Chicago.

Robert's Rules: Robert's Rules of Order is a real manual of parliamentary procedure by United States Army officer Henry Martyn Robert first published in 1876. It was referred to loosely before a debate between two Jenson College professors for entertainment purposes commenced in "Before The Blood: Henry Matthews."

Rogers & Brothers silver-plated utensils: Adele Marseilles orders some of these real nineteenth century utensils for the parsonage from the Montgomery Ward catalogue in "Before The Blood: Bryony Marseilles."

Roman candles: The real name of certain fireworks featured on the late nineteenth century Fourth of July in the fictional fishing village of Munsonville, Michigan, in "Before The Blood: Bryony Simons."

Romanian manele: Real pop folk music from Romania. Harold Matthews briefly dances as if hearing this music in "Before The Blood: Henry Matthews."

Room 303 at The Wisten: The room with one double bed and a private bath that Henry shares with Brumfeldt during their fortnight n Jenson in "Before The Blood: Henry Matthews."

Room 306 at The Wisten: The larger, upgraded room Henry has for himself during his weekend in Jenson when Lord Girard and Brumfeldt are in New York in "Before The Blood: Henry Matthews."

Rose hips: The round part of the rose flower that contains the rose plant seeds. It's located below the rose petals and used in herbal teas, such as the ones John made for Bryony in "Before The Blood: Bryony Simons."

Rosemary: A shrub in the mint family. Its fragrant, needle-like leaves are used for seasoning food. Appears in "Karla Joins In."

Roux: Fat and flour mixed together to thicken gravies, soups, and sauces. Mrs. Parks sometimes let young Bryony whisk the roux in "Before The Blood: Bryony Marseilles."

Row, Row, Row Your Boat: A real nursery song that comes to Bryony's mind when thinking about John's critics in "Before The Blood: Bryony Simons."

Rowan: A real tree or shrub in the rose family with bitter, bright orange red to brilliant red fruit. Rowan wood is a symbol of protection. Appears in "Lycanthropic Summer."

Royal Academy of Art: A real art institution based in London, England, founded in 1768. Dr. Sidney Stone refers to it in a critical way during a meeting of the Munsonville Society of the Humanities in "Before The Blood: Henry Matthews."

Royal Copenhagen Flora Danica: A real, prestigious and internationally renowned porcelain dinnerware. It was originally created in 1761. The intricate florals are still created freehand. Mentioned in "Before The Blood: Henry Matthews."

Rubicon: A real, shallow river in northeastern Italy, where Julius Caesar purportedly led a legion across in early January 49 BC, which ultimately led to becoming dictator for life. The phrase "crossing the Rubicon" means a "point of no return." It appears in "Before The Blood: John Simons."

Rumpelstiltskin: An imp who spins straw into gold for a woman in exchange for her firstborn. The story of Rumpelstiltskin appears in the real 1812 edition of "Children's and Household Tales" by the Brothers Grimm. When Henry heard some weird music his father played, he "saw" Rumpelstiltskin dancing around a bonfire in "Before The Blood: Henry Matthews" Bryony compares the skipping of her heartbeats to a dancing Rumpelstiltskin in "Before The Blood: Bryony Simons."

Rusk: Hard, twice-baked bread. Rusk is dipped or crumbled into soup or crumbled over ham or fish in "Before The Blood: Bryony Marseilles" and "Before The Blood: Bryony Simons."

Sabbath School: Mrs. Parks' name for the religious instruction she provides in the parsonage on Saturday mornings in "Before The Blood: Bryony Marseilles."

Sage: An aromatic plant in the mint family with gray-green leaves. Granny Spencer brews tea with it in "Before The Blood: John Simons." Kellen serves John a sage and onion-stuffed goose in "Before The Blood: Kellen Wechsler." Adele Marseilles soothed Galien Marseilles' sore throat with steeped sage in a clean feed cloth in "Before The Blood: Bryony Marseilles." Henry smelled sage when he first arrived at Arcadia, and he brought a planted potted with it to his sister Etta Markham in "Before The Blood: Henry Matthews." Bryony smelled citron and sage on Henry when he kissed her; John brewed sage tea for her; Bryony ate onion and sage flavored potatoes at Simons Mansion and sage-flavored sausage at Fisher Farm in "Before The Blood: Bryony Simons." Caryn Rochelle buys a candle in "Lycanthropic Summer" that smells like jasmine and sage. John-Peter requests more sage in his dinner in "Visage."

Sapin de Noels: A real French term for Christmas trees. Used in "Before The Blood: Henry Matthews."

Salade Frisée: This classic French salad is made with frisée lettuce topped with poached eggs and croutons and dressed with a bacon vinaigrette. Henry brings this dish as part of his elaborate lunch at William's workplace in "Before The Blood: Henry Matthews." Frisée is also called "curly endive." Frisée has pale green, crinkly leaves and is part of the chicory family.

Saleratus: A real precursor to baking soda. Saleratus was a chemical leavening agent made from potassium bicarbonate or sodium bicarbonate. Used in "Before The Blood: Bryony Marseilles" and "Call of the Siren."

Salicylic acid: A real chemical exfoliant to treat certain skin conditions and the starting point for making aspirin. In "Before The Blood: Henry Matthews," Dr. Sidney Stone uses salicylic acid to treat Henry's asthma by reducing inflammation in Henry's lungs.

Saltpeter or saltpetre: Also called potash or potassium nitrate. Used in gunpowder, pickling meat, and (previously) to treat high blood pressure. Appears in "Before The Blood: Bryony Marseilles" and "Call of the Siren."

Sampler: A real piece of embroidery that showcases one's stitching skills. Lilac Fisher works on one in "Before The Blood: Bryony Marseilles" and "Summer Sisters." Emma Markham completed quite a few in "Before The Blood: Henry Matthews." A sampler with the Bible verse "In the multitude of words there wanteth not sin" hangs in Reverend Marseilles' parsonage office. in "Before The Blood: Bryony Marseilles" and "Before The Blood: Bryony Simons." It's also the only picture that hangs in his office. Marie Clare works on a sampler in "The Phoenix." Old samplers hang on the walls of Fisher Farm in "Call of the Siren."

Santon: Small, hand-painted figure for creches or nativity scenes. Many are displayed at Arcadia in "Before The Blood: Henry Matthews."

"Sava Savanović:" A rea; Serbian vampire novel. Full name is "After Ninety Years: The Story of Serbian Vampire Sava Savanović is a Serbian novella by Milovan Glisic, first published in 1880.

Referenced at a meeting of the Munsonville Society for the Humanities in "Before The Blood: Bryony Marseilles."

Schnitzel: Schnitzel is meat that has been pounded thin. In Germany, this is pork meat. A traditional way of serving it is breaded and fried. Appears in "Before The Blood: Kellen Wechsler."

Schupfnudeln: Real German potato noodles. Appears in "Before The Blood: Kellen Wechsler."

Schwechten piano: A real type of fine piano produced by Berlin-based piano manufacturer Georg Schwechten between 1854 and 1925. Appears in "Bryony," "Before The Blood: John Simons," "Before The Blood: Bryony Simons," and "The Phoenix." Mentioned in "Visage."

Scooter: The name of Brian Marchellis' dog in "Bryony." Also mentioned in "Scotter." It was the name of my dog, used as a placeholder name. But I didn't have the heart to change it when my own dog actually died. Scooter is also mentioned in "Staked!"

Sense and Sensibility: A real novel about family and romance by Jane Austen, which was published anonymously in three volumes in 1811. Referenced in "Before The Blood: Bryony Marseilles."

September 24, 1866: Birthdate of Henry Matthews. Referenced in "Before The Blood: Herny Matthews."

Serfs: A real, poor class of agricultural worker in Medieval times, who could not leave the land without its owner's permission. Kellen was a type of serf to Voll-Bauer. Kellen uses "serf" to describe the type of audience Seymour Cassidy attracted and why Seymour needed Kellen's help in "Before The Blood: Kellen Wechsler."

Shad roe: The egg sac of the American shad fish, a type of herring. Margaret, 1940s Kellen secretary, tries ordering some during a business dinner in "Before The Blood: Kellen Wechsler."

Shelby Cornet Band: The Munsonville Times printed a story that this fictional band would play at a beef stew supper to help raise money to build a church in the small village of Shelby in "Before The Blood: Bryony Marseilles."

Signet ring: A real ring engraved with initials or a design. Lord Girard gives one to Henry in "Before The Blood: Henry Matthews."

"Simon Peter, and Thomas called Didymus, and Nathanael of Cana in Galilee, and the sons of Zebedee, and two others of His disciples were together. Simon Peter said to them, 'I am going fishing.' They said to him, 'We will also come with you.' They went out and got into the boat; and that night they caught nothing." John 21:1-3: One of the earliest Bible verses Bryony Marseilles heard her father read. Appears in "Before The Blood: Bryony Marseilles."

Simons Says: A real children's game of oral commands that should only be followed if preceded by the words, "Simon Says." Any child who follows the command without the prompt sits out the net round. Mentioned in "Before The Blood: Bryony Simons."

Sixteenth Century Turkish map: The fictional couple Warren and Savannah Holloway – and then the also fictional Bartholomew and Edwina Smyth – owned one in "Before The Blood: John Simons" and "Call of the Siren."

Skelly: A miniature plastic, glow-in-the-dark, animated skeleton that serves as a lock-picker for supernatural super sleuth Cornell

Dyer in (so far) "Cornell Dyer and the Calcium-Deficient Bones" and "Cornell Dyer and the Howls of Basketville."

Slatterns: A messy, dirty woman who might also be sexually immoral or a prostitute. Mentioned in "Before The Blood: Henry Matthews."

Snapping crackers: A real, cardboard tube wrapped in brightly colored festive paper and containing a trinket. They're called "snapping crackers" because they make a snapping or crackling sound when pulled apart. Kellen learns about them while overhearing a street conversation in "Before The Blood: Kellen Wechsler."

Snipe: A real, small brown shorebird with a long beak. Served at a Michaelmas celebration in "Before The Blood: Kellen Wechsler."

Snood: A real mesh headgear for holding the hair at the back of the head. The Fisher girls wear them in "Before The Blood" Bryony Marseilles" and "Before The Blood: Bryony Simons." Sally Bass wears one while caring for Pearl Griffith in "Before The Blood: Bryony: Marseille." Henry Matthews wears one while cooking in "The Phoenix." Briana Miller wears one while washing dishes in "Call of the Siren."

Snowdrops: Real bulbous perennial plants with one-inch, bell-shaped, white flowers with a sweet perfume hanging at the end of silvery green, leafless stalks. A legend has God asking the flowers to lend their colors to the snow. All refused except for the snowdrop. So God allowed this plant to bloom first in the spring. Agnes spies them when walking in Central Park with Henry in "Before The Blood: Henry Matthews."

Snow White and Rose Red: A real folk tale by the Brothers Grimm about two sisters who give hospitality to a bear in the middle of winter. Bryony reads the story to Susan Betts in "Before The Blood: Bryony Marseilles."

Snowbell: A stray cat Brian Marchellis adopts in "Bryony." The protagonist of the BryonySeries short story "Snowball."

Snowshoe hares: A real nocturnal hare with large hind feet that changes color during the year – brown in summer and white in winter. Mentioned in "Before The Blood: Bryony Simons."

Sole: A small flat fish with a firm texture and mild "non-fishy" taste. Briefly discussed as a menu item in "Before The Blood: Henry Matthews."

Sommersonnenwende: A real German word meaning summer solstice. Kellen attends a summer solstice picknick in honor of St. John the Baptist in "Before The Blood: Kellen Wechsler."

Song of Roland: A real eleventh-century chanson de geste (song of heroic deeds), author unknown, about a military leader named Roland at the Battle of Roncevaux Pass in AD 778, during King Charlemagne's reign. Possibly France's oldest epic poem or work of literature. Henry reads a portion in "Before The Blood: Henry Matthews."

Song of Solomon: A real canticle celebrating erotic love in the Bible, which is considered an allegory of God's love for his people. Several of its verses as built into the fabric of "Before The Blood: Bryony Simons."

Sonic space traveler 53 engine: A contraption supernatural super sleuth Cornell Dyer claims to own in "Cornell Dyer and the Old Folks home."

Sonnet: A real, fourteen-line poem where each line has ten syllables of alternating stressed and unstressed syllables (iambic pentameter). Mentioned twice in "Before The Blood: Henry Matthews."

Spaetzle: Means "little sparrow." Tiny German egg noodle dumpling. Kellen eats them in "Before The Blood: Kellen Wechsler."

Sparta: A real city-state in ancient Greece. The Spartans were indifferent to luxury. Bryony thinks "Sparta" the first time she sees Owen Munson's fishing cabin on "Before The Blood: Bryony Marseilles."

"Spells to Lure Snakes Out From Hiding:" A pretend book by supernatural super sleuth Cornell Dyer in "Karla Joins In."

Spode China: This real company celebrated its 250th anniversary in 2020. Popular patterns for years include Blue Italian and Christmas Tree. The Spode China used at Spencer Inn in "Before The Blood: John Simons" is white with blue and white flowers.

Squab: A young domestic pigeon, less than four weeks old, with tender dark meat. Henry ate creamed squab at Dr. Hiram Rush and Amelia Rush's party in "Before The Blood: Henry Matthews."

"Straf Mich Gott" Bible: Published in 1602 by J. Piscator in Germany. Name means "God punish me" and was inspired by Mark 8:12: "And he sighed deeply in his spirit, and saith, 'Why doth this generation seek after a sign? verily I say unto you, There shall no sign be given unto this generation.'" Used in many parts of

Protestant Southern Germany. Appears in "Before The Blood: Kellen Wechsler" and "The Phoenix."

Straw ticking mattress: A real mattress made from tightly woven cotton and filled with straw. Appears in "Before The Blood: Bryony Marseilles" and "Before The Blood: Bryony Simons."

Statue of Liberty in New York Harbor: The construction of this is referenced in "Before The Blood: Henry Matthews" and its landmark status is stressed in "Cornell Dyer and the Necklace of Forgetfulness."

Stein's Celebrated Custom-Made Boots: An advertisement for a Jenson business in The Munsonville Times in "Before The Blood: Bryony Marseilles."

Steinway pianos: Any handcrafted piano manufactured by Steinway & Sons. German piano builder Heinrich Engelhard Steinweg founded the company in 1853 in Manhattan, New York. Appears in "Before The Blood: John Simons" and "Visage." Herbert Rutherford's pianos are compared to Steinways in "Before The Blood" Henry Matthews."

Stovepipe: A very tall top hat with wide brim. Appears in "Before The Blood: Henry Matthews."

Strychnine: A real, highly toxic, white bitter white odorless powder that's used as a pesticide and formerly used as a tonic. Appears in "Before The Blood: Bryony Simons" and "Call of the Siren."

Strudel: A real layered pastry in German cuisines with a sweet or savory filling. Mentioned in "Before The Blood: Kellen Wechsler."

Sumac lemonade: Sumac berries have a lemony taste. Sumac lemonade was served at Spencer Inn in "Before The Blood: John Simons."

Summa Theologiae: A real book about Catholic doctrine and the best-known work Thomas Aquinas. Mentioned in "Before The Blood: Bryony Simons."

Sun Kissed Sugar Peach: One of many suntan lotions for sale in "Cornell Dyer and the old Folks Home."

Sunstones: Used as a synonym for lodestone, which has magnetic properties, in "Cornell Dyer and the Missing Tombstone."

Sweet Puffs: The name Nancy Platt gave to the stray white kitten she brought into her home in "Before The Blood: Henry Matthews."

Tabitha: A tabby with a tumor. Appears briefly in "Lycanthropic Summer."

Taffeta: A crisp, smooth, stiff, lustrous plain woven fabric, which was traditionally silk and used for corsets, ball gowns, and wedding dresses. Voll-Bauer's wife wore taffeta when she tended to Kellen in "Before The Blood: Kellen Wechsler." The Smythe granddaughters wore dresses in slate taffeta and in crimson taffeta in "Before The Blood: Bryony Simons." Millicent wore a dress when she greeted Henry for the last time in "The Phoenix."

Tapenade: A real French spread consisting of finely chopped olives, capers, and anchovies. This was served with a plate of crudités and, most likely, spread onto slices of crusty French bread. Was served at Arcadia when Carlton and Elizabeth Mandeville visited in "Before The Blood: Henry Matthews."

Tartar Steak or Steak Tartare: Raw beefsteak that is chopped or minced, held together by raw egg yolk, and seasons with capers and mustard. John Simons and Bryony Simons eat it on separate occasions in "Before The Blood: Bryony Simons."

Teens Today: Fictional magazine referenced in "Lycanthropic Summer"

Temperance Fountain on the West side of Union Square: A real fountain that was donated in 1881 by a wealthy advocate of abstinence from alcohol to encourage people to drink water instead. Mentioned in "Before The Blood: John Simons."

The Ten Plagues of Egypt: Ten calamities God sent in the Old Testament to help free the Israelite slaves. Ten cannisters with a plague each are lined up in the motor home of supernatural super sleuth Cornell Dyer. Appears in "Cornell Dyer and the Missing Tombstone" and "Karla Joins In."

Terpsichore: In Greek mythology, Terpsichore is one of the nine muses. She represents chorus and dance. Henry's cousin Giselle Markham "adopts" Terpsichore as her muse, even though Giselle is a visual artist. Henry deemed the name fitting for Giselle's eyes often danced. Mentioned in "Before The Blood: Henry Matthews."

"The Alchemy of Sir Wallace P. Erkart::" A fictional, ancient book of magic, whose magic molds itself to the intentions of the owner. Appears in "Before The Blood: Bryony Marseilles," "Visage," "Cornell Dyer and the Missing Tombstone," "Cornell Dyer and the Whispering Wardrobe," and "House on Top of the Hill." Mentioned in "Karla Joins In."

"The Apology" by Plato: This real, written account of Socrates' trial in 399 BC by Plato was a book Henry's cousin Archer Markham loved to read in "Before The Blood: Henry Matthews."

"The bride kiss'd the goblet: the knight took it up": Harold Matthews quotes this line from "Lochinvar" by Sir Walter Scott in "Bryony."

"The Brothers Karamazov" by Fyodor Dostoyevsky: A real nineteenth century philosophical novel with murder as its plot and God, faith, free will, and doubt as its main themes. Professor Astor G. Clarke discusses this novel with Henry in "Before The Blood: Henry Matthews."

"The Buffalo Skinners:" Owen Munson sings this real American folk song in "Before The Blood: Bryony Marseilles."

"The Cavern of Horrors:" A real Gothic romantic chapbook published in 1802. Bryony read this book with Rose Fisher the summer they were fifteen in "Before The Blood: Bryony Simons."

"The Christian Faith" by Friedrich Schleiermacher: First published in German in 1820. First English translation published in 1830. A real dogma of the Christian faith from the Protestant perspective. Reverend Galien Marseilles reads it in "Before The Blood: Bryony Simons."

The Detroit News: Founded in 1873, the real publication has won three Pulitzer prizes and is still in publication as of 2023. Appears in "Before The Blood: Henry Matthews."

"The Eleventh Commandment and Other Tales: Fictional book of short mystery stories by Harold Masters. Appears in "Bryony."

'The Fairy Feller's Master-Stroke?'" English artist painted this real painting from 1855 to 1864 while incarcerated for murdering his father in 1843. Members of the Munsonville Society for the Humanities discuss the painting and the murder in "Before The Blood: Henry Matthews."

"The Fate of Fenella by Twenty-four Authors": A real experimental novel published in 1892. Each author, including Arthur Conan and Bram Stoker, wrote a chapter. Bryony read it in "Before The Blood: Bryony Simons."

"The Fish and the Ring": An English fairy tale collected by Joseph Jacobs in English Fairy Tales. Appears in "Before The Blood: Bryony Marseilles."

"The Fisherman and His Wife:" A real folk tale by the Brothers Grimm about the perils of greed and discontentment. Appears in "Before The Blood: Bryony Marseilles."

"The Girl I Left Behind Me:" A real, old English folk song. Because a U.S. Army marching son during the War of 1812. Starts with the lyrics, "I'm lonesome since I crossed the hill, and over the moor that's sedgy." Appears in Before The Blood: Bryony Marseilles" and "Before the Blood" Bryony Simons."

The Green-Headed League: A parody title of the Sherlock Holmes short story "The Red-Headed League" by Sir Arthur Conan Doyle. Appears in "Cornell Dyer and the Howls of Basketville."

The Green Lady: A real folktale from Hertfordshire. A poor girl finds work with a fairy and is warned by the fishes not to eat her food. Appears in "Lycanthropic Summer."

The Hieroglyphics of Horapollo Nilous: Attributed to Horapollo, one of the last priests of the Ancient Egyptian religion in the fifth century. A copy sits in the library at Arcadia. Appears in "Before The Blood: Henry Matthews."

"The Iliad" by Homer: A student at Jenson College read a passage from this epic poem during an orator's contest in "Before The Blood: Henry Matthews."

"The Imitation of Christ" by Thomas à Kempis: A Christian devotional book published 1418 to 1427. Reverend Galien Marseilles and Adele Marseilles read and discussed this book in "Before The Blood: Bryony Marseilles."

"The Irish Harper and His Dog" by Thomas Campbell: Own Munson sang this song from 1853 at the burial of Clyde Fisher's dog in "Before The Blood: Bryony Marseilles."

"The Jolly Cowboy:" Own Munson sings this real cowboy song with the lyrics, "What keeps the herd from running, And stampede far and wide?" as he enters the dining room of Fisher Farm in "Before The Blood: Bryony Marseilles."

"The Kansas Line:" Owen Munson sang this real cowboy song in "Before The Blood: Bryony Marseilles." Mitch Cooper and Eugene Miller sang the song at Munson Day 1892 in "Before The Blood: Bryony Simons."

The Lady, or the Tiger?" An allegorical short story by Frank R. Stockton and first published in 1882. Better experienced than explained. Mentioned in "Bryony."

"The Lambkin and the Little Fish:" by the Brothers Grimm: One of the earliest fairy tales Bryony's father reads to her. Appears in "Before The Blood: Bryony Marseilles."

"The Little Red Lark:" A real, old Irish song from at least the mid-nineteenth century that Kate Miller sings as she prepares to wash a new deceased's body in "Before The Blood: Bryony Simons."

The Lion: A majestic and central character in "Cornell Dyer and the Whispering Wardrobe."

"The Maiden and the Fish," from Portuguese Folk-Tales by Consiglieri Pedroso. One of the earliest fairy tales Bryony's father reads to her. Appears in "Before The Blood: Bryony Marseilles." This particular volume was published in 1881. But Reverend Marseilles apparently has a large volume of fairy tales with themes of fish that he reads to Bryony.

The Man in the Iron Mask" by Alexander Dumas: This final installment of Dumas' real Three Musketeers saga, published in 1850, is based on the unidentified prisoner of state from 1669 to 1703. The prisoner was heled in four different French prisons, include the Bastille." Henry reads a dilapidated version of Dumas' novel while recovering from an asthma attack in "Before The Blood: Henry Matthews."

The Manchester Guardian: A real newspaper founded in 1821 and, as of 2023, is known as The Guardian. Appears on "Before The Blood: Henry Matthews."

The Masters: A real term for European artists from 1300 to 1800. Colin Greene and his wife Elaine Greene displayed copies of famous paintings by the Masters in their Jenson home in "Before The Blood: Henry Matthews."

The Merchant of Venice" by William Shakespeare: A real play written in the late seventeenth century about moneylending and friendship. Henry reads it as a boy in "Before The Blood: Henry Matthews."

"The Mansion" by Henry van Dyke Jr.: A short story about pride, true charity, and self-examination that's often read at Christmas. First published in 1911. Mentioned in "Bryony."

The Munsonville Times: A daily publication for the fictional fishing village of Munsonville, Michigan. Founded by Richard Hasset and Lula Hasset when they moved to Munsonville with their family in "Before The Blood: Bryony Marseilles" and owned and managed by various families over the years. As of 2023, The Munsonville Times is a weekly newspaper. Appears, in "Bryony," "Visage," "Staked!," "Before The Blood: Henry Matthews," "Before The Blood: Bryony Simons," "The Phoenix," "Call of the Siren," House on Top of the Hill," "Julie and the Too-Hard Homework," "Katie and the Big Fear," "Brainy Ann," and "Karla Joins In."

The Mystery of the Cardboard Refrigerator Box: One of the mysteries supernatural super sleuth recalls solving with Sherman Homes and Jim Wipston in "Cornell Dyer and the Howls of Basketville."

The Nordic exhibition of Industry, Agriculture, and Art.: A real exhibition in 1888 that aspired to showcase the finest agriculture, art, and industry from the five Nordic countries: Denmark, Finland, Iceland, Norway[b] and Sweden. Discussed at meeting of the

Munsonville Society of the Humanities in "Before The Blood: Henry Matthews."

"The Old Clock on the Stairs" by Henry Wadsworth Longfellow: Includes the lines, "All are scattered now and fled, some are married, some are dead," which Lord Girard quotes in "Before The Blood: Henry Matthews."

"The People's Illustrated & Descriptive Family Atlas of the World:" Henry purchases a copy of this real atlas at Brentanos in Chicago in "Before The Blood: Henry Matthews."

The Poets of Arabia: Fictional collection of authentic poems by poets of Ancient Aradia. Appears in the library at Arcadia in "Before The Blood: Henry Matthews."

"The Pumpkin" by John Greenleaf Whittier: Boswell Pike recites this ode (first published in the Boston Chronotype in 1846) to the popular autumn fruit in "Before The Blood: Bryony Marseilles."

"The Rainy Day" by Henry Wadsworth Longfellow: Henry and his sister Etta quote this line from the poem, "Into each life some rain must fall, some days must be dark and dreary" in "Before The Blood: Henry Matthews."

The Royal Agrarian Society: Was really formed in 1838 to promote the study of English agriculture. Discussed at meeting of the Munsonville Society of the Humanities in "Before The Blood: Henry Matthews."

The Ruin of the Barmecides: A real poem by ninth century poet Abu Tammam. Appears in "The Poets of Arabia," a fictional collection of poems on a shelf in the library at Arcadia in "Before The Blood: Henry Matthews."

The Sandman: A mythical character who sprinkles magical sand on people to lure them into beautiful sleep. Caitlin Miller introduces the concept to Sue Bass when Sue is very young. Sue eventually uses that term for Luther Hasset in "Call of the Siren."

The Sign of Three Times Three: One of the mysteries supernatural super sleuth recalls solving with Sherman Homes and Jim Wipston in "Cornell Dyer and the Howls of Basketville."

The Singing: Alluring, ethereal, unearthly singing that Sue Bass, and apparently only Sue Bass, has heard since the time of her conception in "Call of the Siren."

"The Sword and the Trowel" by Charles Spurgeon: A real monthly magazine Spurgeon started in 1865 that is still in publication in 2023. Reverand Galien Marseilles was a loyal reader in "Before The Blood: Bryony Simons."

The Third Republic: A real period of time in French history from 1870 to 1940. One of the topics that Kellen discusses over absinthe and frizzed eggs in Parisian cafes in "Before The Blood: Kellen Wechsler."

"The Three Heads in the Well": A real British fairytale referenced in "Lycanthropic Summer" with the verse that begins with "Wash me and comb me."

"The unexamined life is not worth living": This quote by Socrates is calligraphed on a piece of paper and hanging above Adelaide Markham's nightstand in "Before The Blood: Henry Matthews."

"The Young Wife, or Duties of Woman in the Marriage Relation" by William Andrus Alcott: A real book Henry's niece Emma Markham is reading in "Before The Blood: Henry Matthews."

"There is a time for departure even when there's no certain place to go." Henry wrote this quote from Tennessee Williams' 1953 play "Camino Real" and left it on his desk for Melissa to find in "Bryony."

"There is therefore now no condemnation for those who are in Christ Jesus. Romans eight one." Algernon Demars' "comeback" verse to Reverend Galien Marseilles, publicly reassuring him of God's forgiveness during a meeting of the Munsonville Society for the Humanities in "Before The Blood: Bryony Simons."

"There shall no evil befall thee, neither shall any plague come nigh thy dwelling." Psalms 91:10-12: Lilac Fisher is cross-stitching this Bible verse onto a sampler in "Before The Blood: Bryony Marseilles."

There was a Crooked Man: Kellen parodies this Mother Goose nursery rhyme when taunting Bryony in "Before The Blood: Bryony Simons."

Thirteen weeks and two days, to be exact: The length of time that passed after the death of P.T. Barnum's wife Charity to the time he married Nancy Fish. Bryony overhears the phrase at a dinner party hosted by Bartholomew Smythe and Edwina Smythe in "Before The Blood: Bryony Simons."

Thirty Years War: A real, long, cruel seventeenth century war in central Europe with religious conflict at its fore. More than eight million people died from disease, famine and from military battles. Part of "Before The Blood: Kellen Wechsler" takes place during the Thirty Years War.

Thimble: A small metal cap with a closed end to protect the finger form the sharp point of the needle when sewing. Mrs. Fisher uses one when mending a rip in Bryony's dress in "Before The Blood: Bryony Simons." Mentioned in relation to the party game "hide the thimble" or "hunt the thimble" in "Before The Blood: Bryony Marseilles" and "The Phoenix."

Thoroughbred: A real horse breed designed for racing. Savannah Holloway has thoroughbred horses in "Before The Blood: John Simons."

Tiffany silver: Sterling silver wine goblets from the real Tiffany and Co. that were used during a party at Jacob King's Fifth Avenue mansion in "Before The Blood: Henry Matthews." Tiffany & Co. was founded in 1837 in New York City, New York.

Tongan paddle club: Really used by the people of the Tongan Islands as oars, weapons, and in dances and religious activities. The fictional couple Warren and Savannah Holloway – and then the also fictional Bartholomew and Edwina Smyth – own an antique version in "Before The Blood: John Simons" and "Call of the Siren."

Tonic: A real drink often containing the antimalarial drug quinine, soda water, and sugar, thought to perk up one's energy. Strychnine was sometimes used in tonics – as well as other medicinal purposes. The word "tonic" appears in "Before The Blood: Kellen Wechsler," "Before The Blood: Bryony Marseilles," "Before The Blood: Henry Matthews," "Before The Blood: Bryony Simons," and "The Pheonix."

Toujours dans mon Coeur: French for "always in my heart." Caroline Matthews murmurs it to her husband Harold Matthews in "Before The Blood: Henry Matthews."

Townsend Chippendale antique secretary: A real mahogany secretary-desk from the eighteenth century. The fictional couple Warren and Savannah Holloway – and then the also fictional Bartholomew and Edwina Smyth – own an antique version in "Before The Blood: John Simons" and "Call of the Siren."

Treacle: A real molasses-like byproduct from making sugar. Bryony eats treacle scones and marmalade with John in "Before The Blood: Bryony Simons." Treacle was one of the scents Henry detected on Millicent Gothart in "The Phoenix."

Treadle seeing machine: A sewing machine where the wheel turns by way of a foot lever. Appears in "Before The Blood: Bryony Marseilles," "Before The Blood: Bryony Simons," "Katie and the Big Fear," and "Karla Joins In."

Tree of Bards: Ancient bards considered the rowan tree to be their source of inspiration. Caryn Rochelle refers to this term in "Lycanthropic Summer." See also "rowan."

Tree of New Life: Reverend Galien Marseilles' reproachful play on the words Tree of Life, which appears in the Garden of Eden in the Bible. Used in "Before The Blood: Bryony Marseilles."

Trivium: The real study of grammar, logic, and rhetoric. Appears as part of Henry's schoolwork in "Before The Blood: Henry Matthews."

Trousseau: Real French word meaning "small bundle." Referred to any items a bride might need. In "Before The Blood: Bryony Simons," Trudi calls Bryony's wedding clothes her "trousseau."

True Entertainment: Fictional magazine referenced in "Lycanthropic Summer."

Tuppence: A real British pre-decimal coin worth two pennies. Kellen tells a very quiet John in "Before The Blood: Kellen Wechsler," "Tuppence for your thoughts," meaning Kellen is so curious about John's thoughts that he is willing to pay money to learn them.

Turpentine: A real, clear, smelly, flammable fluid derived by distilling resin of living pine trees. Formerly used as distillation of resin harvested from living trees, mainly pines. Formerly used mainly as a paint thinner and an antiseptic. Leopold Russell built his fortune in turpentine and then lost it when turpentine began falling out of favor in the late nineteenth century due to deforesting in "Before The Blood: Bryony Simons."

Turkey Delight: An extremely delicious turkey sandwich, prepared by Mrs. Beaver in "Cornell Dyer and the Whispering Wardrobe."

"Two souls with but a single thought, two hearts that beat as one" by Friedrich Halm. Henry quotes this line from the Austrian playwright's work nineteenth century play "Ingomar the Barbarian" in "Bryony."

Typhoid: A real life-threatening infection typically spread through contaminated food or water. Typhoid spreads through Leland Hills, Illinois, in "Before The Blood: Henry Matthews."

Uncle Barty: Bertrand the Mouse's uncle. Uncle Barty traveled from Indiana to Illinois in 2021 to help search for his lost nephew, Bertrand the Mouse. Uncle Barty has remained in Illinois since Bertrand tends to scamper off, instead of diligently fulfilling his mission to bring the joys of reading to children. Uncle Barty has not appeared in any Bertrand the Mouse books as of 2023. But he does appear at BryonySeries events and in social media posts with Bertrand.

Une vie ou L'Humble Vérité by Guy de Maupassant: Guy de Maupassant wrote this real novel, his first, in 1883. It follows the life of Jeanne, who is lonely because she's lost – or been decided by – anyone she's ever loved. The Munsonville Society for the Humanities deemed it "satisfactory for a first novel" in "Before The Blood: Bryony Marseilles."

Union Spring bed: A real bed sold by Montgomery Ward, Catalogue no. 13, spring and summer, 1875. The bed cost $5 to $6, depending on the size of the slats. Tyler Howe developed the first box-spring bed in 1853. Adele Marseilles ordered one for the parsonage, which ended up in Bryony's room in "Before The Blood: Bryony Marseilles."

"Upon the wicked He shall rain snares, fire and brimstone, and a horrible tempest: this shall be the portion of their cup": From Psalm 11:6 in the Bible. Part of a sermon Reverend Galien Marseilles preaches at Munsonville Congregational Church in "Before the Blood: Bryony Simons."

Velocipede: The real predecessor to the modern bicycle. Bryony and John rose a tandem velocipede during their honeymoon in Chicago in "Before The Blood: Bryony Simons."

Vermouth: Sweet or dry wine flavored with herbs or spices. Bartholomew and Edwina Smythe served it at their dinner party in "Before The Blood: Bryony Simons."

Viking Treasure Locator: A gadget supernatural super sleuth Cornell Dyer uses in "Cornell Dyer and the Missing Tombstone."

Vicente Martínez Ybor cigar: A real cigar founded by Martinez Ybor in 1856, who first manufactured them in Cuba, then Key West, Florida; and finally Tampa, Florida. Kellen smokes these cigars in "Before The Blood: Kellen Wechsler."

Wagnerian opera: Any of the thirteen operas by the real German composer Richard Wagner from 1833 to 1877. The favorite music of supernatural super sleuth Cornell Dyer in The Adventures of Cornell Dyer BryonySeries subseries.

Wash 'n' Dry: The laundromat that Donna Wechsler uses in the 1940s in "Before The Blood: Kellen Wechsler."

Washburn exploded: Also known as The Great Mill Disaster. An accumulation of flour dust inside the real Washburn A Mill in Minneapolis, Minnesota, United States, exploded on May 2, 1878. The disaster resulted in eighteen deaths. Fourteen workers were inside the mill and the other four were at nearby mills who died as the result of the resulting fire. Mentioned in "Before The Blood: Henry Matthews."

Watercress: A real dark green aquatic flowering perennial. Henry is given the choice of cucumber or watercress sandwiches for his wedding menu in "Before The Blood: Henry Matthews." Watercress sandwiches are served at Simons Mansion in "Before The Blood: Bryony Simons." Caryn Rochelle's mother serves watercress sandwiches at her card games in "Lycanthropic Summer." John Simotes adds watercress to a salad he prepares for Melissa in "Visage."

Waterford City's newspaper: Becky Sue Rawlins might be referring to a newspaper in Waterford Township, Michigan, which was founded in 1834.

Waterford crystal: A real, very fine, highly prized cut lead glass named for the town in Ireland where it was first produced in 1783. Amelia Rush insists that Henry's prized gallicas only be displayed in a Waterford crystal vase in "Before The Blood: Herny Matthews."

"We will try the matter and see how it works.": A real phrase used by Robert "Bob" Collyer, an American Unitarian clergyman, who presided over P.T. Barnum's funeral services. Appears in "Before The Blood: Bryony Simons."

Webster's Unabridged Dictionary: This real comprehensive dictionary was given as a prize at the adult spelling bee at the Thanksgiving potluck in "Before The Blood: Bryony Marseilles."

Weekly Book Reviews: Fictional magazine referenced in "Lycanthropic Summer.

Wellington boots: Real fashionable books for men in the nineteenth century. John wore them in "Before The Blood: John Simons."

When Day's Last Light Has Darkened: A poem by Jenson College English professor Astor G. Clarke in his book "Word Gems."

"When Lilacs Last in the Dooryard Bloom'd" by Walt Whitman: Henry lauds death by quoting a line from this poem in "Bryony."

Whippoorwills: A real nocturnal bird with a distinct call. Henry hears them while riding in the woods between Evansville and Arcadia in "Before The Blood: Henry Matthews."

Whist: A real, popular card game in the eighteenth and nineteenth centuries. Guests played a "lively game" of whist at a Christmas Eve party at Abbott Simons' home in "Before The Blood: John Simons."

White soup: Also known as Potage à la Reine. A creamy veal and rice soup, often with the addition of almond paste, and thickened with roux (a cooked mixture of equal parts flour and butter). Appears at a dinner party at Jacob King's home in "Before The Blood: John Simons."

Whitechapel murders: Real unsolved murders attributed to Jack the Ripper that occurred near the impoverished Whitechapel district in the East End of London between April 3, 1888, and February 13, 1891. Discussed at a meeting of the Munsonville Society for the Humanities in "Before The Blood: Henry Matthews."

Whitewash: A real type of paint made from slaked lime (water plus calcium oxide). Was used in the early days of Munsonville in "Before The Blood: Bryony Marseilles."

Wild West Show of Buffalo Bill and Annie Oakley: The real American showman and female sharpshooter performed at the Exposition Universelle (World's Fair) in 1889 in Paris, France. Mentioned in "Before The Blood: Kellen Wechsler" and "Before The Blood: Bryony Simons."

William Stroudley's latest locomotive: The latest locomotive of the real nineteenth century English locomotive engineer appeared at the Exposition Universelle (World's Fair) in 1889 in Paris, France. Mentioned in "Before The Blood: Kellen Wechsler" and "Before The Blood: Bryony Simons."

Windsor chair: A real wooden chair with spindles socketed into a saddle-shaped, solid wooden seat. It first appeared in the U.S. in 1725 and was often used as a desk chair. At least one appears in the green room at Hewes Music Hall in "Before The Blood: John Simons."

Witchcraft Act of 1735: A real Act of the Parliament of the Kingdom of Great Britain in 1735 that made it illegal to accuse people of practicing witchcraft. Mentioned in "Before The Blood: John Simons."

Witchgrass: Found in fields and waste areas, witchgrass is real and has fine hairs that grow prickly as the plant matures. Appears in "Before The Blood: Bryony Marseilles," "Before The Blood: Bryony Simons," "Call of the Siren," and "House on Top of the Hill."

"Wives and Daughters:" A real unfinished novel by Elizabeth Gaskell, which was serialized from August 1864 to January 1866. Adele Marseilles references it in "Before The Blood: Bryony Marseilles."

Wolfsbane: Poisonous purple flowers related to buttercups. Also known as aconite and monkshood (because the flowers resemble the hoods monks wear). Appears in "Lycanthropic Summer." Mentioned in "The Phoenix."

Woofer's dog food: A fictional product for which 1940s Kellen writes an advertising campaign in "Before The Blood: Kellen Wechsler."

Word Gems: The name of Astor G. Clarke's first book of poetry, which he shows to Henry in "Before The Blood: Henry Matthews."

World's Columbian Exposition: A real world fair held in Chicago in 1893 to celebrate Christopher Columbus's 400th anniversary of discovering the New World in 1492. John Simons attended this fair and purchased his Arabian horses. Mentioned I "Bryony" and "Before The Blood: Bryony Simons."

Wuthering Heights: A real 1847 Gothic novel, the first and only novel by English author Emily Brontë. Adele Marseilles read this novel in "Before The Blood: Bryony Marseilles," and compared Algernon Demars' physical appearance to that of Heathcliff, the Byronic male protagonist in "Wuthering Heights."

Yarrow: Pretend magical plant with brownish yellow buds. Appears in "Karla Joins In."

Yellow fever epidemic in Mississippi Valley: A real mosquito-transmitted virus that may cause severe liver disease. A yellow fever epidemic occurred in Mississippi from July to November in 1878. Mentioned in "Before The Blood: Henry Matthews."

Yorkshire pudding: A real pudding baked from flour, milk, and eggs. A favorite of Dr. Sidney Stone in "Before The Blood: Herny Matthews."

Zambies: Former humans that turn into zombie-like creatures with plenty of sunshine and sugar. Appears in "Cornell Dyer and the Old Folks Home."

Zervelat: A real German sausage similar to a large frankfurter but with a smokier flavor. A former favorite of Kellen's in "Before The Blood: Kellen Wechsler."

FINAL MESSAGE

This BryonySeries guidebook may unintentionally omit a particular person, place, or thing (or a book that references it) due to human error.

If you find such an error, email your question or correction to bryonyseries@gmail.com.

We will update the book for the next edition.

Thank you for your cherished readership. It makes the creation of each page pure joy.

www.ingramcontent.com/pod-product-compliance
Lightning Source LLC
Chambersburg PA
CBHW051336020726
47501CB00007B/2122